Strictly SHIMMER

Strictly

SHIMMER

THE NOVEL BY
AMANDA ROBERTS

HARPER

An imprint of HarperCollins*Publishers*
77–85 Fulham Palace Road,
Hammersmith, London W6 8JB

www.harpercollins.co.uk

First published by HarperCollins*Publishers* 2011

1 3 5 7 9 10 8 6 4 2

© BBC Worldwide Limited 2010

The author asserts the moral right to
be identified as the author of this work

A catalogue record for this book is
available from the British Library

ISBN 978-0-00-742501-3

Printed and bound in Great Britain by
Clays Ltd, St Ives plc

Mixed Sources
Product group from well-managed
forests and other controlled sources
www.fsc.org Cert no. SW-COC-001806
© 1996 Forest Stewardship Council

FSC is a non-profit international organisation established to promote the
responsible management of the world's forests. Products carrying the FSC
label are independently certified to assure consumers that they come
from forests that are managed to meet the social, economic and
ecological needs of present and future generations.

Find out more about HarperCollins and the environment at
www.harpercollins.co.uk/green

For all the Strictly fans out there.
Keep dancing, even if you don't know
what the next step is!

Acknowledgements

There are a lot of people without whom this story would never have been the same, let alone been committed to print, so please forgive me for using my moment in the spotlight to say a few heartfelt thank yous.

My family – Mum, Dad, Natalie and Lloyd. Without you I would never have made it as far as Strictly, let alone made it to Strictly.

My friends – Julia, Sally and Allegra. For listening to me fretting, watching me dancing and keeping me laughing. I am nothing without my girls.

And Matt – for dancing with me. xxx

Prologue

The first time I walked onto the dance floor, I had to pretend I wasn't gawping. My eyes must have been spinning like disco balls as I tried to take it all in. I gripped the clipboard I had just been handed as tightly as I could, in the desperate hope that this might keep me calm. Chloe, my new colleague, walked straight across the dance floor as if it were nothing more than a studio, and I trotted along behind her, trying to keep my pulse rate – and my eyes – down.

Nothing could stop me from inhaling the atmosphere though. The springiness of the floor, the way that the audience chairs were all neatly fastened together to keep them in perfect straight lines, the sweeping staircases glistening, despite the relative darkness of the studio. But it was the smell that did it: the unmistakable theatrical smell that I had forgotten existed. It brought back memories of the school plays I'd taken part in as a kid. And here it was again. The set was drenched in it. I took a deep breath and tried to concentrate on what I was being told.

'This is where you'll stand during the show,' Chloe said, pointing up at the only undecorated area on the set. I gasped. It was the least sparkly spot; in fact it was pretty much bare. Directly facing the staircase, it was the one angle that I had never seen on television. But it was unquestionably the one with the best view. And now it was my view. I grinned, then quickly composed myself, attempting to look as serious and efficient as possible.

'I see,' I replied, my brow faux-furrowed. I added a slow nod for emphasis.

Chloe was talking so fast she barely seemed to draw breath, and yet she seemed entirely calm. I knew that she had worked on the show for a couple of years, but I was mystified as to how she was so immune to the magic of it all. The headset she was wearing was the only real clue to her role – without it she could have been a visiting student. She was wearing a pair of baggy corduroy jeans, a v-neck t-shirt and a brightly coloured hooded top. With, of course, a pair of pink Converse trainers. Her face was entirely free from make-up and she had tied her fair hair back into a scruffy ponytail. She looked as if she might have once been capable of being a right laugh, but had been working too hard, taking everything a bit too seriously, for too long. I imagined she was only about thirty, but had an ultra-responsible side to her, which would win out every time anyone suggested something as avant-garde as 'having some fun'.

She was dressed as comfortably as someone who did most of their job on their feet needed to be, and yet she didn't actually look that comfortable in her own skin. Mind you, nor was I. It had become apparent within moments of arriving that I was hopelessly over-dressed for the role of a production runner: a floral patterned tea dress, expensive tights and a pair of patent, leather ballerinas. Overcompensating for my nerves had not resulted in a good look. My attempts to coordinate 'showing respect for the job' (by wearing a frock) with 'practicality' (by wearing flat shoes) had left me looking like I was Chloe's boss, not the other way around. Chloe seemed unconcerned though. She had barely glanced at what I was wearing, so great was her devotion to her holy trio of clipboard, headphones and BlackBerry. She continued to fire facts and details at me like a tennis ball machine. I was frantically scribbling down what I could when a voice from the other end of the stage bellowed, 'Hello ladies! Fancy seeing you here …'

I turned round to see someone galloping down the stage stairs towards us. He too was dressed rather like a student: crumpled jeans, lumberjack boots and a faded dark grey sweatshirt. He had neat dark blond hair and was good-looking in a cuddly, soft-cheeked way.

'Aha, here you are, Matt' said Chloe as he approached.

He was gripping a polystyrene cup in his left hand and immediately extended his free hand towards me. 'Hi,' he said. 'I'm Matt. I'm going to be working alongside you this series.'

'Yes, Matt is a fellow AP. Just been promoted to Assist-ant Producer.'

We shook hands.

'Great, lovely to meet you,' I replied. His hand was warm, and his eyes had a twinkle that made me think he wouldn't be unwelcome in a boy band. He blew onto the steam coming off the top of the cup.

'What do you think?' he asked.

'Of the set?'

'Of course the set! Not bad is it? Not bad ...'

'Not bad, it's incredible!' I replied, relieved to finally find someone I could express a smidgen of my excitement to. Matt grinned.

'Yup, it's pretty special. For what it is.'

Chloe was frowning down at her BlackBerry. She seemed to have forgotten we were there.

'I can't believe I'm actually here,' I continued. 'It seems so much smaller than on TV. But still so ... magical.'

'But have you seen the—?' he stopped mid-sentence. 'Hold on. Just wait there.' Matt darted off between a row of gold audience chairs and disappeared behind the wooden walls of the set. I looked around awkwardly as Chloe tapped away at her BlackBerry.

'LOOK UP!' Matt's voice boomed out from behind the walls. I did as I was told. Three huge disco balls were suspended from the ceiling, dwarfing the hundreds of TV lights that were also dangling from the metallic ropes above. Then, slowly, they began to turn. At first it was a little unnerving. The momentum that their slow turning generated made it seem as if it were the rest of the set that were moving, not them. The effect was magical. They were properly spinning now, casting their sparkly chinks of light across everything beneath them. Their movement made me imagine I was dancing myself, as I remembered all the nights I had got myself to sleep by pretending I was waltzing across a gleaming ballroom floor.

Then, just as suddenly, they stopped. I caught sight of Matt waving from a glass pane high above the stage, above the area I'd be standing in during the performances. He seemed to have gone up to the lighting gallery especially to put on this little show for me. With a quick smile he disappeared from view, then reappeared on the ballroom floor a minute later.

'Just a little something I like to do for the newcomers.' His twinkly eyes were even twinklier with mischief, and he gave me a little bow.

'Wow, thank you. Seeing that was pretty much the only reason I wanted to work here. I think I've peaked. I should probably just leave now.'

I'm not quite sure where the courage for such banter had come from. I seemed to have forgotten all about Chloe, who had by now taken a seat in the front row and was focussed entirely on her emails. She looked up sharply.

'I don't think so,' she said, staring suspiciously at the two of us. 'Come along, Amanda. We've got paperwork to do. Matt – we'll meet you at reception in fifteen. We have to collect Amanda's pass anyway.'

She continued her brusque walk across the set, pointing out cables of different lengths on the floor behind the audience chairs, conscious to make sure that I stepped, rather than tripped, over them. I just about had time to look over my shoulder and wave a quick goodbye to Matt as I trotted off behind her. I was thrilled that I had found someone who seemed as enthusiastic about the job as I was, despite Chloe's apparent attempts to make everything seem as tedious as possible. I followed her along seemingly endless corridors barely absorbing much of what she was saying, as she talked me through the basics of my new job. Deep down I was really only thinking one thing: *I'm here. I'm at* Strictly Come Dancing. *I've made it.*

My heart was still racing by the time we got back to BBC TV Centre's imposing reception area. I had always dreamt of working in live TV but this was the first time I had really grasped how much responsibility it entailed. It had all seemed rather abstract before, when I was just the work experience girl. There was so much to remember. And that wasn't including the names, the labyrinthine corridors of BBC TV centre and the strange unspoken hierarchy that seemed to exist between senior and junior members of the team. Matt had seemed so friendly and approachable, but Chloe was significantly more frosty, despite her relaxed-looking fashion choices.

I glanced up at the huge news ticker running across the glass doorways. There were people milling around reception, generally looking busy, clutching cups of coffee and scanning the faces of those who were seated, trying to work out who their next meeting was with. A small queue had formed at the security desk and it seemed like most people were waiting for their visitor passes to be put together. I spotted Matt at the front of the queue talking to one of the security team. He turned around and smiled at us, holding out a BBC pass with a name and face on it. Mine. 'Welcome to Strictly,' he said. 'You're one of the family now.' *One of the family …*

I smiled back and put the pass around my neck. I felt like a *Jim'll Fix It* guest, glowing with excitement at having been granted my special wish. Except instead of a *Jim'll Fix It* badge, I had a BBC pass. Same difference, as far as I was concerned. Mindful that I should perhaps seem like a glacial model of broadcast efficiency, I maintained a dignified expression. It lasted approximately three seconds, before I yelped 'Yeay!!!' Matt winked at me. Chloe looked as if she was doing her best not to roll her eyes.

'Come on then. We'd better get to the office,' she said.

The rest of the day was a blur of information, responsibilities and titles that I had no hope of remembering for at least a couple of weeks. I was still buzzing from the set visit, so I pushed any anxieties about my ability to actually do the job to the back of my head and got on with taking notes on almost everything Chloe said. Matt continued to pop up through the day, asking if he could get us tea or coffee whenever he was off to the kitchen, and chipping in to clarify some of Chloe's more pedantic explanations. His version always seemed a bit more straightforward. Hours later, Chloe told me that my working day was done, and that she would see me at the same time tomorrow. She had barely finished her sentence before her eyes were back on her BlackBerry screen.

When I eventually left TV Centre and stepped into the London drizzle it was already dusk. I headed for the pedestrian crossing, trying to splash as little as possible of the mulchy grey puddles all over my smart new tights. Natalie, my elder sister, had given them to me for the job interview, and made no secret of telling me that the precious Wolfords had cost her £15 – for tights! The woman was insane, but I did appreciate the gesture. I couldn't doubt the fact that my big sister had really wanted me to get the job, even if she thought Lycra-clad legs would be the key to my success. Either way, the Wolfords had now become a bit of a good luck talisman and I was determined to keep them safe. I decided to scurry across the road and into Westfield Shopping Centre to take back something for supper to say thank you. The rain was coming down a little harder by the time I waited for the traffic to stop at the crossing, so I broke into a run as I reached the pavement on the other side. As I did so, I leapt inelegantly onto an unexpectedly wobbly paving stone, which squelched down into a pool of water, entirely soaking my foot. As I stumbled, I banged into an enormous male chest that I hadn't noticed approaching.

'Youch!' I yelped, and looked up, standing on my remaining dry leg, to see one of the most extraordinary men I had ever clapped eyes on. He had pale hair and lightly tanned skin, but his face was just a blur of attractiveness. Perhaps there was an enormous pair of brown eyes. Most of all, I was left breathless by the Wall-of-Man-Chest, which remained immobile.

'Are you okay?' he asked. I couldn't quite work out his accent. He sounded foreign, but in a non-specific way that made it hard for me to place him. I continued to shake my soggy foot, and in doing so flicked my patent leather ballet pump off and into the puddle I had just stepped in.

'Yes. I, er, the puddle,' was all I could muster.

He looked at my shoe, and slowly bent down to pick it up for me. As he leant forward I copped a quick glimpse of the soft blond hair peeking out above the deep V of his t-shirt. The one leg I was left standing on nearly collapsed. He bent down, picked up my poor bedraggled shoe, shook it off and gave it a quick wipe with a tissue he'd pulled out from the pocket of his enormous hoodie. Then, he handed it back.

'There you go, Cinderella.'

'Thank you,' I gasped. He smiled at me and I managed a goofy half smile back. My tights were suddenly immaterial, as were my shoes: I am quite sure I floated the rest of the way to Westfield.

Chapter 1

By the time I finally arrived back at my sister's flat I was drenched. The faux-fur collar on my coat was matted like an unhappy cat's and drops of rain were dripping off my eyelashes. Any Strictly sparkle I'd had had long since gone, although my memory of the Giant Man Chest certainly lingered.

There was one thought keeping me going, as I finally turned the key in Natalie's front door: fishcakes. Determined to pull my weight while I was a houseguest, I had shunned any form of supermarket own-brand food and had splashed out on some delicious fishcakes, a bottle of wine that cost well over the five pounds I would usually spend, and some fancy dark chocolate. I would be a dream of a younger sister, oh yes I would.

I had deliberately shaken off my umbrella on the porch of their gorgeous south London flat and entered feeling full of optimism and goodwill. Sadly, my happiness was short-lived as one of the shopping bags split and its soggy contents hit Natalie's immaculate fawn carpet. Her head poked round the kitchen door just as I was hurriedly trying to scoop the contents off the floor and into the remaining bag.

Natalie smiled tightly. I was on my knees, frantically scooping like a guilty dog owner in the park. I looked up at her.

'I've brought us dinner!' I said, brushing the carpet breezily with my hand in the hope that the soggy patch I had left would just … go away.

'I'll get a cloth,' she replied and soon re-emerged from the kitchen with a clean, brightly coloured cloth folded into neat quarters.

'I'm so sorry – the packaging must have pierced the bag …'

'It's fine, it's fine.' I wasn't sure that it was.

'Honestly, don't worry about it. But I would really prefer it if you didn't cook fishcakes in the house. I can't stand the smell and in this weather I can't open the back door to get rid of it. I've made some spaghetti bolognese. It's on the hob.'

'Okay, sure. At least try the wine though, it's a nice one.'

'Thanks. But Lloyd and I don't really drink during the week. If you just leave it on the side, I'm sure we'll have it sometime soon.'

I stayed crouching by the soggy carpet a couple of moments longer, as if just *being there* might somehow help clear up my mess. Terrified of the damage my enormous,

2

still damp coat could do in the pristine bedroom I was staying in, I took it off and laid it over the edge of the bath. By the time I reached the bedroom I was shuffling, afraid of each and every clean white surface in there, and convinced that any sudden movement would bring the silver-framed photographs crashing down. Having run a hand across the back of my dress to check for hideous black marks, I plonked myself down on the edge of the downy duvet and let out a mighty sigh.

It wasn't that my fishcakes had been rejected, and anyway I loved Natalie's bolognese. And it wasn't that she had been terse with me about sullying her immaculate home – I'd deserved it. It was that I felt I would never be able to repay Natalie and her husband, Lloyd, for their kindness. I was only a couple of years younger than Natalie but it felt as if she had somehow unlocked a Life Code that meant she was several levels ahead of me in the game called Being a Proper Grown-Up. Well, that and the fact that I owed it to her that I had the job at Strictly at all.

Since graduating from university my life had lurched from crisis to sulk and back to crisis while I slowly drove my entire family mad. I'd struggled this first year: many of my friends were still studying and many were working abroad. I'd felt lost without them, not to mention lonely, and the adult world of work had started to feel entirely out of my grasp. Torn between squandering my savings in London trying to get experience working in TV, and staying at home among the hedges of Surrey with my parents – safe in the short term but pointless in the long term – I had failed to make any proper decisions about anything for the upcoming year.

For a week I would be filled with righteous fury that I had to wait on tables at Sergio's, the local Italian restaurant on the high street. Then I would spend a week agonising over whether to bin the job and take up an offer of some unpaid work experience in a weird, forgotten TV studio in Zone 6. A week later I would fill in a bunch of applications and find myself secretly hoping that I didn't get any of the jobs. After all, that was the only fail-safe method I could think of to stop me from ever finding out if I was really good enough for the competitive world of live TV. And shortly after that the seemingly inevitable job rejections would start to flow in and I would shift from silent terror to full blown adolescent sulk.

I spent a summer at Sergio's trying – and failing – not to splash bolognese on my white waitressing shirt even before the customers had started to arrive. When I could take it no more, I switched to temping in various local businesses. I hadn't accounted for the fact that temps are the only workplace life form given less respect than waitresses. Plus my enthusiasm for trying to work out how to use a different photocopier every week was also waning. After six months my parents were beginning to drop increasingly obvious hints that I needed to move out, and I knew deep down that if I really wanted to work in TV, I was going to have to swallow my fears and make a decision one way or the other.

As the longest and most dreary summer of my life was drawing to a longed-for close, everything changed. I was lying on the sofa as usual, devoting a little time to my now favourite pastime: convincing myself that the nearest I would ever get to a TV studio would be as a novelty act on *Britain's Got Talent* ('Ladies and Gentlemen! The Incredible Sulk!'). Then I heard the phone ringing in the kitchen. Mum, who was expecting a call from her friend Jen, leapt to pick it up. Moments later I heard her call me.

'Amanda! Your sister wants a word!'

What fresh hell is this? I thought to myself. Surely she hasn't found a new way to boss me around already? I only saw her on Sunday …

I took the phone from my mum and held it to my ear.

'Tata dada, tata daaaaa,' Natalie was singing down the line.

'What's up?' I replied, wondering why she was so happy. She's normally a Grade A jobsworth, only interested in her feisty law career and in trying to mould me into someone as ambitious and successful as she is.

'Strictly! Strictly!' she shrieked down the phone, giggling. For someone usually so po-faced, she sounded positively delirious.

'Seriously, what are you talking about?'

'There's a job going at *Strictly Come Dancing*, and Lloyd says he can help you with the application!'

I picked at the fabric on the edge of the sofa's arm. A tiny bit of fluff came away in my hand.

'Jobs don't just come up at Strictly,' I replied. 'They must be impossible to get.'

'Well, this one is being advertised and everything. We're going to come down at the weekend and take a look at your application. It's made for you! No one loves dancing like you do, and now's your chance to be a part of it.'

She was right. I did love dancing, and this did seem like a big opportunity. But did I dare go for it? After the bleak summer I had had, my confidence was at an all-time low, and all I could think was that I didn't really feel like humiliating myself in front of a room full of hot-shot BBC executives. What if I applied and didn't get the job? I wasn't sure I could take any more bad news. And I wasn't sure my parents could take any more of my misery-guts attitude. I was one rejected application away from regressing into a full-blown emo teen. And that was not going to be pretty.

'But I …'

'I won't take it any more. I *can't*. You have to keep going, Amanda. You know you want to do this. I will not be a witness to you wriggling out of it. See you Sunday. And make brownies.' Natalie was right. This was more than just a chance at a dream job in telly, it was a chance to get closer to my actual dream – dancing. Pretty much as soon as I could walk I wanted to dance, but it had somehow always stayed in the realms of fantasy to me.

6

A few days later Natalie and Lloyd had arrived in a flurry of glamorous autumn-wear and all-consuming capability. I had felt strangely nervous when I heard her Audi pulling up outside the house, then faintly amused as I watched her piling poor Lloyd's open arms with a ridiculously huge bunch of flowers, two pairs of walking boots and swathes of cashmere scarves. A moment later ...

'Hiyyyaaaaa! We're here!'

Mum squealed and ran to the back door to let them in. Dad pottered down the garden to greet them. I remained where I was in my bedroom, wishing I had thought to put on something a little more attractive than my usual track-suit bottoms and cardigan. I didn't want Lloyd to think that he was helping a total layabout. I quickly applied a bit of make-up and tried to zhoosh my hair up slightly, then sauntered downstairs.

Saturday lunch passed in the usual blur of misheard conversations and ludicrous anecdotes.

'... so he asked me for legal advice while he was cutting my hair and I ended up with this ridiculous fringe that I never even asked for!'

'... yes, I've painted all of the window sills at the back and then next weekend I'm hoping to make a start on the front of the house ...'

'... so I asked the butcher and he said that it's Mrs Dawson who eats most of the bacon, not her husband!'

'... oh the traffic was mostly fine, and Natalie's new clutch made all the difference when we hit a little congestion coming out of London ...'

I realised I wasn't going to get a word in edgeways and so concentrated on loading my plate with as much egg mayonnaise as I thought I could manage. Oh life, how full of challenge and romance you are ...

'... so what do you think, Amanda?'

I looked up suddenly, a little sad to leave behind my eggy daydream. I had zoned out of the conversation to the point that I hadn't even realised Natalie was now talking to me.

'Hmm?'

'About staying?' Natalie was looking at me expectantly. As, I realised, were my mum, dad and Lloyd.

'I'm sorry, I wasn't really listening,' I replied, sheepishly.

Natalie rolled her eyes. Mum clasped her hands. And Lloyd looked as if this might be a good time for him to take his wife's Audi for another spin.

'Amanda, your sister has kindly offered to let you stay with her if you get the job at *Strictly*. Indefinitely. So that's one thing you don't have to worry about.' Dad was smiling at me hopefully. Despite the tensions of the last year he had always retained a steady faith in me that I found touching to the point of embarrassment. How could he still believe in my abilities in this way? He clearly had no doubt that I would breeze though the interviews and accommodation was my only remaining challenge. I couldn't bear to disappoint him. It was time to swallow my pride.

'Wow, thank you guys!' I smiled at the faces staring back at me. Perhaps if I could convince them I thought I had a shot at the job, I could convince myself. 'That is really kind. Hopefully I won't let you down this time.'

Unbelievably, I didn't. The next couple of weeks passed in a whirlwind of applications and interviews, and before I had a chance to breathe I was walking out of a production office at the BBC, having been told that I was down to the final three for the job. And a fortnight after that I was sitting on the edge of the bed in Natalie's guest room, too scared to move in case I messed up anything, and too tired to begin unpacking my suitcase.

The comforting smell of freshly-cooked bolognese began to waft into the room, but it did little to quell my nerves. I slumped onto the enormous heap of white broderie anglaise pillows, and stared at the ceiling for a while. I had to make this job work, I had to. I closed my eyes and took a deep breath, before sitting up and going back into the kitchen, smiling.

'So, what can I do to help?' I asked casually.

'Unload the dishwasher, get some plates out for the three of us and ...'

'And what?'

Natalie paused, wiping her hands on the fluffy little Cath Kidston hand towel by the kitchen sink.

'Don't mess this job up, Amanda. Just please, don't mess this job up. Just try to relax, and enjoy it.'

'What she said!' yelled Lloyd from his position in front of the TV. 'And no snogging the dancers!'

As if.

Chapter 2

For the next few days I made sure that I was up and showered before Natalie and Lloyd woke up. I crept to the bathroom, praying that they wouldn't hear the boiler, and tried to get out of the house before seven-thirty, having put two teabags into two mugs and left them by the kettle.

They had done nothing specific to make me feel unwelcome, but each time I sat absentmindedly watching TV and enjoying a chocolate digestive, Natalie would loom over me with a side plate, saying nothing, yet everything, with a tight smile.

I didn't want to abuse their hospitality any more than I wanted to feel like an unwelcome guest, so I tried to stay out of their way whenever possible. Consequently, I was the first one in the production office for the initial few days of the job. By Thursday things had changed: I arrived at my usual hour – which would have been cripplingly early for me only a couple of weeks ago – but the office was

11

nearly full. Once I'd hung up my coat I wandered over to Matt's desk.

'Oh, hey there,' he smiled. He slid his arm around the back of his computer monitor to turn it on. Once again he was wearing an outfit that wouldn't have looked out of place on an errant boy band member. The same jeans as earlier in the week, but this time he had some sort of semi-coat, semi-lumberjack shirt on.

'Hi,' I said casually, trying not to betray the fact that I had been momentarily distracted by his chosen look for the day. 'Tea? Coffee? I'm off to the tea bar.'

'I'd kill for a coffee, thank you, lovely,' he replied.

'No problem, coming right up. Hey, what's the deal with everyone being in so early today? Usually I have the place to myself.'

'First live broadcast tomorrow, isn't it? They might not be voting anyone off this weekend but it's the first show. This is calm compared to what you'll see in thirty-six hours.'

'Oh my god, of course. I can't believe it's Thursday already. I'd be sick with nerves if I was one of them. How are they doing? Anyone seen the dances yet?'

'Well, we'll be down there most of the day and we've got lots of rehearsal footage now so you'll find out soon enough.'

'Down on the studio floor?' I asked lightly, secretly thrilled that I was getting to grips with the Strictly lingo.

'Yup,' replied Matt. 'Now then, coffee?'

'Coming up …'

By the time I wondered back from the kitchen Chloe was at her desk, taking her coat off and hooking it over the back of her chair.

'Oooh, I've just put on the kettle,' I said. 'Do you want something?'

'No thanks, we haven't got the time. I just need to check a few emails and then we should get down to the studio floor,' she barked.

Matt appeared behind her and put his hand out for the coffee, making a mock serious face at me on hearing Chloe's tone. She looked up and nearly caught him.

'While I'm doing this, why don't you to go and familiar-ise yourself with the professionals. We don't want any name muddles, people being directed to the wrong dress-ing room, incorrect names on cue cards et cetera.'

I could barely believe this was my job, and scuttled off to the enormous planning board at the other end of the production office, with Matt by my side. On the wall was an enormous collage of all of the professionals and their celebrity partners. Pinned to them were names, swatches of fabric, small lengths of beading and ribbon, images of couture dresses cut from fashion magazines and some newspaper cuttings from stories that had already run about the show. It was part mood board, part reference point and part planner. There was a whiteboard next to it with a table containing the first few weeks of allocated dance styles.

I gazed up at the faces on the collage. Some were familiar, but others were completely unknown to me. It was disconcerting to see a photograph of the notorious female politician beaming down from between an elegant snapshot of Erin Boag and a cute image of Vincent Simone grinning into the camera. There was an instantly recognisable shot of one of the actresses, wearing a pair of dungarees, one of the rap star baring his shiny teeth, and a gorgeous paparazzi image of Flavia Cacace and Kristina Rihanoff walking along a pavement in tracksuit bottoms, hoodies and sheepskin boots chatting to each other. The entire wall was mesmerising, and I found myself staring.

My eyes drifted to the little corner with a handful of new faces. One was marked Artem Chigvintstev, one Robin Windsor and one Lars, but one of the names was obscured by a photograph of the feisty comedian wearing a pair of spectacles on the end of her nose, holding a textbook. Artem and Robin, with their rugged features, would never have suggested to me that they were dancers. And Lars? Well, the picture of Lars just looked a bit like images I had seen in schoolbooks of Thor. Unmistakably Scandinavian, he had dark blond hair, tanned skin and ridiculously dark brown eyes that turned down on the outside corners. He was wearing a dinner jacket in the image, but there was little doubt that he was a big, sturdy guy. All in all, he was a confusing combination of hot Viking and adorable Andrex puppy. And yet, bizarrely, he seemed strangely familiar. I let out a deep sigh, and as I did I caught Matt looking at me. Hands on hips, one eyebrow raised, head tilted to one side, he was staring at me, willing me to drag my eyes from the board.

'Tough gig, familiarising yourself with the new male professionals, hmm?'

'Ha! You can talk. I've seen the way you look at pictures of Ola. You practically have her name scribbled on your pencil case.'

Good save. I wish I could have high-fived myself.

'Oh come on, it's Ola. Everyone's in love with her. It barely counts!'

He had a point.

'Well anyway, who are these guys? Where have they all come from?' I pointed up at the crop of unfamiliar faces on the board.

Matt grabbed my arm and pulled it down to my side again. 'How do you not know this?' he hissed. 'Keep your voice down or Chloe will kill you.'

I remembered with horror that the launch show had taken place before I had got the job, but after I had applied for it. I'd been so nervous about my application that I couldn't bear to watch, so I'd escaped to the cinema and only returned home hours later once the broadcast was over. The holes in my knowledge were suddenly revealing themselves. The first half of the week had been all about technicalities, but now the sudden realisation was dawning that real people were about to start turning up on the studio floor.

15

'Oh man, I'm in trouble. Who *are* they all?'

'Artem is from LA, via Russia and he's worked in the States a lot. He looks considerably tougher than he actually is. Robin looks more exotic than he actually is – he grew up just outside of Ipswich. Jared is all about the boyband look – he's toured with *Glee* and was in *High School Musical*. Then there's Lars. He's a bit of a wildcard. He's Swedish, and he's dancing with Kelly Bracken. Apparently he's very quiet but very charming. And he's pretty much Scandinavia's biggest dance star.'

'Wow, lucky Kelly.'

'She could do with a bit of cheering up,' he replied, with a chuckle.

I was thrilled to have found someone to exchange gossip with. Kelly had famously just turned thirty, and was busy filming her final scenes in the West Country soap, *The Valley*. She had been a lead for ten years, and had become something of a household name while dating her dashing co-star Jeremy Norman-Knott. But despite his reputation as one of the most charming men in TV, he had recently been up to no good with the star of a cheesy reality show. There had been accents. There had been outfits. And there had been a disloyal friend with a phone camera.

No one had come out of the situation well, not even Kelly, who had done a series of daytime TV interviews insisting, 'I'm fine. No really, I'm *absolutely fine.*' For all her tossing her glossy hair extensions over her shoulder she looked more than a little shaken up. She had spoken a little too freely to some of the weekly magazines about how perfect and impenetrable her relationship with Jeremy was, only to find herself regretting her earlier confidence as the full horror of his infidelity revealed itself. She was now a decade older than a lot of the girls she was up against for her next role, still broken-hearted and carrying the weight of a woman who had spent a lot of time reacquainting herself with her Slanket, her *Friends* DVD box set and a freezer full of Ben & Jerry's. If anyone needed a hot Scandinavian to throw them around the dance floor in front of a gobsmacked nation, it was Kelly Bracken. And I was delighted that Matt had realised that.

'You are not kidding,' I replied. 'I hope she turns up looking sensational and shows us what she's really made of.'

'Okaaaaay,' said Matt. 'Sounds like somebody's a little over-invested.'

'Oh, come on,' I said. 'I thought you loved the show as much as I did.'

'Well, yeah, I love the show. Because I love working on live TV, and on something with such a big audience. But my real dream is to work in news and documentaries, so it's not as if I really care about every single dance.'

'Oh.' My voice was quieter than it had been all week. 'I suppose I thought it was a big deal to you too. I feel a bit of an idiot for letting you know how much I love it now.'

'Don't be silly,' he said. 'It's all great fun, but for me just not the dream, you know? I don't really care about dancing. I don't dance at parties or weddings – even the old folk show me up. It's humiliating. And I can barely tell who's doing well or not out there on the studio floor, so I tend to zone out and see it as just work. I like being part of the team that gets the right shot: that's where the drama lies for me.'

'But the disco balls? You gave me such an amazing welcome.'

'Oh well, how could I not have done that for you when you were standing there all starry-eyed with Chloe slowly boring you to tears? You deserved to see it at its best on your first day.'

I was still a little disappointed by Matt's confession but touched that he had made such an effort.

Tension continued to rise for the rest of the day. I was rushed off my feet, taking tapes of the dancers in rehearsal from the production office to the studio floor and back. When I wasn't doing that, I was ferrying cups of tea and coffee, bottles of water and sandwiches to the production team. It was at lunchtime that I made my first trip to the production gallery, the hub of the operation, with its wall of monitors that gave a spectacular view of the set and the dance floor itself. The gallery faced the famous staircase and was positioned directly above the undecorated area of the set, where I would be standing during the show.

Natasha, the director, was in there with her team, looking down through the glass windows like the pilot of a spectacularly sparkly airplane. I was terrified about entering the room, knowing full well that some of the most important people on the Strictly team would be in there, including my own boss. The tension in there would be thick like smog. When I reached the door I carefully put down the tray of teas and coffees I had been asked to take them, then knocked a couple of times.

As I was standing there, Chloe came rushing out of the door, nearly tipping the drinks over.

'Were you knocking?'

'Yes, I didn't want to disturb, or, um, come in during something important or confidential.'

'Are you telling me that you didn't know that the main production gallery door would be sound proofed?'

I suppose, I was really … The thing is, I *did* know that the door would be sound proofed – absolutely every part of a studio is. But in my anxiety to please everyone, and stay as unobtrusive yet helpful as possible, I had, well, I had forgotten. I was an absolute idiot.

'Yes, of course I knew,' I just about managed to stammer. 'But I just wanted to make sure.'

'Riiiight, well you don't need to.' Chloe made a big show of holding the door open for me and calling 'Drinks coming through!' as I entered the gallery. 'And don't put them down anywhere near the equipment. Liquid is lethal around here.'

My cheeks were burning even though no one else had seen our little interaction.

Things became even more tense by Friday. People had started to use fewer words per sentence, and replaced the lost verbs with cups of coffee. And – finally – the celebrities and dancers had started to populate the studio floor. Almost all afternoon was spent on the band rehearsal, which turned out to be the biggest test so far of my ability to remain calm and collected. There were several things that tampered with this aforementioned professionalism.

For starters, it was the first time I had seen any of the celebrities. Sure, I had seen celebrities before – my mum had taken Natalie and me to see countless dance shows in the West End when we were younger. Musicals had been my obsession – every birthday and Christmas the trip to London had been my biggest treat. I had done work experience on some low rent cable channels, which had seen *Big Brother* contestants from years gone by lapping up the final remnants of their fifteen minutes of fame by presenting obscure game shows.

But these were Strictly celebs: a unique mixture of genuine icons, national treasures and sports legends ... all of them doing something that was utterly new to them. It was that rarest of rare things – nervous celebrities, doing their best, but out of their comfort zone. I was transfixed.

The most common reaction to seeing a celebrity in real life is to compare them to the image you have been carrying around in your mind. It's rarely an accurate image, but a kind of composite of your favourite of their screen appearances, the worst paparazzi shots you've ever seen of them, and perhaps a photo or two that you once snipped out of a magazine because you wanted hair, boots or a boyfriend like them. That picture will have been pinned to your cubicle at work, or carried around in your wallet until it's all tatty. But the image is now ingrained and you're left with a semi-false impression of what they actually look like. This is why the first thing that mere mortals say to celebrities is rarely: 'Hello there. It is a pleasure to meet you. I am a great admirer of both your work and your style, and I look forward to many years of friendship with you.' Instead, they might say: 'Oh. Emm. Gee! You are so much taller in real life!' or 'Woah, you're actually REALLY good looking!'

Like I said, it can be a self-respect Bermuda Triangle. Consequently, I was calm to the point of off-hand when I met the first batch of celebs. Matt and I were on another one of our endless caffeine runs, when the show's director asked us to go down to the studio floor and see if anyone else wanted drinks. We left the production gallery and wandered sheepishly onto the edge of the dance floor.

'Hi guys,' said Matt. His gait and his lolloping arms betrayed no shred of nerves as he approached those waiting to dance. A few of them were sitting on the golden audience chairs between the band area and the judges' desk. Everyone was pretending not to be doing it, but they were all looking at each other, trying to size up the competition. These weren't the confident gods and goddesses I was used to seeing on screen. These were real people, and they looked nervous. Flavia and Kristina were using the backs of a couple of chairs for some hamstring stretches. Despite the tension in the air, they looked fabulous, in tight leotards and stockings with gold high heels. I caught myself tugging at my own clothes, trying to make sure my imperfections weren't on display anywhere near them. Meanwhile, one of the celebrities, an ex-footballer who I remember my dad worshipping all through my childhood, was standing at the edge of the floor, running through steps in his head and counting furiously under his breath.

'Hey,' said Flavia, looking up at Matt.

'Can we get you any drinks? Water, tea, coffee, whatever?' he asked.

'Yes, please.' She looked over her shoulder at the others. 'Guys? Drinks?'

Moments later I was jotting down the list of drinks, while not – I repeat NOT – standing there slack-jawed saying, 'But Flavia, you're tiny, so petite and beautiful!' or 'Oh wow, Brett, you sooo don't look as tall in real life as you do on that soap. What are the sets made of? Dolls' houses?'

By the time I returned from the canteen with Matt, each of us laden with a wobbling tray, the band rehearsal was well underway. It was no longer just the celebrities and their dancers standing around – the band were now in position and rehearsing the music with the dancers for the first time.

It had genuinely never occurred to me how important the music was to the show until that moment. But when I put down my tray and looked up to see Kristina deep in conversation with Gnasher, urgently marking out the beats with her fist in her palm, I realised that the relationship between the band's performance and the dancers' was totally co-dependent. A duff note could mean a duff step, and vice versa.

In the meantime, Kristina's partner, a gregarious musician who'd once had a reputation as a bad boy and was now beloved of housewives (including my mum) up and down the country, was clowning around with the others gathered at the side of the stage. Confidently performing faux-elaborate moves while adding a little human beat box to the amusement of the gathered crowd, he had everyone eating out of the palm of his hand. Suddenly, Kristina clapped her hands and summoned him to the dance floor.

This was going to be the first time I had seen any actual dancing, so I was desperate not to head off set straight away. Matt clearly noticed, as when I looked up, he said with an enormous sense of purpose, 'Er, Amanda, please could you check for cups and bottles we need to take back and throw away? Thanks.'

I tried to smile in gratitude, but the minute he had finished saying it he looked away, picked up his tray, his face utterly deadpan. Kristina and her partner took to the stage, and the familiar voiceover began to play on set.

'Ladies and Gentlemen! Please welcome to the dance floor …'

I didn't listen to the rest, mesmerised as I was by Kristina's last-minute stretches. She appeared to be entirely flat at one point. Oh, to be a proper dancer, I thought to myself, remembering the years I had spent making up ridiculous routines with Natalie when we'd been younger.

Suddenly, the music began and the dancers sprang into motion. Immediately everyone fell silent and watched, held by the now-electric atmosphere. The dance seemed so fast and so nimble. I forgot to maintain any pretence of clearing up cups. But, within moments, the spell was broken. The dancers, who had been so confident, had fluffed their steps and were standing, confused, turning towards the band. The ballroom floor seemed larger; the dancers significantly smaller. They returned to their starting positions again.

The nerves had got to everyone. I sensed I should make myself invisible again. I returned to collecting the empties and followed Matt off the studio floor.

'Wow, wow, WOW!' I whispered, as soon as I thought we'd be out of earshot. 'I can't believe how different it looks in real life! I wonder how the judges find anything to criticise half the time, but now it suddenly all makes sense. You can see everything, every breath, every wisp of hair …'

Matt chuckled. 'Come on, Superfan,' he said. There was a pause while both of us heard Chloe calling us on the talkback system.

'Could you head back to the office please? We need you to collect the guest lists for tonight, thanks.' Chloe's voice sounded no warmer. I felt my nerves returning as the temporary shimmer of life on the dance floor quickly faded. As we headed towards the office, we passed a group of professional dancers congregated around a doorway, chatting. They looked anxious and surviving on exhilaration alone. I realised that however tired I was, they must have been up for hours longer than me, doing physical exercise, and the hardest part of their working day was still hours away. The thought made me want to yawn.

In the production office Chloe was printing out lists and spreadsheets with various colour-coded columns on them. It looked like an admin minefield and I sensed it was coming my way. I must have looked horrified because Matt said, 'Don't worry Amanda, it's only paper. We are going to be The Door Police for a while, with the power to allow people into the magical world of Strictly.'

'Well, I wouldn't put it like that,' replied Chloe. 'But I'm afraid I will need you on various doors at various points this evening. Here's the list. The different colour codes correspond to the seating areas and the status of the guests. Obviously the celeb partners are in the front row, so we can get shots of them ...'

'Heh heh, especially the ones who were competitors last year,' interrupted Matt. My celeb gossip database immediately whirred into action as I quickly tried to work out who he was referring to. Chloe raised an eyebrow. There was a shadow of a smirk on her face. Perhaps she had a sense of humour lurking in there after all.

'… anywaaaaay. Amanda, to clarify. Each of the audience members is on a different colour-coded list. They will be given a wristband corresponding to that list on arrival. This way we can avoid sneaky last-minute seat shuffling. The friends, family and key celebs are seated where we can get shots of them, but everyone else is divided pretty equally. It is simply too disruptive to have people swapping around at the last minute.'

She handed me the sheets of A4 and six bags, each filled with different coloured wristbands. She looked me straight in the eye.

'Do not let anyone change their seats. These seats are allocated. Okay?'

'Yes, Chloe,' I replied. I felt as if I was being told off. I wasn't though … was I?

The first show was due to start that Friday evening, so before we were due to take up our door duties, Matt and I headed to the canteen for a late lunch. It had felt a bit like a high school canteen to me all week, but now that I had a clearer idea of what all of our roles were, I wasn't sure where to sit. While we were queuing for our pies, pushing our trays along the three metal rungs towards the till, I noticed a pretty girl about my age. She had dark hair, pale skin and red lips. A cross between Snow White and a fifties cigarette girl, she was one of the most put-together people I had ever seen. Her lips had a perfect Cupid's bow shape, which although created with make-up, didn't make it any less cute. Her hair was cut in a dark shoulder-length bob with a blunt fringe that looked as if it had been cut with a razor. It was shiny in a way that finally made me understand my northern granny's expression about looking 'like boot polish'. She was wearing a black dress with a wide belt, which perfectly accentuated her curvy pin-up girl figure. It seemed fair to assume that she was a celebrity from a show I wasn't familiar with. A kids' TV presenter, perhaps? She gave us a hesitant smile as she approached, picking up a tray for herself.

'Hi there,' she said in a soft Scottish accent. 'Do you mind if I interrupt?'

'Of course not, go ahead,' replied Matt. He was sooo giving her the once over.

'Thanks.'

'How can we help?' I asked. Matt now had his back to me and it was clear that if I wanted to be included in this conversation, I was going to have to include myself.

'Well, I just wanted to interrupt.'

I frowned slightly.

'What I mean is, I didn't have a specific question. I'm new here, only just started, and it seemed to me that you were having the most fun in the canteen, so I thought I'd ask if I could join in.'

I had to admire her honesty. And she was right: Matt and I had just been having a right laugh. Who didn't enjoy piling mashed potato onto someone's plate with a massive catering spoon and then shaping it into a Close Encounters-style mountain? Who could not enjoy that? No one I'd call a friend, that's for sure.

'Well then, welcome to our people,' said Matt. He put his hands together and gave a little bow. 'You are one of the family.'

'Yeay, thank you! I really didn't want to eat with the rest of the make-up team. I've been with them all day, I feel like I need someone, a bit, well, a bit … more relaxed.'

I laughed.

'That's us! Irresponsible, underpaid and too silly to know any better …'

'Excellent news,' she replied, with the kind of crinkly nosed smile that made me think she could be a lot of fun. 'I'm Sally. From make-up. Yes, I do a lot of the fake tans.'.

'In that case I declare you the hardest working woman on Strictly,' I said, picking up a Wispa from the display at the till, showing it to the cashier and putting it onto her tray. 'Let me get you this.'

We spent the meal chatting and joking about the rest of the team, and our experiences with the dancers and celebrities so far. Who we'd seen in action, whose costumes looked exciting and who were our personal favourite dancers. It was the first time all week that I had felt as if I was even vaguely among people like myself. Despite Sally's glossy looks, she had a really warm manner, and I knew that she was the kind of girl I could be great friends with. All too soon the meal was over and Matt and I went to the office to collect our coats before beginning our shift outside on Wood Lane.

We left via the back entrance to the building, passing by the doughnut-shaped courtyard made famous by so many comedies and *Blue Peter* broadcasts. On the other side of the security gate a queue was already forming, even though it was hours until the show began. Matt took one entrance and I took the other. I had queued once to see a panel show recorded here. This time I was on the other side of the velvet rope, and instead of wearing sparkles, I was wearing discreet black clothes like the rest of the production team. It felt like a uniform, a badge to show that I was one of them. I shivered with delight.

Ninety minutes later, I was shivering for different reasons entirely. The thin Converse trainers I had been wearing all week, specifically to fit in, now seemed like the footwear decision of a maniac. It was freezing, and I desperately wished I'd worn boots instead. I dug my hands deep in to the pockets of my Parka, raised my shoulders and did my best to keep smiling.

Luckily the excitement among those queuing was enough to keep my spirits high. Beneath everyone's winter coats I could see flashes of sparkly shoes, satin dresses and jewel-coloured cuffs. Several of the men were holding umbrellas over their wives, gallantly trying to protect their hair and make-up. Each couple looked as if they were on a once-in-a-lifetime date, which in a way they were. And apart from the love-struck there were also some mums and daughters, gossiping and observing every little thing. As I checked people's names off the list they smiled and chatted with me, and I helped them on with their coloured wristbands, making the same joke again and again about whether it would go with their evening wear.

Then, just as I was starting to fade, Matt came up to me and shoved one of his hands deep into my pocket. What the hell was he up to?

'For you,' he said, before darting back to his post. I dug into my pocket till my fingers reached a woolly ball and then realised what he'd done: he had just given me his gloves.

'Thanks mate!' I called over to him. 'What a star!' He waved me away casually.

An hour later, all of the guests were safely inside the building and we had guided them to their seats without too much hassle. As Chloe had warned, a couple of gentlemen determined to show their wives a dream night out tried their hand at changing to a seat in the front row, but Matt and the team were there and we managed to keep everyone happy and correctly seated. I don't know how I concentrated though, as I was constantly doing crazy double takes every time I saw faces I recognised.

Finally, once every guest was seated, and a few final checks were made, I saw on one of the monitors in the green room that the warm-up comedian had taken to the stage. Matt appeared at the doorway, doing ridiculous jazz hands.

'It's SHOW TIME!'

'Yeay!'

'Come on.' He took me by my sleeve and led me up the stairs to the studio floor. Slowly, silently, I followed him onto the set and to the position opposite the staircase where various crew members were assembled. We settled down just as the audience burst into applause to welcome the judges. The men were looking dapper as usual and Alesha was stunning in a black sequined gown with her hair pulled back and up in an elaborate do. I was fascinated to see them interacting with each other, shuffling around and settling down for the performances. Eventually, I started to get calls on the talkback system starting down the countdown before air time. Eventually the theme music began and I knew that the show was now broadcasting live.

I felt a lump in my throat, remembering all of the evenings I had spent watching Strictly over the years – curled up with my flatmates at university, the show an inevitable part of the build-up to Christmas with my family. And now I was here, a part of it.

The celebrities and their dance partners started to appear from the top of the staircase opposite us. Like nervous peacocks, they strutted out, both more glamorous and more human than they ever seemed on television. And so many of them! I had forgotten how many there were at the beginning – I definitely hadn't seen this many of them at rehearsal that morning.

As the theme music reached its climax the dancers had finally descended the glittering staircase on either side, and were now all lined up in front of me like the most bedazzling chess set in the world. They were all smiling, but I could almost see the adrenaline coming off them. Each, in their own way, was revealing his or her nerves. My eyes scanned them from left to right, comparing heights, hairstyles and outfits. As I reached the final couple, I gasped out loud. Because there, next to soap star Kelly Bracken, was Lars, the new Swedish dancer. But he wasn't just Lars, he was the man from the puddle, the gorgeous man I had bumped into outside of the studios, the owner of the Giant Man Chest. It was him. And he must have seen me gasp. Because, at that very moment, as the camera turned away, he winked at me.

Chapter 3

Lars's wink completely threw me, and the show passed in something of a blur. The lights, the movement, the live music and applause all conspired to make me feel as if I was actually part of the performance itself. Even though I was exhausted, by the time the final score began, I was utterly bewitched by the entire thing.

Despite it all, I did try to observe the technical aspects of putting the show together. It all seemed so slick; everyone in their positions seemed so calm. The preceding days were frantic and seemed as if they'd never happened. The only person who seemed to be expending any real energy once the show went live was Anthony, who was operating the Steadicam. I had never done any work experience on a show that used a Steadicam, and while I knew that they were considered the coolest of the cool, I had no real idea why. Until I saw Anthony in action.

The camera itself was not attached to anything ... except Anthony. All of the other cameras in the studio were either on wheels, handheld or suspended from cranes or the ceiling. The Steadicam was strapped to Anthony by means of a giant harness. It was an arresting sight: Anthony, the dad of a giant metal and plastic camera-baby, which he was carrying in a custom-made sling.

But what I wasn't prepared for was the way Anthony leapt onto the dance floor with the dancers during the dance. He had a small set of camera cards pinned to his right, which showed him when his shots were needed. I knew all this already. But the first time that he just stepped up and over the footlights, and onto the floor, I couldn't believe my eyes. Then, following the dance, he joined in with the swoops and leaps, only a few feet away from dancers. What I was so used to seeing as a dance for two, I now realised was actually something even more incredible: a dance for three, one of whom was in a pair of rather sweaty looking khaki shorts and some sturdy, black walking shoes. Again and again, Anthony leapt across the stage getting the most majestic shots. Each time, once he had captured what he needed, he leapt off the ballroom floor just as nimbly and vanished into the audience. By the time the final dance ended, he was sweating buckets and all of his cue cards had been ripped away.

Fascinating though this was – and I cannot make my admiration for Anthony clear enough – my heart was hammering in my chest throughout at the thought of Lars. Obviously, I watched him studiously for the entire time he was on stage. Did he have a nervous twitch? Or just a wonky eye? Could he *really* have been winking at me? I wasn't convinced, and told myself it must have been the result of staring too hard at the lighting gallery. Nevertheless, I was the living embodiment of swoon. I was swoonalicious.

As Bruce and Tess waved goodbye for the first time in the series, and the theme music exploded onto the set once more, the audience burst into delirious applause, and the crew all started to high five and hug each other. I felt numb, tingling from head to foot. This was actually happening to me.

Matt tugged my sleeve. 'To the bar?'

'Oh yes, I'd love to!' Matt had no idea how much I was looking forward to heading to the bar with the cast and crew: a chance to check out Lars, and see if he really had recognised me.

'Awesome. Let's get Sally on the way.'

Ooh, does he have a little crush? I thought to myself, as we climbed a draughty staircase up to the make-up area. We picked up Sally, who was looking resplendent in a black 1950s style shirt dress and a bright red belt, and headed towards the bar. We could hear the music from the other side of the fire doors, and as Matt held them open to let us in, I felt as if we were walking into the greatest party in London that Friday night. The crew, the production team, the celebrities, the dancers and all their friends and family were in there unwinding, gossiping and giggling. I even spotted Chloe chatting to some of the lighting team, looking the most relaxed I had seen her all week.

'Ladies,' said Matt. 'May I help you to a glass of the BBC's finest white wine? Or will you be having something else?'

'Do you know what, Matt? I think I'd bloody love a voddie and tonic. Do you want some cash?'

'No, don't worry.' He put his hand out and rested it on the top of Amanda's arm reassuringly.

'Yep, I'm all about the wine tonight. Thank you!' I replied. Matt headed to the bar and I turned to Sally.

'I am not kidding when I say that that was one of the most amazing things I have ever seen in my life. Have you ever seen a live show before?'

'No, it bloody knocked my socks off too. They looked so great, didn't they? I can't wait to see how they all progress. And isn't it fascinating how you can see how really, really nervous they all look. The telly gives everyone a bit of a confidence sheen, I think.'

'You're so right. You really feel you're living it when you can see it from the studio floor.'

'Yeah! Now I know why my brother is always going on about live venues and gigs. He's always banging on about festivals, and I always sit there thinking. 'Why bother? I prefer watching them from the comfort of my sofa and not from a muddy field.'

'I can't think of enough ways to agree with you about the festivals.'

'But now, hearing the live band, seeing the dancers live … I can see where he's coming from. There's nothing like hearing the beat of the music actually rattling your ribcage, is there?'

From over Sally's shoulder I saw Matt sliding his wallet into his back pocket and picking up the three glasses. He navigated his way through the hubbub towards us. Then, as he approached, I saw another face turn to mine: Lars. He had had his back to me, and I had not realised it was him. The person he'd been talking to, who I now realised was a fan, was walking away, flushed. Left alone, Lars had turned to face me and smiled again. He stepped forward towards me. As he did, he stood in Matt's path, knocking the drinks he had precariously balanced between his two hands. The contents splashed over the edges of the glasses and onto Matt's sleeve.

'Oh my goodness, I am so sorry,' he said to Matt. He seemed very charming. His English was perfect, slightly formal in tone.

'No worries, pal,' replied Matt. 'No harm done.'

'I was just coming over to say hallo to my old friend, Cinderella,' continued Lars. I felt the heat rush to my cheeks, and dug my nails into the palms of my hands. I couldn't speak, and just lifted a hand to my chest.

'Yes, you,' he said to me. 'I rescued you from that puddle the other day. Everything okay?'

Sally had been watching the entire interaction, enthralled, her head flicking back and forth between Lars and me like a spectator at a tennis match. I opened my mouth to reply but she interrupted, sticking her hand out.

'Lars, it's Sally. From make-up. I took care of Kelly earlier, but I think it's my colleague Jeanne who looks after you. Lovely to meet you, I am a good friend of Amanda's, a bosom buddy really. And this is Matt.'

'Well, hallo everyone. It is lovely to meet you. It is good to see that Cinderella is in such good hands.'

'Her name is Amanda,' said Matt, as he handed me my drink.

'Thank you,' I mouthed at him, still too startled to talk properly myself. I smiled at him. I smiled at Sally. And then I smiled at Lars.

'Well, this is just … lovely!' I yelped. My voice sounded weird and high pitched, betraying the intense awkwardness of the situation. I couldn't work out what was making me feel so uncomfortable. Perhaps the fact that Lars had winked at me earlier, or the way that he was being so solicitous, as if we were old friends. Or perhaps it was Matt, who was looking ever so slightly disgruntled.

'Yes, it was lovely to see you, Amanda. Do take care, and I look forward to working with you.' After he said this he looped his arm around my waist and leant in. He kissed me once on each cheek, pulling me in so close that I could feel the heat emanating from his soft, worn t-shirt. I swear that chest was wider than the bed I slept in at university. He gave the others a small wave, muttering 'a pleasure' and wandered off into the crowd.

I let out a huge sigh. Sally was standing facing me, her hands on her hips and her head tilted.

'What. The. HELL. Wasthatallabout?'

'Nothing, it was nothing, we haven't even really met.'

'And yet he calls you Cinderella?' Matt was as incredulous as Sally, although his tone was little sharper.

'I saw him for the first time the other day. I fell in a puddle on Wood Lane, and he helped me up. And cleaned my shoe and stuff.'

Sally grabbed my arm, gripping it like a baby with a rattle.

'And now he calls you Cinderella! That is the hottest thing I have ever heard! Hotter than the sun!'

'Yeah, fairytales. Hot stuff.' Matt took a huge swig from his pint. His sourness was suddenly very unappealing.

'I knooooow. I can't believe he recognised me!' I leant in to Sally, whispering so that no one else could hear us.

'I'm not kidding, Amanda, it's been really nice knowing you this week, and I'm sure you are a really lovely person. But you owe it to all of womankind to do your best here. He is severely hot, you saw the reception he got out there. I want to know more. And you're the woman for the job. M'kay thanks!'

'Yeah, like that's totally going to happen. Yup, definitely.' I shook my head at Sally. Was the woman insane?

'Some men are just born charming, and he's one of them,' said Matt. 'It doesn't mean he's a good person. Or

39

that it's a good idea for you to leap into bed with him. Where's your self respect, woman?'

'Matt, did you not hear what I just said? It is perfectly obvious that nothing is going to happen. Can we all just stop talking about this now?'

'You can stop talking about it. But it doesn't mean I have to stop thinking about it.' Sally gave me a sailor's wink and picked up her coat. 'Well guys, thank you for the drink, but I think it's about time I hit the road myself. Hackney is not going to come to me before bedtime.'

We gathered our stuff and headed to the tube. Sally leapt straight on the Central Line, whereas Matt and I had to wait for different branches of the Circle Line, heading in different directions. For two minutes after an awkward hug goodbye, we sat on opposite platforms, both pretending to fiddle with our phones, until my train finally came. I looked over my shoulder to wave at him as the train pulled away but he was engrossed in his messages, and didn't look up.

Matt's odd tone in the bar made me stop and think for a moment, but it wasn't enough to upset me properly. The evening had been too momentous for that. From the lights to the costumes and the live audience to Lars himself, I felt as if I was finally living the kind of life I had dreamt of last summer when I had been waitressing at Sergio's. Yes, I was exhausted, but I finally felt as if I was a part of something. And that something was special. I might never make it as a professional dancer, like my eight year old self always wanted, but I could still be a part of this world, which was magical enough for me.

As I turned my key in the door, I resolved to tell Natalie what an evening it had been, and make sure that she knew how much I appreciated all she had done for me. But when I entered the flat, the lights were all off. They were obviously in bed. I took my Converses off at the door, mindful not to mess up the carpet again and headed to the spare bedroom. I hung my coat up on the back of the door and turned to the bed. Aaaaaah, bed, I thought to myself.

But there was a small note there, and next to it were my hair straighteners.

Amanda, you left these on. They have marked the carpet. I think we need to chat about this in the morning.

My heart immediately sank. I clearly remembered turning the hair straighteners on before I got into the shower that morning, so pleased that they'd be ready to use as soon as I needed them. But I had, of course, become distracted by my phone and then the decision about what to wear and had ended up running behind schedule. Which meant I never used them at all. They must have been on for hours, and even the safety catch would not have worked until after the carpet had been marked.

The Strictly bubble had burst. No matter what I did, I was always going to be Natalie's irresponsible little sister. I wiped my face, and headed to the shower, where I stood under the hot water for ages, slumped at the thought of such a silly mistake ruining an otherwise dreamy day. As I pulled the covers up under my chin and curled into a tiny ball, I realised there was only one thing for it: I would have to find my own flat, and fast. For the first time in my life, I really needed to not be Natalie's little sister. I needed to be me.

Chapter 4

It was one of those mornings: you're only half awake and you roll over, cocooned and cosy, burrowing deeper into the duvet without a care in the world. And then you remember. Something had upset you the night before, only you're not quite awake enough yet to remember what. You hug the duvet a little tighter, scrunch your eyes shut, and then ... yup, it hits you.

I lay there, pretending to myself that I was still asleep, and trying to fool my body into believing that it was still totally relaxed. But it was having none of my tricks and the minute I remembered the snippy tone of the note from Natalie, I felt the nerves knotting in my stomach once again. I curled into as tight a ball as possible, clamped my eyes shut, and tried to block it all out. I needed to concoct a plan that would enable me to be out from under Natalie's feet for as much of the weekend as I could.

But my older sister is hard to ignore. As I lay there trying to still the anxieties whizzing around in my head, I heard her slippered feet shuffle into the kitchen and her starting to unload the dishwasher. The clanking of the crockery and glasses being put away was followed by the low rumble of the kettle, and finally, the repeated clinks of the teaspoon against mugs as she made tea.

I suppose I knew that she wasn't actually trying to wake me up. I knew that I had been awake already. But every clink and clank sounded like Morse Code. 'You need to find your own place', 'How much more do we have to do for you?', 'When are you going to learn to be a proper adult like the rest of us?' I sighed and rolled over. I could ignore it no more. I needed a plan. And if I had learned one thing that week, it was that plans need coffee. So I pulled on a pair of tracksuit bottoms, and a battered old hoodie that was a favourite for slouching around in, and silently left the flat within five minutes.

Natalie and Lloyd lived in South London near a huge common, which in the crisp, bright autumn air, looked like something from an idealised mobile phone advertisement. There were joggers with matching running kits and spry ponytails which bounced with every step, young dads peering into prams at their unfamiliar newborns, and couples holding hands as they walked through the leaves. All this, and the sun was twinkling down on the lot of them. It was enough to make me want to vomit.

Who were all of these people? How come they were all so self-possessed? Why did they seem to hold the keys to some kind of secret universe of adulthood? What did they know that I didn't, which let them behave like extras from a Scandinavian lifestyle magazine? By the time I had negotiated my way past the brightly coloured buggies outside the cute deli on the other side of the common I was filled with despair, bordering on rage. It was as if last night at Strictly had never happened. The sense of possibility, camaraderie, glamour – it all seemed further away than ever before.

I took my coffee and a pain au chocolat, and sat on a bench on the edge of the common, surveying what now looked like a parade of autumnal happiness. I felt ridiculous to have finally got my dream job only to feel consumed by loneliness and hopelessness. It was so indulgent. What was wrong with me? I took my mobile phone out of my pocket and called the one person I knew could shake me out of this mood: my godmother, Jen.

'Hello?'

'Hi Jen, it's Amanda.'

'Well hello, darling. How are you, city girl? I'm surprised you have time for me!'

Jen sounded thrilled to hear from me, but then she always does. She's been a friend of my parents since they were newlyweds and has known me since the day I was born. While I have never doubted that my mum wants the best for me, I always feel that Jen – mum's best friend – wants the best for me, as well as the most fun possible. She's less inclined to worry about the formalities and more likely to cut to the gossip. As well as being a proper laugh, she is someone I trust implicitly. When I was a teenager she never failed to let me know that I could talk to her about anything I didn't want to discuss with mum, and that it would remain in her confidence. I've rarely taken her up on it but knowing that she is there has made all the difference. She is everything you could want in a godmother.

'So … were you at the show last night?'

'Of course, it's my JOB now, don't you know?'

'Well, la di daa, I am so sorry. Would you do me the honour of letting me know how it is all going? Is it everything you dreamed of? And … are they?'

'Are who?'

'The dancers! You can't kid a kidder, darling. Are they gorgeous? Do you get to talk to them?'

'I suppose so. A bit. Obviously we can't just butt in and pretend we're their best mates, just like in any job. But, you know, we're working together so we have to talk to each other about some stuff. And then of course there's the bar …'

'I knew it! You're partying with them! Please tell me you've met Lars. Is he gorgeous? And what about that cutie Jared?'

'Yes, I've met both of them. And yes, they're both gorgeous. I've probably talked to Lars more than Jared though. He even knows my name …'

'I don't believe it, I don't believe it. I am going to have to get a glass of water.' I heard the kitchen tap running.

'Well, I say he knows my name, but he also knows my shoe size.'

Much to Jen's enormous pleasure, I told her the story of Lars, the shoe and the puddle. She was hooting with delight, and before I knew it, I was doubled up with laughter on that park bench. The Fifteen-minutes-ago Me would have walked by and hated the Now Me.

'So you're having a ball? It's everything you hoped for?'

'Yes, it's amazing.'

'And how's London treating you? Have you got used to city living?'

'Well, I'm still at Natalie and Lloyd's ...'

'Ah. Do I sense a problem?'

'Yeah, a bit.'

'You were never going to be able to stay there forever.'

'No, I know, it's not that. I don't think they're about to sling me onto the street or anything, it's just that I think I have annoyed Natalie with my messiness in the flat. And now everything I try to do just makes it worse. I want to find a place of my own now, but I don't want to seem ungrateful, like I'm running away, either.'

'You've got to take control, sweetie. Tell her the truth. She only wants you to be happy.'

'She wants me to be happy and she wants her carpets to be clean.'

'Of course she does, she worked hard for that house. But she's not crazy, she's just house-proud. And she's also used to her own space. I know dealing with this kind of life crap isn't as much fun as the foxtrot, but you've got to get a grip of it before it gets a grip of you.'

'I know. I just feel as if everyone else knows what they're doing so much more than I do.'

'Oh honey,' Jen roared with laughter. 'No-one knows what they're doing in life, especially the adults. We just get better at hiding that. Now then, you're going to start looking for your own place, and you're going to go back and give Natalie a big hug. Can we get back to hearing about that gorgeous Lars now please?'

I drained the last of my coffee, told her about Lars's mesmerizingly low-cut training t-shirts and headed back to Natalie's, stopping to get two extra croissants on the way. As ever, Jen had made me feel as if the world was there for the taking, if only I bothered to take it.

When I got back to the flat it was silent and Natalie and Lloyd's door was closed, so I put the croissants on a plate and left it on the kitchen table with a note.

I'm so sorry about the hair straighteners. I promise to pay for any damage. Please let me organise dinner tonight?

Then I ran a bath, complete with a generous splash of the bath oil that I had been given for Christmas the previous year. There had never been any point in using it when I was still living at home, as mum's potions and products would always have drowned out the delicate rose scent, and if truth be told, I had been saving it for a romantic rendezvous. But, inspired by Jen's words about grabbing life by the scruff of its neck, I decided Saturday morning was as good a time to indulge as any, and moments later I was luxuriating in Natalie's lovely bathroom, flicking through a magazine and listening to the radio. When I finally got out, I made sure I cleaned up, immaculately wiping the mirrors and neatly folding the bathmat over the side of the tub. I was so fastidious I could have committed a murder in there and Natalie would never have known.

I was wandering back to the spare room when I caught sight of Lloyd in the kitchen, munching on one of the croissants and reading my note.

'Hey, Lil Sis,' he said, with a wink. I loved Lloyd, but I hated it when he called me that. It made me feel like a toddler, hair in bunches, who needed help with my laces.

'Hey,' I replied, clutching my toiletries to my chest, trying not to get any drips on the kitchen floor as I stood in the doorway.

'So you're taking us out to dinner tonight then?'

Yikes. I hadn't actually meant that I was going to take them for dinner. There was no way I could afford that. I had intended the offer to be one of a curry or pizza in front of the telly. But what could I do now? Refuse to take them to dinner, even though I was living in their house, rent-free?

I chewed the inside of my mouth, then replied. 'It's the least I can do. What do you reckon?'

'Well, I'm up for it. Never say no to food. Natalie's just getting up, let's ask her in a minute.'

What I really wanted was to try and get Natalie on her own, to explain the misunderstanding. But my hopes were dashed when she appeared behind my shoulder.

'What are you asking me?' She kissed the side of my head and manoeuvred around me into the kitchen. Lloyd passed her the note. She picked up the other croissant, clearly assuming he had bought it, and read. Seconds later she looked up.

'Awww. Thanks, Chicken. That would be lovely. And listen, sorry about my note last night. I was just really tired, and in a bit of a crabby mood. I should probably not have left it out like that, and just spoken to you this morning.'

She was being so sweet. I realised I might have got myself into a right state for no real reason. I hadn't had my first pay cheque yet; I barely had enough money to pay for my tube fares all week, let alone for a meal for three in swanky South West London. But I knew there was no real way to get out of it, so I hugged Natalie and said 'Great. Just let me know where's good,' and headed back to the spare bedroom.

I flopped onto the bed, wondering how I was going to negotiate this dinner without making everyone concerned feel worse. My phone buzzed on the duvet next to me: a text message. I picked it up and looked at the screen.

BABE! I am in town for the weekend. You around this afternoon?Text me up.xJ

50

It was Julia, one of my best mates from college. Probably the coolest friend I've ever had, she was currently in Milan doing a placement as part of her BA. She was one of the girls I had missed the most over the interminable Surrey Summer, and I was thrilled to hear from her.

> How come you're back? Where are you? Can't wait to see you. xx

After pressing send I didn't let go of the phone, hoping that Julia would get back to me as fast as I had to her. I was in luck.

> Coolio. Soho? An hour? Jx
> See you there. xx

Leaving my dinner apprehensions behind, half an hour later I was on the tube, whizzing up to Tottenham Court Road, my head swimming with all of the gossip I had. We met in an Italian coffee shop on Dean Street that we had been going to ever since I began visiting her during my university holidays. Julia, who had grown up in London, seemed to have known about places like this all of her life. I was sure that her grandmother was one of the original generation of post-war coffee-shop girls who had spent her evenings necking expressos and dancing the jive with men in immaculate suits. We ordered sandwiches and perched on stools at the shiny 1950s laminated bar.

'What the hell are you doing in town then?'

'Massive family party tomorrow – I had it written down in my diary in the wrong month, or I would have told you that I was going to be around slightly sooner. My mum called on Wednesday to check what flight I was on and I realised my mistake. Luckily I had bought tickets for the right weekend, but just written it down wrong or I'd be in serious trouble.'

This was the kind of scrape that Julia got into – and out of – the whole time: I always took dance classes while I was at school, and then at university I carried it on with the local Salsa society, but Julia would just turn up every few weeks to keep me company or to check out any new dancers I'd been telling her about. She never paid any attention to what the instructor was telling us, but managed to fit in with the rest of the class without her somewhat unorthodox technique drawing too much attention to the fact that she barely turned up. In fact, the only reason that she ever seemed to catch the instructor's eye was because she would walk in looking so dramatic, and be so charming that most of the men in the room would be bewitched by her. If I could have had an ounce of her nonchalant confidence when I was not in Salsa classes, I do not think I would have been so devoted to dancing for so long. For Julia, the dancing barely mattered: she brought her personality to the class. For me, I needed the dancing to bring out my personality.

So I didn't dwell on her sudden appearance, having seen her come up against such scrapes before. Instead, we got down to the serious business of two months' worth of news. By the time we had got through our sandwiches, a massive bottle of San Pellegrino, and four coffees, we had just about covered her love life with an Italian boy who was clearly never going to be a long term prospect for as long as he continued to live in his mum's beautiful Milanese apartment, her applications for internships at Italian fashion houses, my total lack of any romantic action over the summer, and my new job at Strictly.

'That is such fantastic news,' said Julia, fiddling with the spoon in her coffee cup. 'I'm so glad you're working on a proper show now. And the dancing! I bet you can't believe it. All those salsa nights at Uni ... Have you actually shown anyone that you can dance yet? I bet you haven't even mentioned it.'

My sheepish expression told her all she wanted to know. She was right. I had told no one about the number of dance classes I had taken over the years, or my passion for actually dancing myself. It seemed so crushingly embarrassing to admit to it when surrounded by the very best in the industry. I didn't mind my colleagues knowing how passionate I was about watching dance, and about the show. If anything I thought that could only be a bonus in the eyes of my bosses, even if it did make me feel like a bit of a dance-nerd around people like Matt. But to admit to being a dancer myself? I'd rather die. It would put me in the position of being such a wannabe, such an opportunist. I didn't want a single person to think that I was only doing the job as part of a dastardly plan to become a dancer. I was serious about my job, and about television. Dance was a passion. I was clear about the two, but I did not want anyone else to become muddled.

'I knew it! Why don't you say something? I bet one of the professionals would take you for a quick spin.' She sniggered. 'A dance … you know what I mean.'

I giggled too, and then opened my mouth to tell her about Lars, but thought better of it. Julia was so feisty, she would build it up into something it wasn't, and I didn't need that kind of pressure. But I was too late; she had spotted me.

'What?'

I waved my hand to try and brush the conversation away.

'Oh come on, what? Tell me …'

'It's nothing.'

'It's not nothing or you would just say. It's clearly something, and that's why you have gone all coy.'

I rubbed my face with my hands, trying to diffuse the situation by not looking at her. She sighed.

'Oh, now there's only one thing for it.' She looked up at the guy behind the bar, catching his eye instantly. 'Could we get two glasses of Prosecco please?'

I sighed, and opened my mouth to protest but I was immediately 'shushed'. As the waiter put two glasses down in front of us, but before he'd had a chance to fill them, I suddenly blurted out 'One of the dancers is completely gorgeous and I have chatted to him a bit and he seems quite flirty, but honestly I don't want you to get your hopes up because nothing will happen, and I can totally tell that Matt thinks he's a bit of an idiot too.' Finally, I exhaled.

'Woah, woah, woah!' The barman stopped pouring, immediately. 'No, not you Lorenzo! Amanda, you. Calm down. Breathe. I only wanted a bit of gossip. Please, rewind. Who's the dancer and who is this Matt and why do you care so much about his opinion anyway?'

The barman moved to pour the second glass, trying very, very hard to pretend he wasn't listening. I could see his smirk, and suddenly felt self-conscious discussing the show in public.

'The less said about Lars the better—'

'So he's called Lars?'

'Yes, but I don't think we should talk about this here ...' I rolled my eyes towards the barman to try and convey my anxiety to Julia.

'Oh Lorenzo won't mind, will he?' The barman winked at us.

'I 'ear too mach in this jab to remember eet all, the gassip.'

'Seriously, forget you heard *anything*,' I replied.

'Okay, okay, let's forget about Mr L. Who's this Matt then? Is he any better?'

'Oh Matt, he's lovely.' I broke into a grin. 'He's a real honey. He's totally helped me this first week, really shown me how things are run, been someone I can talk to, that sort of thing.'

'Sounds cute.'

'Yeah, he's great.' I paused.

'Ri-ight …'

'Oh no, nothing like that. Nothing at all. He's not boyfriend material'

'You're sure? How do you know?'

'Yes, of course, we just work together. And anyway – he's not a dancer. Seriously, it's not even that he's not a professional dancer. He doesn't even dance at weddings. I think he's one of those guys who even at their most drunk can only manage a little bit of swaying.'

'Just checking. You seemed to go a little misty-eyed just then.' I felt the heat rising in my cheeks, as I began to blush.

'It's probably the booze,' I said swiftly, raising my glass to hers. But I knew Julia wasn't going to press the issue, as she knew how much going out with a guy who could dance meant to me. Obviously I knew that a girl like me couldn't demand a Jared Murillo kind of guy, but as dancing was so important to me I had always maintained that I couldn't get serious with someone who was not relaxed on a dance floor. My romantic ambitions weren't as high as those couples who performed scenes from *Dirty Dancing* at their weddings, but I was not going to compromise on a bloke who wouldn't even dance with me at someone else's wedding. I didn't want to be the girl dancing with her friends while her boyfriend nursed a bottle of beer and talked about the football on the sidelines. I wanted someone who would be relaxed, hold me properly and then offer to dance with one of the doddering aunties. For me, that was charm, confidence and chivalry.

'Yes, probably is the booze then.' Did I see Julia wink at Lorenzo at that point, or was I imagining it? Either way, I didn't want to encourage them so I looked down at my watch. It was much later than I had realised.

'Oh my goodness, I've got to get back. I'm taking Natalie and Lloyd out for dinner tonight and we haven't even decided where we're going.'

'How come?'

'Urgh, I'm staying with them. It's my final chunk of news.'

'Oh, urgh. Natalie's an absolute doll, I can't say enough good things about her, but those two are loved UP. I can imagine being in their palace of perfection could get to a girl after a while.'

I remembered what Julia's room had been like at university – the messiest I had ever seen. Clothes, plates, books heaped everywhere. It was a wonder to us all that someone as glamorous as her could regularly appear from a room like that. If anyone would understand the pressure of living with Natalie and Lloyd, it would be her.

'It's just not really working out.' I sipped the rest of my drink, and reached for the hook beneath the bar with my bag on it. 'No real reason, just two sisters under one roof. I think Natalie wants her own space and I—'

'Don't have anywhere else to go?'

'Exactly.'

'Yes, you do.'

'Er, no I don't.'

'What I mean is, I might be able to help.'

'Seriously?'

'Yes, my friend, Allegra. Remember her? She did Italian with me? She's half Italian, now living in London?'

'Yeah, I think so.' I really hoped that she wasn't talking about the girl I thought she was.

'Well, she's living in Shepherd's Bush now, just moved in. Only she was supposed to be moving in with an Italian friend who decided at the last minute that she was too homesick and wanted to go back. They'd signed the contracts and everything, so now Allegra's frantically trying to find a flatmate. I think the other girl said she'd cover a month or so but after that Allegra's on her own.'

'What's the catch?'

'There is no catch! Stop being so doom-laden. Maybe, just maybe, it might work out?'

'You know what, maybe you're right.' I smiled and picked up the bill that Lorenzo had placed in front of us. I noticed that the two proseccos were not listed.

'Excuse me, Loren—'

'Shsh!' he said, with a wink. 'You take-a care, ladies.'

'That was so lovely of him,' I said, looping my arm through Julia's as we walked out onto the street, having settled up.

'He's a doll,' she said. 'He's been keeping an eye on me since I was fifteen.'

'Sweet. I could do with someone like that. Although Matt has been lovely this week.'

'He sounds great.' Julia gave me a nudge in the ribs. I giggled.

'You're evil.'

'No, I'm not. I'm amazing.'

'I know. It's been such a treat to see you.' We were now approaching the tube, where I knew we'd be heading in different directions.

'Listen, I'm going to call Allegra now. Promise you'll get in touch with her?'

'Of course. If I can't be your flatmate any more, I might as well take the next best thing.'

'Ha! I miss you, babe, even in Milan.'

'Yeah right …'

'It's true. Keep in touch. Let me know how it pans out. All of it.'

'Oh you'll hear about it all.'

'Yeay!' We hugged, and descended into the tube on separate escalators.

As my carriage rumbled under the river, I sat fiddling with the strap of my bag, wondering if there really was a chance that this flatmate master plan could work out.

The answer was waiting for me when I left the tube station and felt my phone buzz in my pocket.

Already spoken to Allegra. If you're up for it, text her asap. She's seeing people this week for the room.

I replied immediately, then sent a quick text to the number that Julia had attached. By the time I reached home I was already feeling positive about where 'home' might soon be.

Natalie was snuggled up on the sofa when I walked in, and Lloyd was nowhere to be seen. Natalie looked over her shoulder at me as I stood by the doorway to the sitting room.

'Hey sis,' said Natalie.

'Hey sis,' I replied.

'All good?'

'Yeah, I went to see Julia, she was unexpectedly in town.'

'Lovely stuff. She well?'

'Yeah, great.' I drew breath. I was dreading what I was going to say next. 'Listen, do you guys know where you want to go for dinner tonight?'

I had decided on the tube that I had to be up front about this, especially if I was going to start paying rent sooner rather than later. It was part of my new 'Grabbing Life By the Scruff of the Neck' plan.

'No, Lloyd's out at football. I haven't had a chance to really talk to him about it yet.' I sat on the arm of the sofa, and Natalie turned down the volume on the TV, sensing I was embarking on a proper chat.

'Okay, because … well—'

'… it's okay, I know what you're—'

And with that, the clatter of Lloyd's football boots on the tiles outside announced his arrival home. Like the properly trained husband that he is, he swung the front door open, while staying on the step to take the muddy boots off.

'Evening ladies!' he yelled into the doorway.

'Hiya!' replied Natalie.

Moments later he was in the sitting room, drenched with sweat, his offending boots on the door step.

'Everyone okay? I'm starving! I'm going to grab a shower and a beer from the fridge. Anyone else?'

'No thanks!' said Natalie and I, simultaneously.

Perfect, I thought to myself, now I can speak to Nats alone. But at that moment her mobile rang and she answered it straight away.

'Helloooooo!' she shrieked, sounding thrilled to hear from whoever it was. I sighed and took Lloyd's football boots to the back door, resigned to having to have my financial confession in front of both of them.

When Lloyd had finished in the shower he headed for the fridge and got out a bottle of beer, before wandering back to the sitting room in his dressing gown, rubbing his hair with the huge bath sheet that was now around his neck.

'I tell you what ladies, and I don't mean to be rude …'

'What?' said Natalie, with a slight frown. I sat up in the armchair I was in, ready to scurry away if a domestic was brewing.

'I'm absolutely shattered. I'm not sure I'm up to going out. How about we get a DVD and a takeaway?'

'That's what I was thinking!' replied Natalie, before I had a chance to say anything. 'But only if you want to, 'Manda. I know you wanted to take us out.'

I wasn't sure if it was a set up, an act of extraordinary sensitivity and generosity on their part, or just a happy coincidence. Either way, I concentrated on trying to keep my enormous relief to myself.

'Oh, that's fine,' I said. 'But I'll get it, yeah?'

'Only if you're sure, but it would still be a real treat,' said Natalie.

'Thai? Anyone for Thai? Ooooh, I could do with some noodles.' Lloyd was already up and fishing around in the drawer with the takeaway menus in, holding batteries and spare keys and odd pens. 'Any objections?'

Moments later we were huddled around the menus, planning our feast. It was agreed that Lloyd and I would collect the food, while Natalie went down the road to pick up a DVD. Lloyd seemed no less excited about the food an hour later when we were in the car. He pulled into a side road near the fancy Thai takeaway place on the common, and as I looked at the bars and restaurants rammed with people out for a big night, I felt consumed by relief at the way the evening had ended up. It wasn't just that I had got away with keeping things vaguely under budget, I was also really looking forward to hanging out with Natalie and Lloyd after a week of avoiding them, especially as I had yet to break the potential good news about the Shepherd's Bush flat.

I got out of the car with my wallet and phone shoved into the pocket of my hoodie, and walked along the parade of shops and bars. As I passed a bar I had been to with Natalie over the summer, I glanced in and saw a couple sitting in the large curved glass window. It was her handbag that caught my eyes initially – an adorable clutch bag with a bright, bold cherry motif on it. But then I noticed what they were doing. He had the girl's hands in his hands, and was turning them over. He was really studying them, in a strangely tender way. Her fingernails were immaculate, painted a perfect red, and shaped into neat 1950s tips. I looked up at her, and realised it was Sally. She was looking directly at the man's face. I followed her gaze, and realised that the man was Matt. I immediately felt my pulse quicken. What were they doing? I had no idea that they were a couple. Had they always been together? Had they hidden it from me? I carried on walking, anxious not to be seen, but deciding to try and get a better look on the way back to the car. I was shaken. It wasn't the idea that they were a couple, but the thought that they might have been keeping a secret from me. If they had kept that under wraps, what else could they be telling half truths about? I thought I had made friends in my first week at Strictly, but now I wasn't so sure.

The takeaway was ready, and I paid as fast as I could, no longer caring about the price. My fingers strummed on the counter top as I waited for my payment to go through, and I barely said thank you to the girl behind the till. I was too busy wondering if I should pull my hood up as I retraced my steps to Lloyd. Deciding it was too much, I rammed my wallet back into my pocket and left the door swinging behind me. I approached the bar, my head down, and slowed my pace, ready.

The window was empty. Matt wasn't there, Sally wasn't there, the cherry bag wasn't there. A group of sporty look-ing blokes in rugby shirts were approaching the window corner, congratulating each other at having bagged such a prime table.

I got back to the car and sat down in the passenger seat. I felt strangely defeated. The huge spike of adrenaline I had experienced on seeing Matt and Sally was still washing through my body, except now I had nothing to do with it but wonder why it was there at all. There was no real reason for me to care what they were up to on a Saturday night, so why did I?

'Get a whiff of that food!' said Lloyd.

'Yes, delicious,' I replied, absentmindedly.

When we were back in the kitchen unloading the food, it quickly became clear that they had given us someone else's order. What we had been given was a far fancier selection than what we had actually ordered. I immediately called the restaurant and explained, but the manager was charming about it and said that as it was their mistake, we were welcome to keep everything.

'It's a new girl,' he said. 'She's not quite there yet but we've got faith in her.'

I smiled to myself, wishing I had been nicer to the girl who had served me when I'd been in there. We were in the same boat, after all.

'Well,' said Lloyd, stretching back on his chair when I relayed the manager's explanation. 'It's not the evening we expected at all, is it?'

Indeed it isn't, I thought to myself, biting into my first prawn cracker. Indeed it isn't.

Chapter 5

I used to hate Sunday evenings. Since childhood they reminded me of homework anxieties, boring telly and an overwhelming sense of non-specific sadness.

Lloyd had a different approach to them, and decided that the way to conquer the Sunday Night Blues was to turn the evening into 'an event'. Natalie had told me about this in the past – it was one of the things that she found adorable about him when they had started dating, but I had always thought it sounded strange. It was almost a kind of machismo, him wanting to take on the worst six hours of the week and win. I had never seen him in action, until now.

It was life changing. Once he had returned from his inevitable sporting pursuits, Lloyd spent the rest of the day planning a big roast dinner for early evening. He was rubbing salt and rosemary all over his lamb, hacking up potatoes with an enormous knife, the sort that you only ever get given on your wedding list, and bashing spices around in his mortar and pestle. He loved every minute of it, returning to a kind of caveman state that was more endearing than I had imagined it could be. Meanwhile, Natalie got on with various household chores and I spent the day catching up with emails, talking to mum and dad, and doing some preparation for the week's work ahead. I checked out all the Strictly blogs, what people were saying about the weekend's shows on Twitter and Facebook, and then ransacked my suitcases to try and find something a bit more interesting to wear to work. I still didn't feel I had got it quite right yet. The dress had been too formal, but then some of the other runners, and of course Sally, dressed really well for work. I didn't want to look like a slouch in the fashion stakes, so I set my mind to some serious accessorising, with Natalie's help for a while.

Of course, Lloyd's battle versus Sunday night later saw him emerge the glorious victor. We gorged on the roast and enjoyed a bit of Sunday night telly, and once again the atmosphere was more relaxed than it had been during the week. I felt like my stay with them might not be a relationship-trasher after all. I told Natalie about the potential flatmate vacancy and she seemed genuinely thrilled for me rather than just excited to get rid of me. It was only as my head hit the pillow and the glow of family warmth started to fade that I remembered the fleeting glimpse of Sally's hands in Matt's. Why was it still bothering me so much. What was I going to do about it in the morning?

If only that had been the biggest of my problems by the time Monday morning arrived. Despite my painstaking efforts to keep Natalie's house as ship-shape as she liked it, I broke a cereal bowl while trying to prepare my breakfast (it flipped off the edge of the counter while I was stretching up for the cereal). Then I got drenched on the way to the tube (my umbrella was safely under my desk at work), and sat all the way from Tottenham Court Road to White City with the insistent beat of a middle manager's Bruce Springsteen sprouting from his headphones (noise wasn't the only thing he was sprouting; his ear hair was repulsive). I arrived at TV Centre sweaty and dishevelled, and feeling about as productive as the pair of discarded false eyelashes I saw in the lift up to the production office. But, as the lift doors opened, I took a deep breath. Life, I was coming to get you – ready or not.

Matt looked up as I came in.

'Morning, Princess.'

'Morning, you,' I replied.

'Good weekend?'

'Yes, thanks, you?'

'Yeah, you never guess—'

'Enough chat you two, we need to look at these tapes that have come in from the off-site rehearsals.' Chloe had appeared as if from nowhere, carrying her inevitable clipboard, about eight video tapes, her BlackBerry and a cup of coffee. I reached out to help her get everything onto the desk without major spillage.

'Thanks, Amanda.'

'No probs.' Part of Plan Monday was to get to the bottom of Chloe's frosty attitude. I had chatted to Natalie, who I suspected was utterly terrifying in her own office, about the situation at the weekend, and she assured me that what I was reading as coldness might just be professionalism. I had promised Natalie I would bear this in mind next time that Chloe came at me, but first thing on a Monday morning, it was pretty hard to take.

Half an hour later Matt and I were sitting at our desks, side by side, working through the tapes that had arrived so far. We had to take notes on the routines and how they were choreographed, so that we could refer back to them each week to make sure that none of the routines had ended up looking the same, what with the dancers often rehearsing all over the country and not seeing each other until the end of the week. We also had to make sure that all of the floor was being used over the course of the show, so that the audience got the very best of it.

This was one of my favourite parts of the job, examining the way that dancers were developing their routines and the celebrities were improving as dancers. I had adored the dance classes I had taken all my life, and this little window into the creative process of such high-level professionals was a treat. I could never have dreamed of such an experience when I was taking salsa classes above a pub, and the biggest competition I had ever witnessed took place in a municipal sports hall. Suddenly I was in the thick of it.

The first couple featured were the sportsman I had seen in dress rehearsal the week before and Erin, his elegant partner. They were totally focused, concentrating on every step, with little or no time for larking around. He was treating the routine as an athletic puzzle that needed to be solved, while she seemed effortlessly fluid with almost every movement. Even with messy hair and in nothing more than scruffy cotton rehearsal clothes, she was a pleasure to watch. Her high-heeled feet led his across the floor of the local gym, little flashes of gold beneath the baggy tracksuit bottoms. I tipped my head to one side and smiled to myself, thinking how lucky I was.

I felt a tap on my shoulder. It was Matt. Although we were sitting alongside each other, we each had headphones on, in our own personal little bubbles of concentration. That suited me, as I still wasn't quite sure whether to confront him about what I had seen on Saturday night. It was none of my business, but then, why hadn't he told me? I turned to him and lifted the headphone from my left ear. He was giggling.

'Look at you!'

'Oh, it's gorgeous watching them,' I replied. 'So interesting how they put it all together.'

'Suppose. I just take the notes on where we need cameras and where we need to cut, and I kind of stop seeing the dancing.'

70

'How can you? Look at the shoes, for starters.'

'They always look so odd, those shoes with the exercise wear.'

'I love it. So glamorous. The idea of wearing gold shoes even if you're in stretchy, scruffy, everything else.'

'But it looks crazy.'

'I know, that's the point. The gesture of having something utterly fabulous on, just to practice in. It makes me think of that incredible outfit that Grace Kelly wears by the swimming pool in High Society – barely practical, but completely goddess-like.'

'You could hardly go to the supermarket like that though.'

'Yes, you could. That's what is so magical: that there are still people in the world wondering around on a Monday morning in strappy gold sandals and tracksuit bottoms. It's the kind of knowledge that makes getting out of bed worth it.'

'Whatever makes you happy.'

'It does, it really does.'

'So why don't you just buy some? Seriously, what's stopping you? We're getting our first proper pay packets next week so you could get a pair.' I thought about the rows of boxes that arrived at TV Centre from International Dance Shoes each week, and how simple it would be to buy a pair myself. It seemed as likely as having Aliona's red hair.

'I guess I'm just not that kind of girl.' My eyes returned to the screen, and my headphones returned to my ears. I think Matt replied, but I had spotted Chloe in my peripheral vision and wanted to look busy. She walked past, ignoring me entirely. I carried on with my work.

By lunchtime my eyes were swimming with images of the famous foxtrot and the celebrity salsa, and when I turned to ask Matt if he wanted to go and get something to eat, his seat was already empty. I assumed he was needed elsewhere, as I couldn't see Chloe anywhere either. I decided to go and find Sally instead. As I leant over to pick up my bag, I saw the screen on my phone glow, and realised that I had a new text message.

> Hi, it's Allegra. If you are interested in the room I would love to meet. Are you around Friday afternoon? x

I felt a rush of adrenaline at the thought of my potential new flat, and replied immediately.

> Yes, you're Shepherd's Bush, right? I'm working at TV Centre so could get to you very easily. No probs. Amanda x

It might be a bit of a push to get to the flat and back in my lunch hour, I thought as I shoved my phone into the back pocket of my jeans, but I was desperate. I didn't want to mess Allegra around or let anyone else have a chance to get in there first, so I decided to worry about that nearer the time. Now, lunch. I set off towards the make-up department's offices to find Sally. She wouldn't be doing any actual make-up today, but I knew they'd have a planning meeting with costume design, and I might be able to catch her in time.

The corridors between departments at the BBC are long, wide, and glossy. And, because of the fire doors every hundred feet or so, they are largely sealed in silence. The floors are shiny to a point that you can almost see your own reflection in them, and, most importantly, almost all of them are curving around the circular shape of the building. You can rarely see further than about twenty metres at a stretch. Several times last week I had imagined how much fun it would be to skid down them in a pair of thick winter socks and on one occasion, while I was rushing along behind Chloe, I felt an overwhelming compulsion to simply cartwheel down the wide, gleaming hallway. This time, alone in the corridor, my head filled with the choreography I had been watching all morning. I felt an irrepressible urge to dance. After all, there was no one there. No one would know. It would only be for a few seconds.

I lifted my arms into position, one around my imaginary partner's waist and one on his shoulder. And I began to waltz. Gently, gliding, imagining the band playing in the silence of the corridor, I closed my eyes for a moment and pretended that it was me on the dance floor, being whisked around by a hero in a dinner jacket. The rain outside, the hairy ear man on the tube, the anxieties about Chloe – they all melted away for a few seconds as I spun along the corridor, softly counting the beat beneath my breath. I felt myself dancing in a way that I hadn't done for years – it was as if the corridor was going on forever. In fact, the corridor did seem to have stretched somewhat since I started my little dance. I opened my eyes, still spinning, and realised that I was waltzing straight through a pair of double-glazed fire doors. Which were being held open by a smirking Lars.

I stopped immediately. Already flushed from the routine, my cheeks were now burning with shame. Lars remained stationary, leaning on the open fire door, as I pulled myself together. Then he did a little bow, as if he too were dressed formally for a waltz. He wasn't though: he was in a pair of loose fitting jeans and a white vest top. His arms, which I had never seen before, were almost as splendid as his chest.

'You move beautifully,' he said.

'Thank you. I was, er, just messing around.'

'If that is how you dance when you are messing around in a corridor, I can only imagine how magnificent you are elsewhere.'

I stared at him, placing the cool backs of my hands onto my cheeks in a futile attempt to ease the flushing.

'You're very kind.'

'You're very good.'

'I'm very hungry.'

'I'm ravishing.'

74

'Ravenous, darling, ravenous.' At that moment one of the costume designers appeared from the meeting room we were now standing outside. Immaculately dressed, immaculately coiffed and immaculately manicured, the man, in his mid-fifties and with his spectacles pushed to the end of his nose, peered over them and looked at each of us in turn. 'You are of course ravishing, Lars. But in this instance I do suspect you meant ravenous.' Just as quickly as he had appeared, the designer had scuttled off down the corridor.

'Whatever,' shrugged Lars, and gave me a smile, his chocolatey eyes turning down at the corners. 'I'm going to eat.' He gave me a wink and wandered off towards the canteen.

I stood by the door to the meeting room, my hands still on my cheeks, and waited until Sally finally appeared.

'Hey you!' she said, catching sight of me.

'Hey, thought I'd come and see if you wanted some lunch.'

'Absolutely, I'm starving!'

'Yeah, ravishing,' I replied, under my breath.

'Eh?'

'Never mind,' I replied, already wondering if that exchange had actually happened. Sally and I decided on the sandwich shop rather than the main canteen and sat munching away for a few minutes before I thought the moment was right to ask how her weekend was.

'It was cool, nothing special,' Sally replied. I looked down at the handbag by her feet. It was the same one, decorated with the cherry motif that I had seen in the window of the bar on Saturday night. I wasn't mad, I was sure I wasn't mad. But did I dare ask outright?

'What did you get up to?' I asked, brushing my fringe away from my eyes so as to appear as casual as possible.

'Well, the weirdest thing happened—'

The barista behind Sally dropped a tray of used crockery that he had been carrying back to the kitchen. The cups and plates smashing to the floor were deafening, and splashes of cold coffee sprayed up from the wreckage. Sally jumped in her seat, feeling a spatter of coffee on the back of her tights and leapt to rescue her handbag.

'I'm so sorry, I'm so sorry,' said the barista, who immediately ran to fetch a heap of napkins for Sally.

'It's fine, don't worry about it,' she replied, although I could tell she was flustered.

Eventually the mess was cleared away, and the two of us were offered free coffees, by which time I had had a text from Chloe saying that I was needed back in the office asap.

At the end of the week it struck me that Sally had never got round to telling me what the weird thing that happened at the weekend was. It was my lunch hour and I was on the bus heading down Wood Lane towards Allegra's flat, sitting on the upper deck looking down at the traffic, with the side of my head resting on the window. The week had gone by in a flash. Things were starting to seem more like routine now, and my confidence in my work was growing, but I knew I still had a lot to prove.

I hadn't seen Lars since the waltzing incident, but I had continued to work closely alongside Matt, who was proving to be every bit the dream work buddy. Strangely, the closer we got, the less I felt I was able to ask him about Sally. I tried to drop comments about her into conversation when I could, with my very best 'casual' tone of voice, but all of his replies were in an equally unreadable casual tone. He certainly seemed very fond of her, but he never referred to her as his girlfriend, or even as someone he had had a date with. Yet, I knew what I had seen. I decided to assume that whatever there was between them was in its early stages and they weren't ready to talk about it. I understood that, but it did make me feel a little awkward; as if they were keeping a secret from me, no matter how understandable that secret was.

I looked up and realised that the bus was barely moving. It would probably have been quicker to walk, as we had yet to navigate the entire one-way system. I had chosen the bus as I didn't want to arrive at Allegra's looking flustered and hot, but I was starting to think that I would be just as flustered from the stress of willing the traffic to move a little faster. Cyclists wobbled in front of the bus, a young mother pushed a pram yards from the pedestrian crossing causing us to miss a green light, and people got on and off at every stop. My chances of getting to Allegra and back in my lunch hour were becoming slimmer by the minute. Consequently, when I finally rang the doorbell of the flat just off Goldhawk Road, my heart rate was considerably higher than it would have been even if I had sprinted there in dance shoes.

'Hello?' There was only the trace of an Italian accent in her voice. 'Come on up, I'll buzz you in.' I pushed open the door and crossed my fingers.

I walked into the communal hallway and up the stairs towards the first floor front door. A small, dark-haired woman about my age opened it. Allegra had cropped hair with a blunt fringe. She was wearing ankle-grazing jeans, a navy and white striped t-shirt and old-fashioned penny loafers. She looked both adorable and stern, as if she were daring any admirers to call her a 'slip of a thing'. Her smile betrayed real warmth though, as she reached for my jacket, and showed me into the kitchen.

'Come in, welcome. Shall I take your coat? Can I get you a coffee?' Her manner was quite formal, bur her smile genuine. I realised that her tone might just be a result of English not being her first language, although she spoke it beautifully.

'Oh no, I'm fine. I can't really stay too long,' I replied, following her into a sunny kitchen with wooden floorboards, neat countertops and a circular plastic table at the far end. It was clean and tidy, but not a creamy palace of sophistication like Natalie's. 'I'm just on my lunch break from work, and I don't want to be back late.'

'I see,' she said. Then, suddenly opening her hands wide, said 'So, this is the flat. Take a look around, and let me know if you have any questions. Please, make yourself at home. The room on the end is the one that is available.'

I tentatively wandered down the small corridor to the bedroom that she had mentioned, and saw that it was bigger than I imagined – certainly bigger than Natalie's tiny spare room – and that it had a lovely view onto the flat below's garden. It wasn't fancy, but it was homely. The bed didn't make me shudder like some of the rental properties I had seen at college, and the carpet had no trodden-in chewing gum. More importantly than any of these details, I could imagine myself living in this flat. I wasn't intimidated by inch-deep carpets that I could only imagine myself ruining, it was close enough to work to make life much easier, and it was somewhere I could imagine my mum popping round to without being horrified that I was days from developing rickets or making friends with a rat.

I went back into the kitchen and told Allegra I loved the flat. She seemed pleased but then looked me straight in the eye and asked

'May I ask though, do you have a boyfriend at the moment?'

'No, not at the moment, but, I'm not exactly not looking. I mean, I'm not not looking, and nor am I looking, I'm just … Oh never mind,' I replied. I wasn't quite sure what she wanted to know. 'Why?'

'Well, I am looking for a female flatmate, not two new flatmates. I am not sure that I could live with someone who was with their boyfriend every night.'

'I understand. No-one likes to spend their Sunday evening on the chair watching a movie with the couple on the sofa.' After my time with Natalie and Lloyd I fully appreciated Allegra's anxieties, and the fact that she had asked me outright suggested that she also might not be the kind of flatmate who would leave passive aggressive post-its about buying the next pint of milk. Someone I could live with.

Then, I froze, realising that I had totally assumed Allegra was single. She hadn't corrected me, but nor had she acknowledged what I had said at all. She just looked pensively out of the kitchen window for a moment. I closed my fist, feeling the palms of my hands starting to sweat with nerves that I had said the wrong thing, or that someone else might have taken a shine to the flat – someone less gaffe-prone.

'So,' I said casually, 'how many more people are you planning to see?'

'Only one more person. A guy. Everyone else that I saw seemed like the kind of girl who was a little bit too needy. You have a job you love, you are happily single, you seem like a woman I could respect. This is all good, but perhaps I need to live with a man.'

'Thank you.' Had she just complimented me? I was struck by Allegra both calling me a woman, and someone she could respect. Every other flat-mate bargaining situation I had been in the past had been based on somewhat more trivial issues. Allegra was talking to me like an adult, despite her being tiny, and no older than me. It was unusual, but I liked it. Someone honest and straightforward: now that was a challenge I could rise to. Becoming a man to get a flatmate: not so much. But we started chatting about past experiences with flat sharing, times we had spent with Julia and friends we might have in common. Her frankness was a tonic, although I was still a little unnerved by her self-composure.

I heard a clicking from behind me, I turned and saw that it was coming from a gorgeous 1960s-style retro clock on the wall. A clock that was striking the hour. I was horrified to see that I only had ten minutes to be back at my desk. The calmness of the flat had made me forget the time entirely.

'Oh my goodness! The time! I have to go!'

'Of course, I am so sorry to have kept you.' Allegra didn't seem sorry at all. She didn't seem to understand why I was panicking. I left the flat as fast as I could, barely saying a proper goodbye to her, and ran onto the road. I only had a few stops to go but I knew that ten minutes was the absolute best case scenario, and that I could definitely walk it in fifteen minutes. I decided to walk, and just run to the stop if I saw a bus coming. I suppose I barely need to tell you that a bus whistled straight past me while I was still shutting the front door, and with that I knew I was running back to the office.

Five minutes later I had a text from Chloe.

On studio floor in 5 mins pls thnx. C

I knew that there was no way I could be on the studio floor in five minutes, but I didn't want to admit to her that I was still racing back from lunch. I thought I could buy myself some time by replying though, so I immediately sent back.

Okay, on my way, see you there. Amanda

It wasn't exactly a lie, was it? I *was* on my way ... I might have got away with my half truth if I had not encountered every single red light on the Shepherd's Bush Green one way system. I waited at crossing after crossing while traffic whistled by, sensing the predicament worsening with every passing minute. By the time I got to Wood Lane I was almost sprinting, breathless and too scared to look at my phone, which I had heard buzzing twice more during my trek back. I didn't want to know if it was Chloe chasing me up, and I couldn't face bad news from Allegra about the flat if she had decided to reply immediately.

I smoothed my hair down in the glass-rotating doors of the main entrance and crossed my fingers as I rushed past a group of electricians, winding enormous lengths of cable around the outside of the studio itself. Then I crept around the side of the set, slowly, hoping to create the impression that I had been there all along.

No such luck. It was as if Chloe had sensed me approach, as she immediately spun on her heel from her position in the middle of the dance floor and looked at me, steely-eyed.

'Amanda, good of you to join us. Did you manage to bring the tapes that the team in the production gallery needed?'

I had no idea what she was talking about, and realised with a shudder that the answer must lie on my ignored mobile phone. I felt the eyes of everyone on set turn to me. If tumbleweed grew in West London, a great, big, fluffy ball of it would have wafted past us all at that moment. I opened my mouth to speak, unsure of what would actually come out of it.

'Here they are.' That was not my voice. I looked to my left. There was Matt, holding the materials that Chloe had asked for. How did he know?

'Thank you, Matt,' said Chloe, returning her gaze to her clipboard.

I looked across at Matt, who was ignoring me entirely. Chloe headed off the dance floor and up to the production gallery, and I left the set to return to the office. As I walked behind the Strictly staircase Matt followed me and crept up behind me. Once he was walking parallel to me, he put an arm around my waist and gave me an enormous kiss on the side of my head.

'Mwah! You're welcome!'

I was floored. I think it was the first time he had actually touched me since the day he had shoved those gloves into my pocket. What was he doing? What about Sally? For the second time in ten minutes, I could barely speak. I squirmed away from him, and he immediately looked embarrassed. Every bit of relaxed confidence he had had around me all week suddenly seemed to have vaporised.

'I knew she needed them, I saw her forget them earlier. And, well, I knew you were going to see that flat to day,' he said, almost apologetic now.

'Thank you, thank you so much,' I replied, truly grateful for him saving my bacon when I needed it most.

I put my hand out and touched his forearm.

'I should never have tried to get to the flat and back in an hour. You've been a real friend.'

Matt looked down. I didn't know where to look. We walked to our desks.

Chapter 6

Allegra texted me a couple of days after my visit and to my enormous surprise she announced in her characteristically formal way, that she would love to live with me. A week later I received my first proper pay cheque, and moved in to the Shepherd's Bush flat the following weekend. I was thrilled. Finally I felt like I was a proper part of city life. My own flat, my own job, my own Oyster card …

Lloyd drove me up from his and Natalie's flat on the Saturday morning and gallantly carried my boxes of books and CDs up to my room, while I trailed behind him with coats and shoes. I spent the weekend settling in, and then on Sunday afternoon Natalie appeared at the door, with a bottle of wine and an enormous lasagne in a beautiful dish.

'A housewarming present!' she announced, 'For you two on your first Sunday night!'

Lasagne was as much of a speciality for Natalie as Sunday nights were for Lloyd, so I knew how much the gesture meant. She came in for ten minutes to look around, immediately suggesting the perfect arrangement for the furniture in my room, and then gave me an enormous hug before saying she absolutely had to leave me to it. I could tell she didn't want to though, and was taken aback by how much of a sentimental loony she was being about it all. She was almost as bad as mum.

'You don't need me any more! I can't bear it!!' she wailed. 'I know I'm behaving just like Mum but I'm just so proud of you. It's gorgeous here and I know you're going to be very happy.'

Allegra looked on bemused as Natalie wiped the tears from her eyes, hugged me again and then leapt into her Golf and drove off. I was thrilled to have such a delicious ready-made supper in the kitchen, but as I went to put it in the fridge, I caught sight of Allegra's one recipe book – a scrapbook of hand-written notes in her own and her mother's handwriting – and realised that perhaps lasagne wasn't such a treat for her. Either way, we shared the meal and the wine, and spent the evening chatting. I soon realised that for someone so softly spoken, Allegra was very sure of herself and her opinions. Having grown up in a big family with older brothers, she was thrilled to be living away from the nest and making her own way in the world. Studying feminist theory and literature she had all sorts of thoughts on womens' representations in culture, and she was gently emphatic about them when we were watching trashy TV together. She absorbed it all, but as far as she was concerned, nothing was as good as Buffy the Vampire Slayer.

Once I was settled into the flat, I got to know what Allegra's likes and dislikes were: that milk left out of the fridge for more than ninety seconds repulsed her, that I should never mention Buffy series 4 and that she showered every day at exactly 7.30. Meanwhile at work, I had learned to keep my head down and keep Chloe as calm as possible. However, there always remained a vague threat that something I didn't know was going on which would stress her out to a degree that she would develop her BlackBerry twitch and go that strange, tense shade of pink.

Sally had had a couple of weeks' holiday that were booked before she got the job so it was just me and Matt. We were getting along nicely together, almost as if that moment when he kissed me had never happened, although occasionally it would replay itself in my mind. Meanwhile, there was another constant ticker tape running at the back of my head: Lars. We'd bump into each other from time to time, and none of those moments ever passed without some kind of wink or smile. He seemed endlessly amused by me, but also genuinely interested in the fact that I was such a dancing enthusiast. So many of the rest of the crew were just fans of the show and saw it as a job in live TV, but for me it was all about the dancing techniques, which formed a perfect arc across my working week. For the first few days we'd examine the tapes that were coming in from rehearsals and help to set up the staging for the weekend, then on a Friday the dancers and professionals would start to appear for band rehearsals and dress rehearsals, then, on Saturday – the real thing.

Where others saw shots, heard beats or planned frames, I saw dance steps. The week became a blur of potential steps, all building towards that magical hour or two when we finally saw the couples step out in front of the audience in all of their splendour. And every weekend I thought the same thing: I would sell my top teeth to be able to take part in the show, I would love to dance with one of the professionals, I would kill to try on one of the dazzling bespoke dresses … but I would probably die of nerves on the night of the live performances.

The studio is so much smaller than it looks on TV, which means that every week when I would watch the show from the edge of the studio floor I never failed to be mesmerised by how close we were to the action. The week that one of the actresses got her foot caught in the hem of her dress; the unsure magician counting out his steps under his breath; the audible gasp when James Jordan lifted his partner in a breathtakingly gorgeous routine – I saw them all, I heard them all, I sense the mood of the room change with each and every step. It was like living in a childhood dream without having to share a room with Natalie.

In short, I was in heaven. It was Halloween week and I was starting to feel that any day now I was going to be presented with the keys to the City of Adulthood. Maybe it wasn't so hard after all!

When I arrived at work on the Saturday the decorating was in full swing. The show was going to have a stronger theme than ever before and I couldn't wait to see what they had done with the costumes. Sally had only arrived back on the Thursday and was immediately plunged into a world of false fangs, fake grey hair and spookily opaque contact lenses.

I handed Chloe a cup of coffee when she arrived. My attempts to find the jolliness that I was still convinced lay within her were ongoing. Okay, so my attempts were not that successful yet, but I was determined I wasn't going to give up on her for a while.

'I can't wait to see everyone in costume!' I said, turning the mug so that the handle was facing her to pick up.

'When did Halloween become such a big thing? Why are we being so American about it all this year?' she said, in reply.

'Oh, I don't know. I hadn't thought of it like that. It'll make a nice spectacle though ...' My wavering voice betrayed the fact that her sharp reply had already hit my confidence.

'Is the show not enough of a spectacle for you as it is?' Now I just wanted to chew my own fist off. Why, why, why did I even try to make small talk with Chloe? Why was she missing the gene to just engage in a little banter, and why had I been given a double dose of the gene to try so hard? What did I think I was going to gain from it? But above all that, I was hurt that she knew me so little after all these weeks of working together that she might think I was not impressed enough by the show – nothing could be further from the truth.

'Of course,' I muttered by way of an olive branch. 'This is one of the most incredible experiences of my life.' Even that sounded like an apology.

Chloe's mood seemed to lift when show time eventually did roll around and the consensus was that the Halloween special was a true triumph. One of the contestants had done a genuinely moving dance as a statue which had come to life for one night only, another pair had performed an electrifying tango, and one of the cast's older contestants had revealed Anton to be a dancer with as much strength of character as actual strength.

But that night I decided not to go to the bar with the rest of the team: even though I had been looking forward to it, I felt the dreaded burning sensation at the back of my eyes and throat that suggested my body was either bravely fighting off a cold, or standing at the front door, about to compliment one on its shoes and invite it right in. I thanked my lucky stars that I lived so close to the studio and hopped on a bus, leaving Matt and Sally in the bar together with some of the others from production.

Once I was home I made myself a Lemsip and picked up my phone to look at the little batch of texts and calls I was starting to get regularly from those who knew I was working on the show. There was always one from my mum, and it was never without some wild exaggeration such as

> Anton is simply the most gentlemanly gentleman EVER TO HAVE WALKED ON EARTH don't you think??????!

I usually had a couple of little comments and giggles from Jen, who never failed to ask how I was, and then there were some comments from friends either wanting to know which of the dancers were single, or cheeky requests to know who had not made it through to the next round.

Obviously I ignored all of the requests, knowing that my job was simply not worth risking to reveal a thing, but I replied to most of the lightweight gossipy queries that I could. I usually just avoided the actual question and tried to keep people happy with non-specific nuggets of information such as

> Costumes for next week are AMAZEBALLS!

Jen I would usually reply to properly, or even email with more news about life in general. And as for my mum, I could usually keep her entertained with a quick

> I know! Incredible!

or

He's just like that in real life too!

But that night mum's tone had changed: I sensed ambition. Instead of just comment or support, there was a sinister new undertone ... the unmistakable whiff of hinting.

'Oh, it looks like so much fun! I wish I could be there to see you all in action.'

Yeah right, I thought to myself, I bet you do. Now, my mum is without doubt incredibly supportive – she was always there at parents day and she never failed to turn up at school plays or sports days. But she has never been one to keep things to herself once she's actually there. In fact, she used to turn up to things and then sound genuinely horrified if I did not win every single race that I was entered in, or have the most lines in every play that I was taking part in. The idea of her at a live performance was frankly terrifying. Luckily, I had a watertight get-out clause.

It is so amazing, I can't believe it is my job. But it's hard work too! Such a shame you can't come and see the show in action. The tickets are impossible to get hold of! Ballot is done weeks in advance. Love to dad and speak soon xxx ...

That should do it, I thought to myself. Safe for now. Or at least I hoped so.

A few days later Sally and I were queuing for coffee and I decided to broach the subject of audience tickets with her. We had been discussing the merits of various types of facial jewellery, where the rhinestones that she had taken to sticking on the contestants' faces came from and what the best kinds of glues for keeping them safe were. I loved having these kinds of conversations with her as she always took the subject seriously, but never patronised me for not knowing the answers to the bizarre questions I usually found myself asking. Of course, it was pretty much impossible to doubt Sally on anything to do with make-up as she always looked so immaculate herself. Today, she was wearing black, three-quarter length clam diggers, a bold, red and white checked shirt tied at the waist and a pair of red patent leather heels with enormous hearts stuck to the front. They looked as if they could have been made by Disney but she assured me they were only M&S. As ever, her make-up was neat and pretty – perfect 1950s flicks on her upper eyelids and bright, red lips with a dramatic cupids bow. She was telling me about her mum's recent conversion to false eyelashes when I spotted my chance to ask about families visiting, and leapt in.

'It's impossible, isn't it?' she said immediately. 'Everyone assumes that because you're working on the show you have a limitless supply of tickets, as if you're Willy Wonka or something.'

'Exactly, that's what's happening to me too.'

'People ask you how you're job's going because that's polite, and then you're doomed. If you tell the truth they either think you're showing off, they pump you for info you don't have, or they demand tickets. And if you keep it to yourself, they think you're ungrateful and you haven't realised what an incredible job you have.'

'Yes! I can tell that some of my school friends think I'm maybe being a bit aloof about it, or are worried I'm not enjoying it, but I sometimes think that if I tell them the truth I might go on and on about it and never stop.'

'I feel your pain, sister.' Sally got the mug of tea she had been queuing for and chinked it against mine. 'Sucks to have our problems.'

'Good point. It's not the worst thing in the world, but it is frustrating.'

'The only way I ever got around it was when my baby sis came to the studio for band rehearsal. I didn't even mean for her to, she just had to come over once when I locked myself out of my flat and had to drop off keys. I managed to co-ordinate it with lunch, and took her up to the studio floor. I swear I thought she was going to pass out, she was that excited.'

'Ha! I can imagine. It feels like a lifetime ago when I saw it for the first time. My head nearly exploded with excitement.'

'Yeah, it's that bizarre feeling of seeing something so familiar through new eyes. I love it out there though, I really do.' We were wandering back to our desks – well, me to my desk and Sally toward the make-up room – and I felt awash with relief that there was someone else my age on the team who was as much of a fan as I was. Matt always seemed keen to let me know that while he loved the show, he was destined for something more worthy.

Matt … I hadn't mentioned him to Sally for a while. As the first few sips of caffeine hit me, I decided to be bold.

'Me too. It so cool that you get it like I do. Matt always seems a little above it all, and Chloe's just interested in getting the job done. I sometimes wonder if she even sees the dancing at all.'

'I don't see as much of Chloe as you do, but she certainly seems to let the stress get to her. I suspect it isn't that she doesn't care about the dancing, but that she really wants the audience to experience as much of the excitement as we know is taking place. Or maybe she just drinks too much coffee? And as for Matt, he pretends to be above it all, but I know he loves it really.'

'Really?' I turned to look at her, her glossy ponytail bouncing as we walked down another interminable corridor. How do you know? I thought to myself.

'Yeah, he's just a big softie, isn't he?'

'I suppose you would know better than me,' I replied boldly, pressing my fingernails into the palm of my hand, holding my breath for the reply.

But the reply never came. Because before Sally had a chance to draw breath the double doors in front of us flew open and Kelly, Lars' celebrity partner, came exploding through them, shouting into her mobile phone.

'How can you do this to me? Now of all times?'

She was approaching us at quite a pace. Wearing black leggings, a metallic leotard and what I suspected was Lars' hooded top, she was stomping down the corridor in fury. There was a brief pause while she listened to what the person on the end of the line was saying, and then: 'even if you don't love me any more, can't you even respect me? Respect what you've done to me?'

Sally and I looked at each other. She couldn't miss us. She would always know that we had heard this conversation. We looked forward and continued walking. Our paths crossed as Kelly began to shriek, 'You will regret this. I swear you will regret it. You are going to wake up in the new year and realise that I was the best you could ever get. I am a PRIZE. You had me, you had a PRIZE and you lost me. You THREW me away.'

I kept my eyes to the floor, desperate not to look as if I was listening in. I was of course enthralled, and secretly thrilled that Kelly was finally standing up to the grim Julian Norman-Knot, assuming that's who she was talking to. I bristled with knowledge that Sally was in the same boat. Then, as Kelly passed through the second set of fire doors, she dropped the sports bag she had over her shoulder, and its contents started spilling out onto the corridor.

'Do. You. Need. A. Hand?' mouthed Sally at her. She ignored us, one hundred percent focussed on her conversation.

'You have humiliated me. You have made me lie for you. You have broken my heart and then made me doubt if everyone else around me is lying. And you don't seem to care.'

Sally and I looked at each other, then stooped to help scoop up the contents of the bag. It became clear that the zip had broken, possibly under the strain of the amount the bag was holding. I grabbed at socks, dance tights and random items of sports kit made from t-shirt cotton of various colours. Sally discreetly made a stack of the numerous celebrity weeklies, turning them from the pages that they were open on (pages all featuring either Kelly or Jeremy) and returned them to the front covers.

'It ends here. No more interviews. No more lying. Leave me alone. Just leave me alone.' The anger in Kelly's voice was fading. I held the broken zip together and Sally tried to tug it, to at least create a semblance of the bag being back together.

'Please. Just leave me alone now.' Kelly was now slumped up against the wall, with Sally and me kneeling in front of her. She ended the call and looked up at us. A tear rolled down her heavily made-up face, leaving a pale, foundation-free trail down her cheek.

'Thank you, girls,' she said. Her voice was now barely a whisper. 'I don't know what I'm going to do.'

'You're going to be fine!' said Sally. She tentatively put her hand out and rested it on Kelly's upper arm. 'You're an amazing dancer, and everyone loves you.' Kelly gave her a weak smile.

'I don't mean about the competition. I mean about my life.'

'Well, you *are* an amazing dancer, and everyone *does* love you.' Even as I was saying it, I realised that my desperate words of consolation might not help. I could almost see them tumbling out of my mouth like the contents of Kelly's sports bag. Even as I finished the sentence I wished I could cram them all back in again.

'Maybe it's enough for you, dear. But I need more than dance. And not everyone loves me, as Jeremy has very clearly demonstrated.'

'I know. I'm sorry. I just, it's just that, we all want, I hope the competition helps. As a distraction? And then—'

Sally shot me a look. I shut up. Kelly took a deep breath and lifted her glossily manicured nails to her face. I remembered Sally telling me the week before that the shade was one they had blended especially for her. She wiped beneath her eyes.

'Well, thank you, ladies. I would appreciate it if we could keep this to ourselves.'

'Of course,' replied Sally. 'But you take care, and you know where we both are if you ever need, you know, anything.'

We all knew that that would never happen. But we all knew that that was what Sally had to say. The corridor divided and we all went our separate ways. I sat down at my desk, opened my emails, and realised that once again I had failed to get a straight answer out of Sally about Matt. I promised myself that this would change by the end of the weekend.

Chapter 7

It was 1pm when the text message arrived. Up until that point the day had been utter bliss: the first weekend when absolutely nothing had gone wrong. If dress rehearsal days reflected the real thing, Saturday's show would be perfection. All coffee remained unspilled. All nerves remained unfrayed. All tempers remained unlost. I felt as if I was part of a well-oiled machine, moving seamlessly from task to task. We all knew what we were doing, we were all doing it well, and we were all doing our jobs with relish. Tonight, the show would surely be perfect.

Matt and I were printing out the camera cards to give to each of the cameramen when I heard the buzzing of my phone vibrating on my desk. I saw Chloe at the desk opposite mine, tapping away at her emails. She was on her BlackBerry so much, and she never hesitated to contact me via my personal mobile, so I figured that she wouldn't mind me picking it up. If only I hadn't ...

> Darling, am in Westfield with Jen. Dying to see you
> and I have a present. Can we deliver to your office?
> On our way. All hugs, M xxx

My mother was on her way. To TV Centre. To see me.

I did a little gasp as I read the message. I'm no fool, I understand just how efficient the security measures at the BBC are. It's a scrupulous set-up. But ... they'd never had to deal with my mum before. My stomach lurched. I hoped it was just hunger.

> I don't think I'm going to be able to see you.
> Security. And so busy.xx

I needed to nip this situation in the bud. The BBC could not cope with my mum and Jen waltzing up and down their corridors. And there was a real risk that they might actually waltz, as I had already proven. I looked up over the edge of the partition surrounding my desk. Chloe remained focussed, Matt remained at the printer.

> Nonsense darling, I've been in before to see Lloyd.
> Am sure the gentleman at the desk will be charming.
> See you in 20-ish mins!

She seemed to think that there was only one gentleman on the desk at the BBC. And that he might remember her from last time. Did she also still think that it was still 1955? I now knew that my stomach did not want food, but an easy life. I must have been frowning at my phone as Matt shouted over at me: ''Sup, Roberts?' He had taken to calling me 'Roberts' lately.

I held my finger to my lips and mouthed 'Shshsh!'

He mouthed back 'What?' and I gestured to the door. We both headed outside. The minute the office door was shut behind us I grabbed his arm and whispered, 'My mum is in Westfield with her mate and she's threatening to come over and drop something off for me, I told her that she can't come and that we're all busy and that security is really tight, especially on show days, but she doesn't seem to understand and she has just texted back to say that she's sure it's all fine, she's heading over now and she is pretty much definitely going to turn up and cause a scene, any minute now, and I can't bear it because this is the only week when so far I have managed not to do a single thing to either humiliate myself in front of Chloe, or at least do something actually wrong, or something that has just annoyed her in an intangible way and I don't know what I'm going to d—'

'AND BREATHE!' Matt grabbed me by my shoulders and then smoothed his hands across them, as if stroking imaginary antimacassars on my hoodie. I felt my shoulders lower an inch as I finally exhaled.

'What is the actual problem?' he asked. 'Is your mum that much of a liability? She's not going to get in anyway if security can't get hold of you.'

102

'She'll cause a fuss. She thinks that turning up at work is just like school Parents' Day and everyone will be thrilled to see her and want to tell her how I'm getting along. I remember when she showed up at Natalie's office a few years ago and told her boss she liked her haircut, but it was unnecessarily severe. Natalie sobbed on the phone to me for about two hours.' Matt was smirking.

'She sounds fun. I think we should let her in.'

'Seriously, I can't take it. Not today. Everything's going so well.' Matt replaced his hands onto my shoulders.

'What is the worst that can happen? She will be a bit overenthusiastic? She'll say something that will get Chloe's back up?'

'Well, yes, and—'

'And what's the best that can happen? I know how much she loves the show, I know how much you love the show and I know how much she loves you. So inviting her up would be a big deal for her. It *is* time for lunch anyway, no-one would miss us for a bit.'

'Us?'

'Yeah, if she's soooo bad then she'll need both of us to chaperone her, won't she? The Mumwranglers.'

'Have you got time? What about the camera cards?'

'Of course I've got time. We can go down and get her, whizz her around the office and then take her to the studio floor.'

'You would do that?'

'Roberts, what makes you happy makes me happy. We're all part of the Strictly Family now remember.'

'The last thing I need is more bloody family …'

'Zip it,' he said, leaning on the office door and holding it open for me. 'Text her back and say we'll see her in reception in five.'

I didn't need to. When I looked at my phone there was a text message already there.

In reception! So excited!

It was the number of bags that they had that stood them up in comparison to the rest of the professionals in the reception area. They each had three, stiff, cardboard bags on each side of them, and were standing like little icebergs amidst mini-oceans of Christmas shopping. And then, once I had absorbed the noise, it was the volume that struck me.

'Darling! My Strictly gal!' My mum truly had a voice for the stage. She gave me an enormous bear hug, despite being four inches shorter than me, then outstretched her arms at Matt and gave a huge sigh as she said 'Well … and who is this?'

'Mum, this is my colleague Matt. I've told you about him before, you remember.'

'All good things, I hope, Mrs Roberts,' he said holding out his hand. When my mother offered hers in return he took both her hands in his and smiled like a game show host. 'It's a delight to meet you. And I love your nails.'

I rolled my eyes at Jen, who I could tell was on the point of intense giggles.

'How are you, Amanda?' she said and gave me a smacker of a kiss on my cheek.

'Not too bad,' I replied. 'And what a treat to see you!' She smoothed my hair and whispered in my ear 'We aren't intruding horribly, are we?'

'No, don't be silly. It's so good to see you. Just don't let mum get too frisky.'

'She'll behave, I'll see to that.'

I introduced Matt to Jen and the four of us headed for the lift to the office with the mountain of shopping bags. I winced when a department head I recognised from elsewhere in the building had to wait and take a second lift because the purchases were simply taking up too much floor space. But Matt kept the conversational ball in the air expertly by talking them through the week's costumes.

'So, dress rehearsals today, ladies. The costumes are pretty spectacular this week ...'

'What's Flavia wearing?' asked Jen. Flavia had long been her favourite of the professional dancers and she longed to see her on tour.

'It's a bit of a change this week, as she's in trousers,' replied Matt. 'They're doing a jazzy kind of Quickstep.'

'Oooh, that's a bit feisty isn't it?' I was thrilled by the way that the girls were experimenting with costumes more than in previous years.

'It's not as feisty as Katya's outfit,' explained Matt. 'She's got a little sequinned cheerleader's outfit for her chachacha. It's got her partners' name emblazoned on the back like a proper cheerleader, and she's wearing legwarmers, dancing with a rugby ball, the lot!'

Mum grinned at me. I could tell she was struggling to take it all in. 'Are there also some more traditional floaty ball gown type dresses as well?' she asked.

'Oh yes, of course!' I replied. But Matt was already explaining …

'Natalie is wearing a white floaty number, which has silver strands all across her back, and Aliona is doing the Viennese Waltz in a pale blue, or pale green … I think it's a pale green dress which is tight around the bust, but hangs in a breezy style below.'

Matt's descriptions were starting to run out of steam. I could sense him running out of vocabulary with each dress.

'Empire line dresses,' said Mum.

'Exactly!' replied Matt. 'I knew you'd know. And they're lovely.'

I caught Jen's eye. We were as entertained as each other by Matt's valiant attempts to talk dresses.

I led Mum and Jen into the office and helped them to stuff their loot underneath my desk, while Matt stood on indulgently. Then – with much fanfare – Mum produced the present she so urgently needed to drop off: an iron.

'Now darling, I know you think I'm crazy—'

'Think?!' said Jen, smirking.

'—but it's one of those things you only buy once or twice in a lifetime and spending money on an iron is *so boring*, so I thought I should do it for you. You see? I'm not trying to be boring, I'm trying to stop you from having to deal with boring-ness.'

'Thanks Mum, that's really sweet.' I was genuinely touched by the gesture, as it contained all of the back-to-front logic that I was used to from my mum. I gave her a quick hug, and then Jen pressed something into my hand. It was a small box, beautifully wrapped.

'Shall I open it?'

'Of course, it's for you.'

'Now?'

'Of course now, you noodle!'

Slowly, I undid the ribbon and opened the stiff, navy-blue cardboard box. There was a crumpled layer of tissue paper and within that lay a heavy piece of gleaming metal. I pulled it out. It was an exceptionally glamorous keyring.

'Oh my goodness! I can't believe it! It's so fancy!' There were more hugs and squeezes as Matt looked on indulgently. Luckily most of the rest of the office seemed to have gone to get something to eat.

'Well I thought I should keep a *Tiffany's* one aside until you buy your first place, but you can't have your first front door keys and nowhere lovely to put them.'

And that summed up the difference between mum and Jen: they had both given me something that they thought was both necessary and would make life a little more lovely. What different things though …

Matt leaned in to our huddle with the air of a man thrilled to be part of a conspiracy.

'Ladies, shall we … hit the dance floor?'

Mum and Jen looked at each other, and then looked at me. I thought they were going to explode. Mum's mouth was trying so hard to fight the biggest grin of all time. The corners had gone all wobbly and she was squinting her eyes in a desperate attempt to look serious. Her excitement was at surface level, ready to burst out at any point.

'Can we? Can we really?'

'Of course, Mum, but please – a few rules. Only go where we say, don't wander off. Don't try and start talking to people. I know that sometimes they look as if they're talking to themselves, or to you, but they are talking into the headsets that we're all wearing, so that we can hear each other wherever we are on the set. And please, please, please don't say anything embarrassing. Okay?'

'Honestly, Darling. I don't know what you think I am going to do. I'll be a credit to you, I promise.'

I looked down and saw that Mum was wearing one of her favourite pairs of shoes – gold pumps. This visit was no impulsive decision, she had been planning to meet the stars and dancers all along. I pointed her to the office door and we started leading them down the corridor.

The walk to the studio seemed to take forever. At almost every fifty metres along the way, mum and Jen wanted to examine the photographs of stars and shows.

'Look Judy, it's the newsreaders. Don't they look great?'

'Oh yes, it's a lovely shot. Doesn't her hair look charming like that? I wish I could get mine to behave in that way.'

108

This time it was Matt who caught my eye. We managed not to giggle. Just.

'We saw the dresses on the way in too.'

'Oh, they were magnificent,' agreed Jen. 'I can't believe how tiny some of them are.'

I remembered the dresses from series gone that were on display in the reception area. I had stopped noticing them already, but it had only been a month ago that I used a different door every morning so that I could appreciate a different dress each time. For the first week I had been enchanted by the tiny, pistachio-green dress, covered in bead dropper rows, that one of the contestants had worn for a jive with Vincent Simone. I had never thought of the soap star who had worn it as particularly tiny, but the dress seemed fit for a doll, and particularly feminine compared to the imposing façade of BBC reception area. Then I had gone through a few mornings of fascination with the extravagant sapphire salsa dress that Camilla Dallerup, the 2008 winner, had worn. The dresses stood so solemnly in their glass cases, it seemed almost impossible that they had actually been there for all of that drama and passion, they they had once been warm from the exertion of bringing the dance to life. But every now and again as I walked past one and a bit of beading caught the light, I remembered. What Mum and Jen didn't know was that the best was yet to come.

Eventually we came to the staircase that led to the studio. Matt led the way and Mum and Jen followed, holding their

BBC passes out in front of them like old-fashioned press passes in a 1970s cop movie. I walked behind them, trying to hurry them along a bit. The minute that we go to the back of the set Mum adopted an overwhelmingly camp stage whisper.

'Oh darrrling, I feel like a star already!' It was a miracle they couldn't hear her in the LWT studios on the other side of town.

Matt led them around the back of the silver chairs, and up onto the gallery looking down over the dance floor. We silently took seats on the banquette that was perched opposite the judges' desk. Surrounding the desk was an assortment of dancers and celebrities in their rehearsal clothes. Jen grabbed my wrist and smiled at me.

'WOW!' she mouthed, then 'thank you.'

A couple took to the floor. It was Vincent and his partner, an actress of about Mum's age, who was looking pretty sensational after a month of non-stop training. They took to their positions and the band started playing. Mum visibly jumped.

'Oh my goodness!' she whispered, pointing at the band. 'I didn't even see them there! I am so used to not looking at them, and they're so good … you kind of forget that they're playing live.'

'Well they are Mrs R, they certainly are.' Matt was loving every minute playing Mister Charming with Mum.

'I can tell that now – they're sensational!' Mum was sitting at the very edge of her seat, peering down to see the band. Vincent and his partner twirled across the floor, making every step look effortless. It was a sensational routine, a paso doble that was making the absolute best of her acting skills. The two mild-mannered people who had taken to the dance floor a minute ago had now vanished, and it felt almost shocking to see a dance so intense taking place live, with so few people watching.

'Well, I never!' she said as the routine ended with its dramatic flourish. She turned to Matt. 'I have never seen anything like it. I suppose you're immune to the excitement now.'

'Matt doesn't like dancing,' I said.

'Hang on a minute,' he replied. 'I never said I didn't like dancing.'

'Yes you did, the week I started. I have had to curb my enthusiasm around you ever since.' This was true, and I was rather chuffed to have a moment to tease Matt on the matter.

'Hey. I didn't say I didn't like dancing – I said I didn't dance. There is a difference you know.'

Mum and Jen were silent, watching the discussion take place over their heads. Below us, the band were practising individual bars, and the conductor was having a discussion with Vincent.

'I'm sure you said you didn't like dancing.'

'I don't!'

'Well then.'

'What I meant was, I don't like it when it's me doing the dancing. To be honest nor does anyone else in the room.

111

Of course I like watching dancing. How else would I cope on a show like this?'

I was starting to feel a little confused. I was sure that Matt had always maintained that he didn't like dancing. Was he changing his tune? Or was my memory playing tricks? Either way, I had a creeping sense of unease when I recalled all the times I had tried to rein in my glee at seeing one of the couples trying out new steps. I never wanted to seem uncool in front of him, I now realised. Why did I care? He didn't even want to be working on the show beyond this year ...

'You seem to be coping admirably, especially with unexpected guests like us around,' said Jen.

'Ladies, it's no great hardship to work on a jewel of a show like this one. I'll make that Pulitzer-winning documentary one day ... One more dance?' He nodded his head down towards the dance floor, diverting our attention away from him. Lars and Kelly were walking solemnly onto the floor.

'Ooh look, Jen, it's Lars!'

'Hmm,' mumbled Jen, then looked at me. She wrinkled her nose and eyes in a secret little half smile. 'Isn't he lovely?'

'Kelly is so beautiful in real life. She was always in wellies in that soap and now look at her.'

I remembered Kelly slumped in the corridor sobbing the week before. She looked like a different woman in Lars' capable hands. They took their places, and the music began. I had been expecting another delicate ballroom dance. I was far from the mark. The couple were performing a red hot salsa, kicking and flicking in perfect synchronicity, and clearly loving every minute of it. I realised I had seen the routine on the tapes earlier in the week. It felt like a lifetime ago.

'Well, she's cheered up since that business with Jeremy, hasn't she?' Mum's stage whisper was getting louder now. I sensed that it might be time to move them along, but I was reluctant to break up the fun. Matt was staring at the couple, looking utterly bemused each time that Kelly returned smiling to Lars's arms.

'It looks like a bit of Nordic charm can go a long way, doesn't it?' said Jen to Mum, nudging her in the ribs.

'Too right, Jen.' They giggled together as the dance ended. Kelly was staring up at Lars' face. Her chest was an inch from his eyeline, rising and falling from the effort of the routine. But Lars was barely betraying any emotion at all, leaning over her, looking into her eyes with what could only be described as—

'Such a steely gaze,' said Mum, interrupting my train of thought. She was right.

Kelly was still panting when the couple finally broke their entwined embrace. The other couples gathered at the side of the stage and burst into a spontaneous round of applause. The high standard of their dance was obvious to everyone.

'If that doesn't get a ten tonight I don't know what could!' shrieked Mum, all pretence of a stage whisper now vanished. 'Bravo!' Mum and Jen were now clapping along with the rest of the crowd at the edge of the dance floor. Everyone on set had stopped, mesmerised. The other runners, the technicians who had been moving wires and adjusting lights, the costume and make-up team members who had come to see that everything looked okay on stage. Each and every one of them – and us – were stopped in our tracks.

Then, almost in slow motion, I saw Mum raise her fingers to her lips. She wasn't going to …? Oh my god, she was. Now standing, she pursed her lips and blew an enormous wolf whistle. How had she ever even learned to do that? Jen was now standing too, both of them entirely caught up in the moment. I caught Matt's eye and we giggled at each other, then I turned to look down at the dance floor. Slowly, the others had stopped their applause and now most of them were looking up at the four of us.

Lars, whose back had been turned, now turned his head around as well. He looked me straight in the eye. I froze. Partly because he looked so devastating in his workout clothes, with his hair already styled and a thin sheen of sweat on his arms from the exertion of the dance. And partly because this was the single most embarrassing moment of my life. I felt lightheaded, as if I was looking down from a height considerably greater than the one I was at. I think I actually did feel my toes curling up in my shoes. I winced, scared to meet his gaze. But instead of looking angry, he grabbed Kelly's hand and spun her around. The two of them did a deep, gracious bow and curtsey, complete with broad smiles. Mum and Jen squealed. My fate was sealed. I was the Greatest Daughter of All Time. Everyone else could just step back, including and *especially* Natalie, and no one would ever be able to provide a treat like this ever again. I closed my eyes and allowed myself a couple of seconds to wallow in the glory of the moment.

When I opened them I noticed an extra figure in among the cluster of dancers: Chloe. She was holding her ever-present clipboard, wearing her headphones and staring right at us. Slowly, she raised an eyebrow. I looked at Matt, who was already on his way downstairs.

'Come on Mum, it's probably best you got going now. That's my boss down there, so I should get back to doing my job.'

'Oh, do let me say hello?'

'Well, if we pass her. But it's best if we get going really.'

'Whatever you think is best.'

'I think it's best we get going.' I picked up her handbag from the banquette beside her and started trying to shuffle them along towards the stairs. When we reached the bottom Matt was already there talking to Chloe.

'... and so we're off now!' he was saying breezily.

'Is this Chloe?' asked Mum, extending her hand to say hello. 'I'm Amanda's mum!'

'Hello, yes, I understand who you are.'

'How's she getting along?'

Mum, please it's not parents' evening. Leave it. Move on.

'She has become a very valuable member of the team,' said Chloe. It was a thrill to hear her say that, even if it was through gritted teeth. She certainly wasn't smiling.

'That's wonderful news! It's her absolute dream job, you know? Ever since she was a little girl, all she has ever been interested in was dance. We used to take her up to the West End every Christmas and birthday. It was all she ever asked for. I can't believe she hasn't been up on stage yet herself. I'm sure she's itching to!'

By this stage even Jen could tell that they were overstaying their welcome, and had a gentle hand on the small of Mum's back. Chloe was staring back, a rictus grin on her face. I was mortified that mum had given away my dancing dreams after I had been so specific about not revealing them.

'It was such a treat to see some of the rehearsals too. I can't thank you and your team enough. It could have been Amanda of course if only she had applied herself. She's a natural, an absolute natural.'

Chloe's eyebrows were now raised, quizzical. Matt was staring wildly, no longer able to tell who was amused and who was furious. I knew how he felt. My heart was hammering faster than any of the salsa steps we had seen and I could feel sweat beginning to form on the back of my neck. How was I going to get Mum out of this corridor and back towards the tube? I was genuinely beginning to believe that this conversation would never end.

'Well, Mrs Roberts. I can quite imagine. Amanda has a lot of natural talents. But for now, I think we'd like her back so she can start using them with us again.'

'Oooh, how embarrassing, have I been banging on?'

I wanted to weep, I really did.

'Not at all. I just wish that my mum was able to come and visit me at the set too. But we really do need to be getting on now. So if we could have her back …?'

'Of course, I am so rude. How silly of me. Now then, which way am I going, and thank you again.' And then for the first time in my six weeks at Strictly, I saw Chloe break into a warm, open-hearted smile.

'Honestly, it was our pleasure. Like I said, I wish I could do the same for my mum.' She looked at me, and at the door, so I hurriedly shuffled them both along and got them back to reception as soon as possible. After huge hugs and many thanks on everyone's part, Mum and Jen finally wandered off onto Wood Lane. As the revolving door finally swung around behind them I let out a huge exhale of breath, and Matt gave me a huge, bear hug.

'Thank you!' I exclaimed. 'I am now Queen and Princess of all daughters.'

'You're welcome,' he said, picking me up off the floor and twirling me around. An image of my feet in gold dancing shoes flashed across my mind. 'Now let's get back to work before Chloe's magical mood wears off.'

Matt put me down. We stepped back from each other. Suddenly the space between us felt enormous, and radiating like the air above a road on a sunny summer's day. What had just happened? I adjusted my BBC pass around my neck and headed back to the studio floor. I needed to speak to Sally. Soon.

Chapter 8

The rest of the evening had a strange, floating feeling to it. I wasn't really sure how I had managed to get away with the visit from Mum and Jen going as well as it had, and I was so glad that Matt had persuaded me to let them come. I thought that I already had my dream job, but that evening it felt as if it had got even better. Even Sarah's patience with them had come when I had least expected it, and given an extra gloss to the event. It all left me feeling a little ... no ... I didn't dare say it ... but ... I felt the first whispers of Christmassiness.

Shortly before the show started I had five minutes to pop my head into make-up and see how Sally was getting along. She had missed out on the Mum-visit drama and I was feeling a little unusual about sharing it all with Matt and not telling her.

I was adamant that I was going to confront Sally about her relationship with Matt today. There was now a constant vague buzzing at the back of my mind, like the pale awareness that a wasp is trapped in the next door room. The buzzing was called Matt.

'Good evening ladies!' I knocked gently on the door to the make-up room. Ola was sitting in the make-up chair that Sally was working on, having her final touches applied for the professionals dance. 'Just wondered if I could get anyone any teas, coffees or drinks?'

'Oh you star,' said Sally. 'I am gagging for a cup of tea.'

'Ola?'

'Oh yes please, darling. Could I have some water.'

'Water it is.' I went off to find a cup of tea and a bottle of water from the area by the stage doors where I now knew everything was stored. There were about sixty small bottles of water, all lined up in neat rows, each labelled with a dancer's or celebrity's name. I remembered how bizarre the system had seemed when I was new to the team. Eventually Chloe had explained to me that everyone used to drink from everyone else's water bottle, and all it took was one cold to knock out most of the cast and crew for a week. Labelling the water was a quick and easy way around it. In addition, I always thought that it made the water bottles look rather sweet, as if they themselves had been named. By the time I had finished my little daydream about water bottles called James Jordan, I was back at make-up, delivering the drinks to the ladies.

'And how are you all?'

'Fine, fine, everything is remarkably under control today. No last minute rhinestone dramas so far.' I gazed at the countertop that Sally was working from. So. Much. Glitter. As Matt once said, it looked as if a unicorn had just sneezed on it.

'Was that your mum before?' asked Ola. 'She looks just like you.'

'Your mum was here?' said Sally.

'Yes, she was in Westfield with a friend and she came by to drop off a housewarming present. Then we took them up to band rehearsal for a while. It was wonderful.'

'Oooh I bet they loved it!'

'Yes, I think it was even more exciting than they had imagined. We saw some wonderful dances, I can't wait til the show begins.'

'Who did you see?' asked Ola.

'Vincent and Penny, and Lars and Kelly.'

'Doesn't Kelly look amazing today?'

'More to the point, doesn't Lars look amazing today?' said Sally with a wink at me.

'Well, yeah, they are both gorgeous.' Suddenly, all I could think of was that moment – Lars looking down at Kelly, both of them panting from the exertion of the dance.

'So, do we all fancy Lars then?' asked Beth, one of Sally's colleagues, who was tidying up her area next to where we were standing. 'The viewers all seem pretty convinced.'

This was true. As the series had progressed, Lars had gone from being someone who felt like my own secret discovery to the hands-down hunk of the show. From teen-agers to housewives, he was getting almost as much coverage as a pop star. Magazines, celeb websites and now paparazzi were following his every move. And they were becoming ever more intrigued by what was going on with him and Kelly.

'Yup,' replied Sally. 'I think that's just a stone cold fact. We all fancy Lars.'

'What about you! You're taken!' I blurted out. As I was still saying the words, I realised how much I was giving away by stating that. It was the buzzing. It was getting louder, I just had to know what was going on.

'I most certainly am not off the market where Lars is concerned!' said Sally, hands on hips.

I drew breath to answer, my fingers and toes buzzing. I was finally getting to the bottom of things. And then, through the talkback system in my headphones, I heard Karen.

'... could we have Amanda to the studio floor please? Amanda to the studio floor ...' and once again I was whisked into the world of the live show. From start to finish I was as excited as the first time I set foot on the studio floor. As the music started to play and Bruce and Tess took to the steps, I felt the perfect combination of being as thrilled as ever to be there, but like I finally belonged. The show went flawlessly – I was getting so slick that I managed to pre-empt most of the problems that could have cropped up, the dancers were all magnificent, and Matt even remembered to collect my camera cards we had been working on when Mum announced her arrival.

But what made getting the practicalities right was that I could really sense the genuine passion coming from the contestants this week. The competition had reached the stage where real talent was starting to emerge from some of the celebrities, and people's confidence was rocketing or plummeting. After each dance I could see that the muscles, the frowns, the tiny beads of sweat meant more than ever before. Even the dresses were starting to look more magnificent than I had seen before, largely because some of the key celebrities had now slimmed down to so much more of a dancer's shape with the rigours of the training regimes they were taking on. The kaleidoscope of colour and sparkle seemed brighter and bolder than ever before and it felt as if the energy the dancers were putting onto the dance floor was crackling through everyone in the studio. And, all along, there was something else fizzing away at the back of my mind – I had to talk to Matt and Sally. Had they had a thing that had just not worked out? Was it just that one date that I saw them on? Or was I being an idiot for having invented the situation, and let it ferment in my mind over a few weeks.

But I forgot about all of that when Lars and Kelly finally took to the stage. It didn't matter a jot that I had seen it before. It was just as incredible as the rehearsal I had witnessed earlier. They were moving in perfect synch, fast but controlled, and maintaining strong eye contact throughout. I felt my feet moving along as theirs moved. I realised that I had seen the dance so many times on the tapes we had been going through earlier in the week that I almost knew it myself. I saw each step before it happened, I felt it in my feet as they did it. For the first time, I wished it was me up there on the dance floor.

I felt the electricity of the dance flicker through the audience, and then they were on their feet in a tidal wave of wild applause. I could see people grabbing each other's arms and nodding in agreement that this was the best dance that they had seen. Then Alesha stood up, followed by Len.

Kelly and Lars held their final position for as long as they could without acknowledging their applauding fans. As they held their position, I imagined being in it myself. What did it feel like to be leaning back in Lars's arms? What was it like to be held by him? Could you smell his skin when you were that close to him? Could you hear his breath? Could you feel it on your face?

I pulled at my top, thinking that the studio lights were exceptionally hot that evening. I remembered slamming into Lars's chest that day on Wood Lane. The moment had been too brief to remember properly, but the memory was still there, like an old bruise that you aren't sure how you got. I cherished it, and tried not to replay it in my mind too often in case I somehow wore it out. I blinked and saw Matt to my left, looking intently at me. I brushed off my face and carried on applauding with the rest of the audience.

As the couple stood up Kelly burst into bittersweet tears, and it hit me with a jolt that being in Kelly's position might not be that great after all. She looked good on the dance floor, but the dance floor could deceptive. Sally and I had had a glimpse of the crumpled wreck that she was hiding from us the rest of the time, and I knew that that girl was not a girl I wanted to be. Her hand slid into Lars's as they took their position before the judges. It had to be said, it didn't look too bad for now though, especially when the judges gave the couple exceptional scores, even better than Karla and Artem, who up until that point had easily been the best of the night.

I put my hands in the back pockets of my jeans, and as I did, I realised that the box containing the keyring from Jen was still in my left back pocket. It didn't quite fit in the pocket, and was poking out of the top. I knew that all it would take was me bending over to move out of the way of a camera or to pick something up and the box would pop out and onto the floor. But I knew I couldn't stand around holding it while we were broadcasting live in case I dropped it or was needed to do something urgently. So I took it out and discreetly bent and placed it under the edge of a bit of staging, making a mental note to go back and get it later. It will come as no surprise that the energy the rest of the show created and the high spirits among all of us meant that I walked off stage at the end of the broadcast and forgot about the keyring altogether.

As soon as I was officially off duty, I made a real point of going to find Chloe to thank her for being so patient with Mum and Jen.

125

'It meant a lot to them,' I explained. 'You know what fans are like …'

'Yes, I understand, it's a real treat to be able to make someone's day like that.'

'And I know that it was officially during working hours, so thank you so much for allowing for that.'

'As I said, it's really not a problem.' Chloe didn't look cross, but she didn't really seem comfortable either. It was the first time we had ever discussed anything beyond what needed to be done on the show right then and there. We were both in uncharted territory, but Chloe seemed noticeably more uneasy about it than I was. She was not someone who oozed cheeriness on an everyday basis, and she certainly didn't seem upset in any way, but her usual quirks of fiddling with her BlackBerry, avoiding eye contact and speaking in short, sharp bursts were all more pronounced than ever.

I remembered the advice that Natalie had given me weeks ago about how to deal with her. Perhaps all of those frowns weren't anger, or disappointment. Perhaps they were nothing at all to do with me. Perhaps the reason that she was so slavishly addicted to checking her phone was nothing to do with a Spartan work ethic, but because she had other issues churning away in her life. All of those mornings that I had sat on the bus, determined to 'crack' her stern ways seemed a bit wasted now. Perhaps a smile might have been enough. Considering this made me feel compelled to put my hand out and touch her arm in a sort

126

of reassuring gesture, but I knew better than to do something so wildly patronising to my boss in a bar full of our colleagues. Either way, I saw a vulnerability in her that I hadn't really noticed before. She looked down, then made proper eye contact for the first time in our conversation.

'I'm just glad it all worked out,' she said quietly. 'I would love for my mum to be able to come.'

Why couldn't her mum come? That is of course the question that any sane person would ask in that situation, but I was prevented from doing so by Anthony still sweaty from his SteadiCam exertions, asking us if we'd like a drink. As Chloe turned to meet his gaze, I saw that what she had been fiddling with during our conversation was her keyring. Suddenly, I remembered my gift from Jen, languishing under the edge of the set, and realised I had to run to get it immediately.

I excused myself for a minute, and dashed to the lift, nearly skidding on the gleaming wood of the corridor. I jabbed and jabbed at the lift button, and the doors opened painfully slowly to reveal Matt and Sally.

'Not coming to the bar?' asked Sally.

'No, I've left something on set, have to run and get it.' I hastily took their place in the lift and started jabbing at the corresponding interior buttons. The doors began to close.

'See you in a minute then?' I could hear Sally asking, as the doors finally met. I knew it was too late to bother answering. I willed the lift to descend as quickly as possible, as I knew I only had a matter of five or ten minutes before the crew appeared to start dismantling the set. It was only there, constructed and in place from Thursday to Saturday, before being dismantled and put into huge lorries and stored on the outskirts of London for the rest of the week. There was usually a tiny window of time before the team started to take it apart, and I knew my time was limited. A small, navy blue cardboard box did not stand a chance against a team of strapping men and one of the most famous sets in country.

When the lift finally reached the ground floor I sprinted past the doors to make-up and past the pop-up spray tan tent. I deliberately skidded around the corner to the entrance to the set and clattered up and behind the wooden construction as fast as my legs would safely take me. I ran straight across the dance floor from the stairs end to the end where the crew worked from. I stepped off the dance floor and crept my hand around. There it was. The box. Safe and sound. I pulled it out from its resting place and whipped off the lid to check that the contents were safe. Of course they were. The keyring was there untouched. Despite being already out of breath from getting there, I let out a huge sigh, and felt my shoulders slump with relief

It was only then that I realised how alone I was. The set suddenly seemed much smaller without the crew and the audience filling it with noise and energy. I looked behind me, and saw that the gallery was empty, as were all of the seats. It was so quiet I could hear my own breath. I almost felt as if I could hear my own heart beating, like the opening to one of the latin dances. I had the place entirely to myself. It was definitely the first time, and I was quite sure it would be the last. I put my keyring into my bag, which I put on one of the chairs on the front row, and stood, entranced, deciding to savour it a moment.

Flashes of the night's show played again in my memory. The band, the applause, the dresses. Lars and Kelly, in each other's arms after their dynamic salsa. My feet started to twitch. I knew I knew the steps. And I knew it would be madness to try them. But some kind of salsa madness got hold of me, from my feet up. I ceased to think straight, overwhelmed by the size and silliness of my opportunity. Without troubling myself with any more sensible behaviour, I did what the dance fan of the last fifteen years in me would have wanted.

I walked back to my bag, got out my iPod, and found the salsa track that I sometimes listened to while running round Hyde Park. I pressed play, turned the volume up high, took my position and started to dance Kelly's salsa part. The music shot through me like a tequila, and my body seemed to take on a life of its own. I knew the routine even better than I realised, and, knowing it was only 90 seconds long, I revelled in every single move. Of course there were some steps I couldn't do while dancing alone, but for all the rest I was good enough that Craig himself would have been proud of me. The kicks, the hips, the breaksteps: bang on. As my arms made the final flourish I knocked the white speakers from my ears, and stood alone, the silence only broken by my own heavy breaths.

Then, from nowhere, a slow hand clap. First just the one, which startled me. Then another and another. A slow, almost sarcastic round of applause. My head whipped around, horrified at the thought that a crew member had caught me. Why had I been so reckless? But it wasn't a crew member sitting at the bottom of the iconic staircase. It was Lars. Now dressed down in some loose fitting jeans and a deep v-neck cashmere jumper, he was sitting on the bottom step, smiling at me.

'Oh my goodness.'

'We meet again,' he said, slowly standing up.

'What are you doing here?'

'What are *you* doing here?'

'I just came to collect something I left during the broadcast.'

'Well then, so did I.' Was he telling the truth? It was impossible to tell with him where the difference lay between smirking unkindly and flirting wildly. Was it both, or neither? We stood there, staring at each other. My chest was still rising and falling after the exertions of the dance. I desperately wanted it to be still. I tried to stop it by holding my breath, but that just made me looks as if I was sticking my cleavage out for no good reason. Mortified, I grabbed my bag, blurted out 'Please don't tell anyone, please' and ran past him to get off the studio floor. He did not move. I felt like less than nothing, a naïve little wannabe who had been utterly humiliated.

As I ran to the lift and started pressing its buttons frantically all over again, a thousand worst-case scenarios starting playing out in my imagination. Had Lars been the only one to see my carnival of self-indulgence? Were there more senior members of the production staff who had caught me? Had I put my job in jeopardy? If my job was at risk, what would Natalie and Lloyd say after they had done so much to help me? How would I pay my rent? It would break my mother's heart to know that I had been so stupid the very same day that she had had such a wonderful time here. Maybe she would even think it was her fault? And then, what about the friends I had made here? What about Sally? And what about Matt?

And it was as that thought crossed my mind that the lift doors opened and Sally and Matt stepped out again. Their expressions changed quickly from a cheerful 'We've found you!' to something more concerned.

'What's wrong?' asked Sally immediately, worried by my stricken face.

'I think I have just ruined everything with a salsa! Everything!'

It was time to take a deep breath and explain the situation properly.

Chapter 9

For a moment, all three of us were silent. We left the lobby area outside the lifts and stepped out of the building. There were several, huge red trucks parked at the back exit to the set, each with the image of an old-fashioned movie camera on them, and the words SET TRANSPORT. A fleet of burly looking men were flooding into the building as we headed out to stand in the loading bay. The area was like an aircraft hangar, freezing cold and bleakly ugly.

'What's the problem, Sweetie?' Sally tipped her head to one side and put her hand on my shoulder. She looked so sweet and so concerned. I briefly felt aglow at how lucky I was to have made a friend like her. Then I remembered the problem in hand.

'Oh god, it's so embarrassing, and it's going to sound so totally ridiculous saying it out loud now.'

'Just spit it out! You looked so freaked out when we saw you.'

'Yeah,' agreed Matt, who seemed noticeably less concerned about me than Sally. He was standing a couple of paces behind her, his hands jammed deep into the pockets of his jeans. He was stomping his feet a little, as if to ram home the point that it was freezing out there. Sally, wearing a pair of gingham pedal pushers and a pink polo shirt, didn't seem to be feeling the chill. Or perhaps she just didn't feel she needed to make the point so very clearly.

'You know the gorgeous keyring that Jen, my god-mum, gave me? Well I had it in my pocket earlier and I realised during the show that it was probably going to fall out or I'd lose it or something, so I hid it at the edge of the set. I nearly forgot about it and so I ran back to get it before they started taking everything apart ...'

As I said that, the scenic ops team started to walk behind Sally and Matt, carrying the audience chairs towards the trucks. For the past two months I had always assumed that they were gold, but seeing them away from the studio lights, I realised that they were actually silver.

'... and I got there in time. But then ... then ... then I looked around the set, and I realised that I had the studio floor to myself, for what would probably be the first and last two minutes of my life, like, ever.'

'Right ...' Sally was starting to look even more concerned. And even more cold. On the other hand, my cheeks were still burning with shame, my heart was hammering and even my feet were feeling a bit sweaty with stress. My stupid, sweaty, treacherous feet. I hated them.

'So I got my iPod and I—'

'Oh no, don't say it.'

'Well, yes, I knew the sals—'

'You did not.'

'I did, I did.'

'Er girls, what are you talking about? What has she done? What has gone wrong?'

'Who caught you?'

'Lars.'

'Caught you doing what?'

'His salsa?'

'Yup.'

'From tonight.'

'Yup.'

'Oh. Emm. Gee. Did he see the whole thing?'

'I think so, yes.'

'How do you know?'

'PLEASE will someone explain what has happened?'

'I turned around and he was at the bottom of the staircase.'

'Oh man.'

'GIRLS.' Matt ran a hand through his hair, exasperated at the pair of us. Sally turned to him, now looking equally frustrated.

'Lars caught Amanda doing his salsa on the studio floor. By herself.'

Matt winced, as if someone in stilettos had just trodden on his toes.

'Why would you do that?' I drew breath to try and explain.

'Because it's her dream,' interrupted Sally. 'It's her dream to dance, and it's her ultimate dream to dance the salsa. With Lars. Have you not listened to anything she has said since you met her?'

'Yes, but I just didn't realise she would actually do it.'

'Well nor did I.' This was getting worse by the second. 'I didn't mean to do it; I haven't had some weird Fan Plan all this time. I just got down there and had the place to myself and couldn't help it.'

'What, one thing led to another, did it?'

'Yes.' This pushed Matt towards a smirk of ludicrous proportions. He rolled his eyes. 'You're not even kidding!'

'No, I'm not. It was truly the most embarrassing thing that has ever happened to me.'

'Ha! I can imagine.' There was an actual snigger from Matt now.

'Oh don't worry honey.' I was awash with relief that Sally was there. 'I don't think anyone else saw.'

'I know, I know. But what if they did? I am just so ashamed that anyone might think I only wanted to work here because I am some kind of rogue fan. I have tried really hard to maintain a level of professionalism, even though it is such a big deal for me to be here. Plus, also, the fact that I, um, shouldn't have actually been doing that there anyway ...'

'Look, let's just work on the basis that it was only Lars. We have no way of finding out if anyone else saw, and even if they did, remember that everyone is usually more interested in their own life anyway. At this time on a show night most of us are much more concerned by what we're having to eat when we get home than by what you got up to for ninety seconds when you had the set to yourself.'

Matt was now just scowling to himself, clearly in despair at the way that Sally was actually taking me seriously. Two men carrying an enormous part of the backdrop walked behind him, momentarily making it look as if it were him on stage. For a moment, I wished he was. Then maybe he might understand.

'I hear what you're saying, Sally, but I just want to D. I. E.'

'Move on. There will be fresh gossip next week. Let's just go and have a drink and forget about it. You didn't do anything that wrong professionally; it's just been a fleeting moment of embarrassment. It was in front of one person.'

Yes, but what a person, I thought to myself.

'It was nothing compared to what the celebrities go through each week. You saw some of them at the beginning – they were terrified!'

Sally was right. I had never realised how completely exposed they were until I had been there for the live shows. The moments while they took to the stage as the taped package about their training played to the television audience was excruciating – there they were, only a metre or two from audience members, standing still, sometimes alone, under the studio lights. Those moments before the music began were always so revealing. I thought of Kelly and how gutsy she had been to get up and do that salsa when the rest of her world was falling apart.

'Drink now? Please?' said Tom, with a beseeching smile. It was hard to refuse him now that he had stopped his mini sulk. His way of getting over things was so endearing. I could take a leaf out of his book and learn to move on a little faster from time to time. He took his hands from his pockets and put an arm around each of us. 'Come ooooooooon!' We formed a giggling huddle and headed up to the bar.

The first person I saw when we reached the entrance was Kelly, with Lars. They were standing in the doorway, with their backs to the room, so no one else would have been able to see that behind their backs they were firmly clasping each other's hands. Matt was leading Sally and me, and seemed oblivious to the situation.

'Excuse me, mate,' he said as he leaned around Lars's shoulder. I saw Sally's careful gaze on me when Lars tapped Kelly gently on the bottom to get her to let us pass. As I walked past them I saw that Kelly was beaming with pride, and the couple were still receiving congratulations from almost all of the rest of the team for their spectacular effort. It was their night, I told myself – Lars had bigger things to worry about than me living out my little fantasies on his turf. What he was going through would surely make him oblivious to my silly personal soap opera. My brain was more than happy to accept this information, but my heart … Well, my heart was stuck in a kind of wistful gridlock. It was somewhere between longing, shame and sadness, but with a tiny sparkle of delight that came from knowing that whatever the consequences might turn out to be, I had nailed the salsa on that dance floor.

On the far side of the bar Chloe was talking to Anthony the SteadiCam operator. He actually looked considerably leaner and more elegant without the bulky equipment strapped to him. Seeing him stripped of it made me wonder how he ever managed to carry it at all. Whatever he was saying seemed to be pleasing Chloe though. She had her head back, roaring with laughter in a way that I had never seen before. As I watched Sally head to the bar to get our first round, I scanned the room, and realised what a lovely group of people these were. I let myself believe it was all going to be okay. We were working as a team, and we all loved the show. It seemed that there had been no professional harm done, and the prickly sense of embarrassment I had inflicted on myself might just subside after all. Then, I looked round and saw Matt, watching me as I gazed around the room.

'Happy now?' His voice had an edge to it. I wasn't sure if he was teasing me or genuinely asking.

'Yes, thanks. You?'

He shrugged. 'S'pose.'

'What's wrong?'

He squirmed a bit. That passive aggressive 'oh no everything's fiiiiine' face was something I would expect from a teenage girl, not him. Suddenly I felt rather judged. And I didn't like it.

'Seriously, what is wrong?'

'Nothing, nothing.' He waved his hand nonchalantly.

'Don't brush me off like that. What's wrong? I am not going to ask a fourth time.'

He shrugged. 'I just don't get what a big deal you had to make of salsa-gate. I think you need to … calm down a bit.'

'I know, I agree. It was really embarrassing. I feel silly already for making that fuss when I saw you guys.' I *did* agree with him, but now I just wanted this whole awkward situation to be diffused as soon as possible.

'Were you embarrassed because of us or because of Lars?'

'Well not you guys, you're my mates.' Although I was beginning to wonder just how good a friend Matt really was if he was prepared to keep his relationship with Sally on the down-low while subjecting me to such scrutiny.

'No, I mean us as in the crew. The team?'

'Of course you guys. I already explained: I don't want my snatched moment of living out my dreams to get me in some kind of professional trouble.'

'So it wasn't just a Lars thing?'

'Well it was *mostly* a Lars thing … Because he was the one who saw me.'

'It's not *Upstairs Downstairs*, you know. We are all part of the same team, dancers and crew alike.'

'I know that. Why do you keep banging on about this?'

'It's just that you keep saying you're worried about your job, and I think that what's really getting to you is how embarrassed you are that Lars caught you.'

'I've told you. It's a bit of both.' We were now talking in urgent stage whispers, like an unhappily married couple trying to keep the volume down in front of the children. Matt raised his eyebrows sceptically at me. In fact, it was sceptically and sarcastically. One eyebrow sceptical, one eyebrow sarcastic. This was turning into an argument. Why was this happening? I thought we had been through all of this fifteen minutes ago, yet now I felt as if I was watching our friendship dissolve like a sandcastle caught in the tide. I didn't want to fight with Matt. I didn't think he wanted to fight with me. And yet he seemed to be genuinely furious with me. I shot a look across the bar to Sally. She was only just leaning in to place our order. As I turned back to meet Matt's gaze he let out a little sneering snort of laughter. Something in me snapped.

'What? I don't get it. What exactly are you so pissed off with me about? Are you accusing me of having a silly little schoolgirl crush? Or accusing me of having impossible dreams that are somehow embarrassing to try and achieve? If there's anywhere I should not have to bother to hide a lifelong passion for dancing, surely it's here? Or is it him?' My arm flailed out as I went to gesticulate at Lars, only just catching myself from making a gesture that others might notice.

'This is my first job. It's all pretty much amazing to me. I haven't had time yet to develop lofty ambitions to direct coverage of world news events or groundbreaking documentaries watched by seven tweedy professors.'

Matt's mouth was now opening and shutting as if he was about to begin rebuttals, but no sound was coming out. I whipped my head back and saw Sally handing a bank note over the bar.

'Like I said ... I don't think it's your career that you're worried about.' His eyes were narrowed as he looked at me. He was fiddling with his fringe. 'You're a born team member here. You're amazing at your job, everyone loves you, and you're picking it all up faster than I ever did. But I find it kind of embarrassing to see you losing it over some dancer.'

'But I—'

'I mean, you don't even know anything about him, and yet you behave as if there's something going on between the two of you. It's like you think a bloke is hot just because he can dance. I know that the Latin's really sexy but you know it's not *actually sex* don't you?'

'How can you even—?'

141

'He's a nice enough guy but there's *nothing going on*. He's just at work here. Why do you care so much about what he thinks? Why get this het up about things?

Hot tears were prickling my eyes. All it would take was a blink too many and one might roll down my cheek. This was a different person to the friend I had known for the last few weeks. Here was a man unrecognisable from the one who had been such a gentleman with Mum and Jen only a few hours ago. I had never seen this sharpness before. I felt frightened that I had put so much trust in someone with such an edge. I looked over Matt's head and saw that Sally was now making her way through the crowd back towards us.

'Why do you care who I fancy anyway?' I said, very quietly. 'Or what I do with my career? It is not as if *you* are following *your* dreams. You're more than happy to sneer at dancing, and talk about how your ambitions are so much loftier than being here. But it's not as if you're stuck on the show. I mean, oh boohoo, poor you, having to work on one of the biggest shows on TV. And even if you did want to move on … have you actually tried applying to do anything else? You're too scared to even approach other departments in case you're rejected. Just the same as you're too scared to try dancing in case you look like an idiot.'

Sally was getting very close now. I had no idea if I could count on her as a friend or if she would assume the role of ally and girlfriend of Matt when confronted with the

142

choice. But regardless of the position she took, I knew that I had to fight my corner. I had spent all summer wafting around at home wondering if I would ever get a job, and I had spent the first few months of my time at Strictly creeping around, almost apologising for my presence. Somehow those few moments on the dance floor had shown me a tiny chink of confidence I hadn't known I had. I took a deep breath, feeling stronger than I had done all year.

'Well, you know what? I'm not embarrassed any more. At least I have been honest about myself. I *did* try dancing and I *did* look like an idiot, and guess what? I survived. I'd rather be me than someone who never took to the dance floor.'

Sally approached us, holding out the three drinks she was clasping together. The atmosphere was thick; she could not help but notice it.

'Here you go guys, what's going on?'

'Nothing. It doesn't matter.'

'Oh, it does matter. It matters to me.' I had the bit between my teeth now. I wasn't prepared to let this one go any more.

'What matters?'

'Well,' I took a deep breath. 'Matt here thinks I am pathetic for having a 'schoolgirl crush', and that I need to grow up a bit. I think he needs to take a look a bit closer to home before he starts lecturing other people on how to run their lives.'

'When did this become about me? I'm not the one leaping around on dance floors I don't belong on.'

'It became about you when you stood here looking furious with me the minute that Sally went to the bar.'

Sally frowned. Like me, she must have assumed that this conversation was over when we got back to the bar.

'Hey, you two—'

Matt threw his hands up. People in the bar were now starting to notice how heated our discussion was becoming. All of the burning shame I had just about managed to convince myself I had avoided now seemed to be rushing at me like a charging bull.

'No, Sally, it's fine. I have said my piece. We can have our drinks like grown-ups now.' I raised my glass at the two of them. 'Here's to a successful show.'

Matt's scowl was going nowhere.

'Fine.' He raised his glass reluctantly. 'Cheers.'

Sally rolled her eyes.

'Why are you guys even having this stupid fight? I thought you were friends.' I took an enormous swig from my wine glass. It seemed to go straight to my head.

'Yeah,' I said, with the same kind of sneering laugh that Matt had turned on me only minutes earlier. 'Well I thought you two were friends too. Until I saw you at Grists's.'

The hubbub of the bar continued around us. I heard Chloe's unfamiliar laugh from across the room. And yet the silence between the three of us seemed louder than all of it.

Matt turned to me, his eyes narrowed. Sally looked at Matt, and then at me.

'What did you say?' she asked. Her voice was very quiet. She was leaning in slightly.

'You heard. I saw you. I know what you were up to.'

I gulped the rest of my wine in one go. It hit the back of my throat like a warm syrupy punch. We were standing, so I had nowhere to slam the glass down, but I wanted to. I really, *really* wanted to. I waved it around a little bit, weakly, instead.

Sally looked at me incredulously. 'I honestly have no idea what you are talking about.' She seemed to think I was joking about something. I started to feel as if all my big talk might have been a terrible mistake. 'You've both lost me now.'

This had now turned into the longest and most exhausting night of my life. Everything seemed to be catching up with me. The enormous sense of empowerment that I had felt while confronting Matt a few minutes ago was now trickling away. I felt deserted, and facing the two of them I felt rather vulnerable. I had a mental image of Cary Grant in *North by Northwest*, alone on the prairie as an unexpected plane dived at him.

'Never mind. Never mind.' I waved my empty wine glass around fruitlessly again. 'It's just that I have known for weeks that you two are seeing each other. I have tried not to ask you outright, and I have tried to be discreet about it. I don't know why you never said anything, and of course it's your prerogative to keep your private lives private. But whenever I've tried to approach the subject neither of you have given me a straight answer, so I assumed that for some reason you wanted to keep it a secret from me. Or you didn't trust me to keep it a secret from other people.

My glass was starting to wave more and more now. If it had had any wine left in it, it would have been spilled long ago.

'I don't know why you have kept this secret, but it's hurtful to know that your friends are holding truths from you, especially as I confided in you so early on about Lars ... and now you're throwing that back in my face. It shouldn't be hurtful, it should just be your business and my business – I understand that and maybe me bringing it up makes me a bit pathetic, but there it is. It has made me feel weird for weeks. And every day it edges a little closer to being hurtful. I feel exposed, like a fool for admitting to being passionate about something while you're being discreet about something else. It's too much.'

I drew breath. Matt and Sally were standing there silently. Neither of them had shown any sign of interrupting me during my little outburst, as if they knew that the more space they gave me the more of an idiot I would make myself look. Matt crossed his arms and gave an enormous sigh.

'I have had enough of this. You are an absolute mad woman. I cannot cope.' He leaned over and placed his glass on the table we were standing behind. 'I am going home to get some sleep. Hopefully tomorrow I will wake up and this will all prove to have been some kind of a bizarre nightmare.

'But—!' My arms – and glass – were now flailing in a way that it was impossible to conceal from others in the bar. Matt just shook his head, looked down and quietly left.

'See you next week, have a good weekend.' And with that he was gone.

I shivered, suddenly feeling as if someone had replaced my blood with fresh stuff straight from a chiller cabinet. A feeling of dread crept through me. Something had gone horribly, perhaps irredeemably wrong, and none of us seemed quite sure how it had happened. Sally was still standing there, glaring at me.

'Where the hell did that come from?' She was actually speaking through gritted teeth. It was as if opening her mouth any wider would mean she were incapable of not screaming at me.

I paused, trying to think of what to say next.

'Why would you think that?'

'What?'

'All of it, just all of it.' She moved her hands to her hips, looking fully like Rizzo now. 'Why would you think we were a couple? Why would you just assume that? And more importantly, do you really think I am the kind of person who would keep something like that from you? That I would listen to your confidences and not share mine, even a tiny bit?'

'But I saw you. In Grists's bar on the common. You were sitting in the window, holding hands. It was total date hands.'

Sally rolled her eyes. Her shoulders dropped an inch.

'Seriously? That's what you're talking about?'

'It was pretty obvious what was going on. I was walking to get a curry from two doors down. That place is really near my sister's.'

'Really obvious was it? Obvious that we were having a quick drink downstairs before Julia from costume's birthday party? Which was being held upstairs? I suppose it must have been really obvious given that *you have never met her.*'

Eek. I now knew that Julia was one of the team from last year who had stayed good friends with Sally and Matt. I had even heard them mention since that they had been to her birthday party. I didn't know that that was where it was held, or that it had been that night.

'But you were holding hands.'

'Yes, we were. For about four seconds.'

'It was date hands.'

'Yes, I know. Because I was showing him what had happened on a date I'd been on earlier in the week. I was asking him if he thought that it was a good sign. He didn't understand what I was explaining, so he asked me to show him. That's why we were holding hands, for a few seconds: as an example. Clearly I should have asked *you* for your opinion, not him, given that you have such strong intuition and opinion on the matter.'

The sensation of my blood having been replaced from the chiller cabinet was long gone. I now felt completely frozen with horror at what I had done. I could suddenly see with complete clarity that one fleeting moment on a weekend a few weeks ago when I was feeling a bit blue had spiralled in my mind and become something quite different. My ridiculous insecure mind. All that time, I had been assuming that there was some big secret being kept from me, when there was nothing there at all. It was nothing to do with me. I clasped and unclasped my hands.

'Oh Sally, what have I done?'

'I don't know, but I think being caught doing the salsa is now the least of your worries.'

'I'm so sorry, I was just so sure of what I saw.'

'Yeah, you saw what you saw but you just added your own interpretation to it. Not cool, Amanda, not cool.'

'I know, I'm so sorry.'

Sally sighed and then shrugged.

'I guess you thought I was someone I'm not. Well it turns out that you're not the kind of girl I thought you were either. And I don't even reckon it's me who is the most upset by this.'

She leant down and picked up her coat and bag.

'Have a good weekend. Think things over, yeah?'

Sally left the bar and I looked down to collect my own bags. Across the floor I could see Kelly, still in her gold dance shoes, sharing a joke with Lars and Chloe. I didn't feel like laughing.

Chapter 10

As the night bus made its stately way around Shepherd's Bush roundabout and on to Goldhawk Road, each bar, each pub, each restaurant seemed to be spilling a larger crowd of ecstatic party-goers than the next. The gangs of smokers, the would-be lovers, even the groups of girls in their short skirts and heels, dashing to make the tube – they all seemed to be hitting that Big Night Out party nirvana all at the same time. Looking down on them from the top deck of the bus home, I had never felt further away from them in my life. As we waited at traffic lights at Hammersmith Grove I watched a couple about my age talking outside a pub. She had her back to the wall, and one knee bent, her leg forming a neat triangle against the wall. He was facing her, hands in pockets, until he put his left hand up against the wall and leaned in. It was definitely a first kiss. I felt invasive watching them, but on a stationary bus there was little else to look at.

I felt overwhelmed by a sense of lonely longing, wondering when that was ever going to happen to me again. At that moment it seemed utterly inconceivable that I could maintain a proper friendship, let alone put myself in line for a snog any time soon. I rested my head on the bus window and finally the tears I had been holding back for the last few hours arrived. I wasn't even crying, it was just sad, silent tears. Every time I blinked my face became a little more damp. With no one to talk to there were none of the gulping gasping sobs that so often characterise a good cry. This time it was tears and tears alone.

We reached my stop and I got off the bus. As I walked the two roads from the stop to my front door my imagination, which was now behaving like a melancholy but competitive child, spiralled at the sight of cosy rooms with their lights on. I saw televisions flickering from behind blinds and curtains and imagined happy couples entwined on expensive but immaculately maintained modular sofas. They had probably done all of their washing up and were just finishing watching a moving but improving foreign film before heading upstairs for early night. The houses I passed with all of their lights off were clearly home to couples already curled up together in bed. Or still out, at a fabulous party that was almost definitely as good as Truman Capote's Black & White ball. Of this I was quite sure by the time that I reached home, still wiping my face with the sleeve of my cardigan.

I closed my eyes and took a deep breath as I turned my key in the front door of the building, praying that Allegra was either out (at a fabulous party, of course) or in bed. It was by now after midnight, but I strongly suspected that if she was in Allegra would not have gone to bed by now. She was rarely in bed before 1am, preferring to stay up drinking strong coffee from the stovetop mocha she had brought from Milan and smoking furtive cigarettes on the kitchen balcony. She seemed to think I didn't know about the smoking, as she never did it when I was anywhere in my flat other than my bedroom, and even then it was always on the balcony. But the smell and the occasional white menthol cigarette butts by her rosemary plants were clues enough – it did not take Miss Marple to piece the picture together. When she had these late night coffee and fags sessions she would read and work on her thesis rather than watching TV, so I was never bothered by any noise either.

The flat door was only a few inches open when I saw that the sitting room light was on. Allegra was still up. I closed the door quietly and gently rested my head on it. I closed my eyes, steeling myself. I just wasn't in the mood to chat, especially as the chances that my make-up streaked face would give me away were high. I walked up the stairs slowly, quietly, hoping to make it to my bedroom unbothered.

No such luck. As I passed the sitting room I saw Allegra's legs up on the sofa, but at the crucial moment she leant forward, meaning to catch my eye as I crept through the hallway.

'I thought that I had heard you,' she said with a small smile. 'How was the show?'

It would have been rude to ignore her after that. For all her unlikely reserve, Allegra had proved to be a truly good person and an ideal flatmate. She was tidy, but not so tidy that she did the washing up in a way that felt like an accusation about the last time that I did it. She was interesting but not in an exhausting way that meant I couldn't just catch up with EastEnders if I wanted to. And she was kind. She remembered things about my life; she cared. And this inspired me to want to do the same. Conscious that I was getting through my new London friends faster than my family got through Quality Street at Christmas, I decided to sit down for a bit of a chat with her.

'It went fine,' I replied, moving a stash of fashion magazines from the armchair in the corner and plonking myself down on it. 'It was the best one yet actually.'

'I saw the second half. It looked great. Are you okay?'

My smeared face had indeed given me away. I scrunched my mouth up to one side, mindful that an excess of kindness could bring on the sobs that I had so far avoided. Compared to the manic energy and riot of colour and emotion I saw at work, Allegra's was a profoundly still, calm presence. She was wearing a pair of tight khaki cotton trousers with zips on the sides, a brown vest top and a large, open denim shirt. Her feet, up on the sofa, were bare but her toenails were painted with a discreet pale pink gloss. It had never occurred to me that she was the kind of person who might paint her toenails before. She was slowly turning one of her chic Scandinavian coffee mugs in her hands. Her effortless continental sophistication made me consider how unpleasant I must look. The small matter of my streaky face aside, I could feel my hair starting to stick to my scalp, forming a bit of a groove where my talkback system headset had been for hours. I had an unidentifiable stain on my jeans and sensed that I was emitting that non-specific but undeniable Smell of Work. A combination of stress, sweat and canteen food perhaps?

'Yes, I'm okay,' I replied. I knew I didn't sound sure.

'But you look terribly sad. Have you been crying?'

I nodded slowly, and another tear plopped onto the cushion I had put on my lap as I had sat down.

'Has something gone wrong at work?'

'You could say that,' I said, just before the first of the gulpy sobs made a leap for freedom from somewhere near the back of my throat. I was off … Exhausted by the crazy range of emotions that the day had thrown at me and consumed by relief at being safely at home in such a calm environment, I unleashed the full story of mum's visit, the show, my salsa moment and then the Matt, Sally and Lars drama – the misunderstandings, the crushes, the non-existent crushes and the mess I had made of everything. I explained to Allegra how mortified I was to have made the ridiculous assumption that I had about Matt and Sally, but also how offended I was that Matt felt he could have any kind of say at all in who I took a shine to.

Allegra listened to everything, sitting very still on the sofa. I could not have asked more of her if she had been a fully qualified agony aunt. I wished she had been around for some of my more shameful teenage mistakes. She let me tell the whole story at my own pace, only occasionally butting in with the occasional 'Of course, Matt simply does not have the right to judge like that', 'These emotions are of course understandable,' and at one point a slow, sad 'Oh Amanda, oh dear.' She was no more impressed by my imaginative interpretation of what I had seen at Grist's than Sally and Matt were. By the time I had reached the end of the sorry story she was nodding thoughtfully at her own knees, listening intently. Then she looked up and said softly 'You must be clear in your mind where the professional ends and the passionate begins.'

'It isn't that easy though, is it?' I replied, twisting and untwisting the soggy tissue I had had in my hand since the bus ride home. 'I am passionate about my job, and I also want to be a good professional. That is what has got me into this mess.'

I waited for Allegra to give me some life-changing nugget of advice. The benefits of having such a considerate and qualified flat-mate were only just starting to make themselves known to me.

'It's not such a mess, and it will unravel,' said Allegra with a sigh. What? I didn't want any existential wafflings from her! I needed to be told actual specifics of how to mend things with Sally and Matt, and ideally how to get Lars to fall discreetly in love with me as well. Did Italian feminists not know how to do this?

'And anyway,' she continued, 'it's not the mess that people make of things that is important. It is how they get out of that mess that counts. And I am sure you can do that.'

This really wasn't the kind of thing I had been hoping to hear at all. I wanted some kind of recipe, an ancient fable and perhaps a devastating fashion tip.

'I suppose so,' I answered glumly. Then, a thought. 'Would you like to come down to the show one weekend? You could come to the bar afterwards and meet everyone, help to smooth the rocky waters?'

I loved the idea of having Allegra on side, with her splash of continental insouciance. Plus, I felt as if I needed all the friends I could get for the next week or two.

'That would be lovely. It would be charming to meet your colleagues, and I think I should meet this Lars. I do not think that it is a good idea for you to date some dancer.'

The words 'some dancer' prompted a pang of protectiveness for Lars. He wasn't just 'some dancer', he was one of the best in the world, and he was also a wonderful man.

157

The image of him smiling up at me, Mum and Jen flashed across my mind again.

'Perhaps I could bring one or two of my friends to meet you, although I cannot come next week—'

'It's okay, next week we're in Blackpool anyway.' I could barely get my words out fast enough; I was so keen on my plan to get Allegra to help me with things at work.

'Well, then, yes. Hopefully in two weeks I will be able to make it. But now, Carina, I have to go to bed ...'

Allegra had taken to addressing me with the Italian 'Carina' as a term of endearment within a couple of weeks of me being in the flat. At first I had thought she was utterly oblivious to my actual name, and just kept getting it wrong.

At first she had stuck to Amanda, for at least the first weekend. And then, after a few days, she started to slip in the odd 'Carina.' The first couple of times it was after I had said something funny and I assumed it was some kind of expression of glee. But then one Saturday night when we had shared a rather strong bottle of wine she addressed me as Carina and I felt I simply had to answer back.

'Allegra,' I had said.

'Si si,' her eyes were heavy-lidded from the strength of the wine. It was the most relaxed I had ever seen her.

'You do know that that's not my name, don't you?'

'Eh? Amanda? Do you prefer me to call you a nickname?'

'No, Amanda's fine. But you keep calling me Carina by mistake. It's quite unnerving. I don't know who that is.'

And with that, she roared with laughter more than I could ever have imagined. It was contrary to everything I had learned about her so far. She was usually the most self-contained person I knew, completely at odds with the usual stereotype of Italian dramatics. But that night, she seemed fully Italian.

'Carina!' she gasped. 'I do not think that that is your name! 'It is a term of endearment for you! It is like 'darling'. I cannot believe you thought that!' I blushed. What else could I do?

Once we had sorted out that it was the same as her calling me 'darling' or 'sweetie' I found it hugely engaging. So much so that I had almost lost track of what she was saying.

'... because I must be up early in the morning as I am heading back to Milan for a few days. My father is very sick.' Allegra stood up and started to puff up the scatter cushion she had been leaning back on.

'Oh I'm so sorry, I had no idea. Here's me babbling on about my inconsequential problems and your dad is ill. Is it a recent diagnosis? Is there anything I can do to help?'

'No no, nothing you can do. He has been sick for some time but he has a big operation next week and so I am going home to help my mother to care for him for a few days.'

Now that I bothered to look, I saw how tired Allegra looked. I had fallen for the trap of thinking it was terribly sophisticated to be so slim and languid, but now saw that it wasn't worth it if it was simply masking a churning mass of sadness and anxiety.

'What about your studies? Will you get terribly behind?'

'It is a possibility, but my priority must be to take care of my family.' She headed into the kitchen and put her coffee mug in the sink with a side plate she had had some biscuits on. She started to run the taps. I felt for her, heartened that she had a sense of priorities so close to mine. I could not imagine how I would cope with the pressure of family illness. She seemed to be managing admirably.

'Of course, and thank you for being such a kind friend at a time of such sadness for you. Promise to call if you ever need anything, or even if you just want to chat. Leave all of that; I will take care of everything.'

I shushed her out away from the sink and towards the bathroom.

'Sleep well, Allegra, and have a safe journey.'

'I will Carina, and so shall you.' She smiled and closed the bathroom door.

Allegra was wise, but as far as the idea of me sleeping well went, she was way off the mark. Yes, I conked out almost immediately after my head hit the pillow, exhausted from my crying workout. But I was awake two and a half hours later, sweaty, twisted in the sheets and unable to find a cool spot anywhere in the bed. For the rest of the night I drifted in and out of sleep, jumping at every sound I could hear, endlessly shaking out the duvet, trying to find a way to relax.

My dreams became progressively more psychedelic and unnerving throughout the night. They featured a freaky combination of dresses, dancers, and colleagues, all inter-cut with shows I had been to see as a child, shows I had performed in as a child and costumes I had seen on televi-sion. There was a constant background soundtrack – a sort of sinister playground ride version of the Strictly music, and I kept waking up with a start, panicking about confrontations that had never happened. Lloyd was fight-ing with Chloe, my mum was cross with Kelly, Allegra was giving Matt a piece of her mind. Everything was a huge jumble – it felt as if my brain had decided that the best way to do its filing was to throw everything up in the air first, and then begin processing it afresh.

At 6am I heard Allegra's taxi buzz the bell and listened to her quietly head downstairs with her suitcase. I texted her, wishing her a safe journey and all the best for her father's operation. I rolled over and lay on my back, wondering how on earth I was going to fill a wintry Sunday without making myself feel utterly blue alone in the flat all day.

I got as far as realising that I should probably do some housework before I must have exhausted myself at the prospect, as at 8am a text reply from Allegra woke me from a fresh batch of freaky dreams. It was only when I saw Allegra's name appear again that I remembered something I had rattled past the night before: this week, we were off to Blackpool.

Chapter 11

Blackpool. Just the thought of it made me feel that there could be a fresh start. A different venue, a different atmosphere, and a few days away from the rut I had got into at work.

The show was going to be broadcast from the Tower Ballroom the coming weekend, meaning that we were all heading up there for a few days – dancers, celebrities and crew, the lot of us. The combination of a seaside resort and so many of us trekking up en masse brought to mind the feeling of a school trip: cool girls sitting at the back of the bus, one poor unfortunate puking into a bowl and someone losing their purse full of pocket money. I was convinced I was going to forget something so I spent much of Sunday laying out which clothes I would need to take, and writing elaborate notes and traps made of Post-its that meant I could hardly walk from room to room without seeing tiny fluorescent squares shrieking 'HAIR STRAIGHTENERS!', 'MOBILE CHARGER!' or 'TOOOOOTHPASTE!' at me.

163

I was resigned to the fact that one thing of vital import would be left behind, but once I had done the requisite housework, I focussed my attentions on trying to make sure that what I did forget was as low down my list of essentials as possible.

After these home-based tasks, I decided to take Jen up on the offer she had made the day before, and popped round to hers for tea. Unlike my parents, who rarely came into central London, Jen only lived in Chiswick and was much more available at a moment's notice. She didn't have a calendar swinging from the back of one of the kitchen cupboards, filled with plans and birthdays like Mum did. Instead, there was a big blackboard on one of her kitchen walls, which was always covered in barely intelligible squiggles and scribbles. Shopping lists for parties that had happened four months ago, suggested dates for theatre trips that had never happened, and birthday reminders for people who she was going to see that day anyway all fought for space amidst cut-out newspaper cartoons that amused her, receipts for things she probably shouldn't have bought and photographs for friends and family which she had pinned to the edges of the blackboard with blu-tack.

When I arrived it was just getting dark, so I pottered around the house after her as she drew curtains and turned on pretty little side lamps until the kitchen and sitting room were twinkling with cosiness. I leaned against her big range cooker while we waited for the kettle to boil and explained the dramas of the previous night all over again.

Less enigmatic than Allegra, Jen wasted no time in laying out her thoughts on the matter.

'Well for starters that Matt has no right to tell you who to fancy, but I think I know what his problem is. And as for Lars, he's TBGL to trust.' I didn't recognise the term but Jen was on a role. 'And good on you for seizing your salsa moment, but remember, honey – it's a once in a life-time thing. You can't start making a habit of it or you'll just get caught by someone who does matter, or you'll get a reputation for taking the mick, which, as we all know, you really aren't. I understand how much this job means to you, and while matters of the heart always seem like the most important thing that are going on at any given time, it's your career you need to focus on.'

While she was talking, I watched Jen pour the kettle's contents into a brown teapot, and get a selection of biscuits and shortbread from a tin which was decorated with images of the then newlyweds Charles and Di. The things that tin must have seen … She put the treats onto a chunky plate that I recognised as one I had decorated for her as a child, over a decade ago. I followed her into the sitting room, kicked off my shoes and curled up on one of her enormous leather sofas.

I knew that what Jen was saying was right, but I also accepted her advice with a pinch of salt as there was a degree to which she was saying what would suit her. She had lost her husband a few years before, much to her – and my whole family's – devastation. Since then she had thrown herself into her successful career as a ceramics designer. Mum and I had sometimes worried about her working too hard, and wondered to each other if it was just a way for her to deal with her grief, but then again I admired her career and had looked up to her all of my life for being someone with independent finances. That was all well and good but I suddenly found myself thinking *Wait, what had she just said?*

'Jen, what on earth is TBGL?'

'Oh darling, if you don't know that by now you certainly need to.'

'Well, what is it?'

Jen put her cup of tea gently down on a side table. There was barely space for it amidst the photo frames stuffed with images of happy summers from years gone by. She looked at me, dead in the eye. I noticed how tired she seemed. I hadn't noticed it before, and hoped that I wasn't boring her.

'It means Too Bloody Good Looking. It's a curse.'

'What are you on about? How could a person possibly be too good looking?'

'Very, very easily. It's a terrible think to happen to a person.' She bit into a Hobnob pensively.

'Oh, *really*.' I reached in for another biscuit.

'People who are devastatingly good looking rarely have to develop other skills, let alone a proper personality. Attractiveness can get you so far that often much else gets left behind. It can be a tragedy.'

166

'You sound like those supermodels who say that their life is a disaster because people are too scared to talk to them on account of how beautiful they are. Oh boohoo, that's what I say.'

'I don't doubt that that does happen to them, but I see your point. What I am talking about is how lazy good looks can make people – emotionally and intellectually.'

'I suppose real beauty can be quite hypnotic.'

'Exactly. I'm talking about properly gorgeous people, not just nice looking people who can manage to get a brush through their hair and wear clothes that don't smell of wet dogs and left over curry.'

'I see. So basically, what you're saying is that Lars is out of my league.'

'No, quite the opposite. I suspect that he's not even in your league. Because people that gorgeous are rarely as interesting or funny as the rest of us mere mortals.'

'But he's hilarious! I already told you about that time that—'

'Yes, I know all of that, and I'm not saying that he's not a nice guy. Of course he is, he seems lovely. But that's it. He's probably just a nice guy. And you deserve more than that. You deserve someone who thinks you're a goddess, someone who is filled with passion and ideas and will support you with yours. Lars just isn't the kind of guy you go out with. And that is a stone cold fact.'

Now, I knew Jen was talking sense. Jen was the One I Went To When I Needed To Hear Some Sense. But where

Lars was concerned, I still felt a kind of static buzzing in my head whenever people tried to convince me of anything other than his total and utter all-consuming immortality. It reminded me of the feeling I'd sometimes get when I was on the hunt for the perfect pair of shoes to wear with a specific frock. I'd start looking in shops and magazines and almost immediately I would see exactly what I wanted. Except usually the perfect shoes would be the £400 ones, meaning that for the rest of my hunt I just came across shoes that slightly irritated me by not being as amazingly stunningly breathtakingly perfect as the ones I had seen early on. Lars was my £400 pair of shoes, and anything else just seemed a bit tacky in comparison.

Jen broke my momentary daydream just as I was starting to imagine Lars as a pair of perfect gold dance shoes.

'Don't get sulky on me now, madam.'

'I'm not! I'm daydreaming. I do take your point, but you know how it is.'

'My memory might not be what it was, but I certainly remember what it's like to be crippled by a crush.'

'I'm not crippled!'

'If you're falling out with your friends over it, then I'd say that's a minor disability.'

'Well, yes, but I am also falling out with them because of the 'date hands' thing.'

'And that was entirely your responsibility, so the sooner you apologise and start mending your bridges there, the better.'

'You're right. I'm dreading seeing them tomorrow, and I will definitely apologise. The whole thing makes me feel sick. What a mess.'

'At this point, it seems that the only person turning it into a big deal is you. You can diffuse this.'

'Yes, and I think going to Blackpool will help. A change of atmosphere, change of pace.'

'Exactly. Now tell me this: what are you having for your supper? You need to be fighting fit for tomorrow.'

When I admitted that I hadn't even thought about it, let alone got myself to the supermarket to actually buy anything, Jen went to her freezer and fished out a frozen lasagne, which she then wrapped up in a freezer bag and presented me with on the condition that I didn't let things slide like this again. I promised solemnly, we gossiped about the rest of the family for a while, then she dropped me at the train station for me to zoom back into London. As she drove off, I waved goodbye, grateful to have such a wonderful godmother.

The atmosphere in the office on Monday morning was hard to read. In general, spirits were high after the success of Saturday's show and we were all excited about Blackpool, if a little fraught by the extra work it would involve. But it was hard for me to feel that energy through the crispy air of politeness that Matt and Sally were giving off in my direction.

There was a sense that this was the calm before the storm, that everyone was keeping a lid on things for now as it was for the best, but any one of us could blow at any minute. There was a clipped efficiency in Matt's voice when I arrived at my usual time to find him already at his desk.

'Hey, how are you?' I said, with as broad a smile as I could muster. I hung up my coat on one of the pegs by the door and turned around to hear his reply.

'Fine thank you. Good day yesterday?' The little nicknames, the teasing, the banter. They were all obvious in their absence.

'Yes thanks. Good to have a rest.'

Matt simply raised his eyebrows.

'What did you get up to?'

'Sleeping mostly. You know how it is.'

'Can I get you a coffee?'

'No thanks, just got one.'

'Okay.' I felt so sad at our forced politeness that I wanted to go into the kitchen and wail over the sound of the boiling kettle. I missed my friend, his cheery smile, and his calming ways. I missed his silly jokes, I missed his sarcastic asides, and I missed his hand on my arm as he emphasised a point. It really was as if someone very dear to me was simply not there any more. But I was determined not to cave in. Today was for making things better, not worse. It was clear from his brisk tone that Matt was not interested in discussing emotional issues in front of anyone else in the team, so I simply played along with our polite little charade and vowed to find a quiet moment to make my apology as soon as possible.

By late morning I figured that the atmosphere was calm enough that I could sneak down to the make-up office and say hi to Sally. As I walked in she was there with her boss, poring over old 1970s dancing images, looking at the hair and make-up from the Tower Ballroom's most famous days. I knocked on the open door to alert them to my presence and they both looked up.

'Hello there, sorry to interrupt,' I began as politely as I could, so as not to get Sally in any trouble with her boss, Jackie.

'No problem, how can we help?' said Jackie with a smile.

'I was just wondering if Sally knew what time she was going to take her lunch.'

'You're welcome to head off now, if you'd like,' said Jackie. 'We're pretty much done here.'

Sally looked at her watch.

'It's a bit early,' she said. 'I'm not sure if I'm really ready—'

'No worries, I was just wondering,' I interrupted. I didn't think I could bear to hear her say out loud that she didn't want to take her break with me. To lose one friend over this misunderstanding would be bad enough, but both? I felt a lump in my throat.

'That's not what I meant,' she replied.

'Oh, okay.'

'Look, why don't I come and find you in a bit? Say 45 minutes?'

Yeay! It wasn't quite as bad as I thought. Except, now of course I felt bad for interrupting her.

'Great.' I replied, with a grin.

'I'll text you, yeah?'

'Perfect.'

Within the hour we were sitting in the canteen, a plate with a steaming baked potato in front of each of us. Mine was covered in a heap of baked beans and grated cheddar. Sally's had a mountain of tuna and cottage cheese on top of hers. My stomach was in knots as I steadied my nerves to apologise to Sally.

'Listen,' I began.

'It's okay,' she replied. I looked up at her.

'Hmm?'

'It's okay. I think everything got a bit out of hand on Saturday night. All of the emotions of the show – we were all so tired and we've been seeing hardly anyone but each other. We got a kind of cabin fever and took it out on each other.'

'You really think so?'

'Yeah, I do. I think you were an idiot to have made the assump—'

'I know. I really mean it, I am so *so* sorry. I behaved like an utter brat. Please know that I am truly sorry.'

'I believe you. Really, I think the less we say about it the better. You were silly to have made the assumption, but I can see how it could have happened, I suppose. And I can understand why these things can seem like a big deal.'

'Oh I could *hug* you. Thank you so much for understanding. You know I didn't mean to intrude, I just became consumed by the idea that you two were hiding something from me.'

'Well we weren't, so give us the benefit of the doubt in future.'

'I will. Well, at least I definitely will with you.'

'Why, what's wrong with Matt?'

'Nothing. Nothing *really*.'

'That's clearly a lie. What's the problem?'

'I'm sure it will all work out in the end, but for now he is doing that thing where you are all jolly and polite, but only as a way of showing how angry you really are. That kind of breeziness that I've seen my mum giving my dad a dose of, or you sometimes see fizzing away between couples in Ikea. The whole 'Oh I'm FINE, why would you even ASK, given that you don't CARE' vibe ...'

'Ha, you do realise that you just compared the two of you to an old married couple.'

'You know what I mean. He's just not left me with that much of an opening to apologise, even though he said some pretty nasty stuff to me too.'

'You can't just wait for him to lead you around the dance floor, as it were. You've got to take command of the situation. Having said that, I do understand how crap boys are at talking about their feelings. I've just learned not to ask with Date Hands. He is always where he says he's going to be, and he's never less than brilliant fun on a date, so how can I complain if he doesn't want to open up to me about the innermost secrets of his heart? For now – I'm not that bothered. Let's just have a bit more fun and get to the heavy stuff later. We're still young; stop trying to look for the answer to everything'

'Yeah, you're right. On all counts.'

'Good luck Missus. And now can we get back to talking about this?' She held up a copy of that weekend's paper with a contestant from another reality show unveiling a truly bizarre new haircut. I giggled, putting my hand to my mouth in shock.

'I KNOW,' said Sally with a chuckle. 'That kind of thing would never go on under my roof.'

'Is it a wig?' I grabbed the paper from her hand and held it close to my face to scrutinise the picture.

'I don't think it is. I think she has actually had that haircut. And you think you've got problems …'

We dissolved into giggles and I felt a little lighter knowing that I had at least salvaged one of my friendships.

As the afternoon plodded on I kept a sly eye on the situation in the office at all times, trying to work out if there might be a moment when I could talk to Matt alone. The sun slowly dipped below the horizon and I started to feel overwhelmingly sleepy despite it being only shortly after 4pm, and I realised that the general buzz caused by the

Blackpool trip meant that I would not be alone with Matt until the end of the day.

I stayed focussed on my screen, flicking between answering emails and checking out the plans for the weekend's show. Eventually the office began to thin out as people started to head home. As I peered over my partition I could see that Matt's head was still bowed as he concentrated on his own screen. Finally, well after 6pm, Chloe took a personal call on her BlackBerry which resulted in her saying that she had to leave now too. She seemed cheerier than usual – as if when not looking at the screen of either her laptop or her BlackBerry, she might be a little more engaged with life than usual. She had a bit more lightness to her. Or maybe it was just me, finally getting to know what had always been there a little better.

'Have a lovely evening,' I said as she slung her rucksack over her shoulder.

'And you,' she said. 'Don't stay too late.' It occurred to me that I was living in topsy-turvy times if Chloe was encouraging me not to do too much work and Matt was ignoring me so he could get more done. Finally, as the door shut behind Chloe, I started to log out of the applications I had open on my computer. I stoop up, looking over the desk partitions between us.

'I'm going to head off now too,' I said. 'Unless there is anything I can help you with.'

'No, thanks, it's all cool,' said Matt with a tight little smile.

'I'm sorry.' He looked up again. I noticed for the first time how long his eyelashes were as he looked out from beneath them.

'I'm sorry about everything,' I repeated. 'I shouldn't have said those things about you. About Sally, about your dancing, about any of it. I'm really sorry if I have messed things up between us.'

'Forget it. I have.'

'Have you though?'

'Yeah sure.' He couldn't even meet my gaze.

'I have never been less convinced by anything in my life. It's a good job you are not a lawyer.'

'Let's do it this way. If we keep saying everything is fine then maybe soon it will be.'

'So you're saying it's not fine?'

'No, I'm saying I don't really want to talk about it. Least said, soonest mended and all that.'

'Fine, but remember this: I *am* truly sorry. It was just the wine, and the tiredness, and the everything getting all mixed up together—'

'Amanda.'

'Okay, I'll stop. But. You know …'

'Yes, I know.' Matt broke into his first genuine smile of the day, but still he looked a little sad.

'Friends?'

'Friends.'

'Oh yeay, because you have been such a good friend to me since I got here.'

'Friends it is,' he said looking down at his keyboard. Then he picked up a Kit Kat from his mouse mat and chucked it at me. 'Here you go Roberts. I never got round to eating this at lunch time.'

I caught it and waggled it at him.

'Call it a peace offering?' he said.

'To friends.'

And with that he picked up his bag, opened the office door for me, and headed out after me. I was getting better and better at Mondays.

Chapter 12

Three days later we were on a coach speeding up the M1 to Blackpool. I say speeding, but we weren't. It was more of a sedate trundle, in a coach that I was fairly sure had seen more of the UK than I had. The school trip vibe was in full swing among the Strictly team; we were all tingling with nerves and excitement. Matt was sitting alongside some of the lighting guys, and Sally and I were sharing a row, flicking through endless celebrity weeklies together, discussing potential outfits and rumoured flings. At the back of the coach a gaggle of the costume ladies were working their way through fashion magazines, tearing out ideas and gossiping about weight loss secrets of the stars they had worked with in the past. We were a little travelling Strictly bubble, and I was on cloud nine to be a part of it.

Dusk was falling as we approached Blackpool. The coach driver pointed out the tower to us from miles away and the slow approach towards the twinkling lights had a uniquely British kind of romance.

'It's like the Eiffel Tower!' I gasped. 'Sort of …'

'Durrr, that's what it's modelled on,' said Matt, craning his neck around to look back and pull a stupid face at me.

'I'd never realised how imposing it was. You don't get any sense of that from the photos.'

'I know what you mean,' chipped in Sally. 'It's blummin' massive. Blackpool doesn't look great in the guidebooks when you're used to looking up cheap flights to Mikonos, but when I came for the first time last year I was really knocked out by how strangely magical it is.'

I agreed. I had not been expecting it, but I was getting a real sense of the glamour and excitement that was a part of Blackpool. I rested my head on the coach window and looked down at the streets of guesthouses we were now starting to pass.

As we waited at a crossing I saw an elderly woman step out of her guesthouse and start sweeping the step. She looked tired, worn even, but I admired the way that she was keeping her property. Moments after she started, a man of her age came out of the building. He was wearing slacks, slippers and a tank top over a plaid shirt. He put his arm around her, took the broom and gave her an enormous kiss. A sense of sadness crept up on me. For all the glamour of the ballroom, the thought of ending up with a man like that seemed just as enticing from time to time.

'You should be more excited, Roberts,' said Matt with a grin. 'We're in the home of ballroom in this country.

How have you not been here every summer since you were a kid?'

'I don't know, I guess my parents weren't as excited by sprung dance floors as I was in the nineties.'

I was reminded of the day trips I had taken to Brighton with my family as a child. The towns seemed so similar, as if they were siblings. Matt chuckled to himself, as the coach headed further towards the centre of Blackpool. I was now pinned to the window, trying to absorb as much of the atmosphere as possible. It was an uncanny combination of full-on glamour and near-derelict buildings, seemingly within a few blocks of each other. There were row upon row of theme pubs, a mobility scooter hire shop on almost every corner, and most importantly of all, signs advertising shows and dances plastered outside the majority of the venues. I felt as if I was coming home – this truly was the land of the dance floor.

As we pulled into the hotel and I caught sight of the sea for the first time, I felt a genuine frisson of holiday excitement. I could almost smell the brine, the candyfloss and the polish on the dance floors. All of those dreams that had been fulfilled here, all of those longed-for dances, all of those embraces masquerading as holds. I felt that we were dancing in the footsteps of generations of dancers.

My dreams that night had nothing on the psychedelic torment of Saturday night but I still slept fitfully, startling at every unfamiliar sound from within the bowels of the hotel, struggling to work out what temperature I wanted the small room to be, and above all, wildly excited about where we were. I was awake by 6am, sitting propped up against the four huge hotel pillows, watching rolling news in a trance and wondering how my belongings – now scattered all over the floor – had ever fitted into the overnight bag I had brought with me. I slightly wished I had something fabulous and sequined so that we could all go out dancing after the show on Saturday, but alas I had the same wardrobe as ever.

Several of us met downstairs in the hotel's restaurant for breakfast, bleary-eyed and slightly unnerved to be seeing each other at such an early hour, so fresh from bed. It wasn't so much the early start that made breakfasting together seem this intimate – we had all seen each other at all hours before – and nor was it the actual breakfast – loads of us ate at our desks at work the whole time. But it was the fact that there was nothing between our beds and our plates. Usually we had all commuted into the office, but that morning there was no way of getting around the fact that we were fresh from our bedrooms. Some of the men still had wet hair from the shower, some of the women's make-up looked considerably fresher than it tended to after twenty five minutes on the Central Line and we all smelled icily of toothpaste. Of course, no one said a thing about it, but I suspected we all knew. We ate our cereal (or giant fry ups, in the case of the gents) without mentioning it. In fact, we were stumped for our usual conversation as well. With no commute to banter about, and not much to say about the walk down the hotel staircase, we had little to say to each other, and ate largely in silence.

It was both thrilling and disappointing to see that Sally looked even more immaculate than ever. There was a part of me that had sometimes hoped that her precise 1950s lines would look too harsh first thing in the morning, but no – they simply looked as if she was in high definition. Chloe looked much the same as ever, not just looks-wise but because of her preoccupation with her BlackBerry. I had checked if she had a Twitter account weeks ago and she didn't (or at least, not under her own name), and given that the whole team was right there under the same roof, I struggled to know what it was that was of such fascination or importance that it kept the thing stapled to her at all times. I decided that she must have a very active Facebook community, although it seemed doubtful.

One of the last to make it down to breakfast was Matt, who appeared to have slept as well as I had. His hair was freshly washed, and he had attempted to style it, although there was a clump sticking out at the back, shooting off in a direction entirely independent to the rest of his 'do'. He was wearing clothes I had never seen before: loose, comfortable jeans, and a chunky-knit navy and white woollen jumper that made him look as if he could happily head to the sea for a day's fishing. In his hand he had a soft pale blue scarf. I recognised the scarf as the one that was often hanging from the back of his office chair, or crumpled in a heap to the side of the set. It seemed as familiar an old friend as he did.

I was getting up to fetch myself a second cup of coffee when he entered the dining room, so as I passed him I gave him a dig in the ribs and asked my usual: 'Coffee?' As I nudged by him I noticed how lovely he smelled. None of the overwhelming spray-smells of the two cameramen I had been in the lift downstairs with, but a more subtle hint of grass and clean linen. This was new.

'Go on then, Roberts,' he replied, and pulled out a chair on the opposite side of the table I had been sitting at. As I walked off towards the coffee counter I heard him ribbing Sally about the hot-pink diamond print sweater she was wearing.

I don't really know what possessed me to do what I did when I came back with the two cups of coffee, but the freshly laundered Matt smell that I had caught a whiff of when he came in seemed to have done something curious to my sense of confidence. So I walked back, carefully avoiding spillages from the coffee cups, and then leant in to put Matt's down before him. As I did, I took a deep breath. I was right, he smelt lovely. So, as I was leaning over his shoulder to deliver the coffee, I turned my face and gave him a smacker of a kiss on his right cheek. I have no idea what had come over me, but the weekend-away vibe of us all being in the hotel together had somehow seeped into my pores. It was only a couple of weeks ago I had been thrown by him hugging and kissing me, and now I was doing the same, utterly unprompted.

At the very moment that my lips touched his soft, freshly-shaven cheek, I realised that what I was doing was inappropriate for a world of reasons. Firstly, we just weren't kissy-kissy friends. We never did air-pecks, we barely hugged, we were arm-punch and back-slap kinda pals. Secondly, from my vantage point as I kissed him (which was mostly a very close up view of his nose); I saw Sally's eyebrows shoot up and suddenly remembered that I was in front of my colleagues. Mercifully, I could not see Chloe's response to what I had done, but the cameramen had not escaped my notice. And thirdly ... why on earth was I doing this?

As I lifted my mouth away I decided that the only possible thing I could do now was to just keep talking, without pause, for a minute or two, so that no one else could. That would work, wouldn't it?

'Mwah! Kiss me quick!' I doffed my imaginary beach hat while slightly wishing I were dead. 'One coffee for you Mister. Now then, I'm off for another slice of toast, so can I get any of you good folk a little something extra while I'm at it?'

Now I was backing away from the table and talking like my dad when he was feeling nervous around my mum's parents at Christmas. What had got *into* me?

'No? Nothing else for anyone? Not even a tiny pot of hotel jam?'

Oh god, shut up Amanda, just shut up.

And with a final flourish I backed into a member of the serving staff and sent the full English that he was carrying clattering to the carpet. I longed to clatter to the carpet myself, as I offered profuse apologies and help clearing up. It was of course mortifying, but had the momentary benefit of diverting everyone's attention from my ludicrous show of affection and towards the beans slowly congealing into the swirly corporate patterns decorating the floor.

The speed with which we had to head to the set was the only thing that saved me from the horrors of breakfast time. We were on a coach to the Tower Ballroom within twenty minutes and conversation had moved on to the day's rehearsals ahead. The approach to the foot of the tower was exciting, but only as exciting as a short coach trip involving all of your colleagues and an enormous car park could possibly be. On the other hand, nothing had prepared me for the majesty of the ballroom itself.

After weeks of seeing routines being rehearsed for the Strictly dance floor, to see the Tower Ballroom in all its glory was incomparable. The first thing that Sally and I did was walk out onto the sprung floor to feel its springiness.

'It's made of all different kinds of woods. I was reading about it on my phone in the hotel room this morning,' she said.

Matt came up and joined us, with a couple of the others.

'It's incredible, isn't it? Mahogany, oak and walnut – over 30,000 blocks.'

185

Sally rolled her eyes at me, as if to say 'Men and facts, eh?'

'I'm ashamed to say I don't even know when it was built,' I replied, looking up and trying to take in the height of the ceiling and its intense goldness. To say it was extravagant would be like saying that I enjoyed the odd spin around a dance floor. I tapped my foot on the floor, and felt the delicious give that it had. I did a little jump, and as I landed felt exquisitely cushioned.

'Dreamy,' I muttered to myself.

'It looks kinda Victorian,' said Sally. 'I think I was thinking more of 70s kitsch.'

'This tower, ladies, is a part of the World Federation of Great Towers. Oh yes indeedy. Such a thing exists. Created in 1989.'

'All this gold though, dude. It's like the Victorians were outdoing Versace before Versace was doing Versace.'

'When did you become Norris McWhirter?' asked Sally.

Matt had his head tipped back and was looking at the ceiling. I could see his Adam's apple on his tilted throat.

'That's a quote from Shakespeare, from a poem called Venus and Adonis,' he continued.

'Wow, romantic,' said Sally, spinning around and trying to soak it all in. I said nothing, just looking around me, stunned to be there at all.

'Those chandeliers are also some serious bling.'

'Yeah, they get lowered to the floor to be cleaned. It takes more than a week to do them.'

'Seriously, Matt, I thought I was a bit of a Blackpool geek this morning in the hotel. How do you know all of this?'

'I used to come here as a kid. I had a book of facts I got with my pocket money one year. I loved it. I was kind of obsessed by it.'

'Sweet,' said Sally. 'Bet you never thought it would come in this handy. I don't really remember seeing you much here last year.'

Matt didn't have a chance to reply as the dancers and their partners were starting to arrive for band rehearsals, and I was soon busy buzzing around after Chloe. The enormity of the Tower Ballroom in comparison to the usual set slightly overwhelmed us all. The dancers were having to make an extra effort to fill the space, us runners were exhausted from the extra distance we were covering and the band were making adjustment to how they usually played as well.

I was sitting on one of the red, velvet-covered chairs to the side of the stage, going through plans for Saturday night, when Lars and Kelly took to the stage. They looked like an actual couple as they walked onto the floor, and I felt a tiny niggle of jealousy. It was hard to dislike Kelly as she had been nothing but kind and vulnerable around me, but each time that I saw them arm in arm, jealousy simmered somewhere inside me. That jealousy was not a little stoked by my knowing that once again, I had memorised their routine as a result of watching their rehearsal videos and seeing their preparations so far.

Kelly was wearing a pale pink ball gown, emphasising her tiny waist and enhancing her not inconsiderable bosom. It wasn't as full-on Vegas-style glittery as some of the costumes I had seen the others in, but it had more of a delicate shimmer to it. The fabric looked as if it was shot with something slightly metallic, and caught the light with every spin. She was wearing high gold shoes and had her hair up on the top of her head, with a few tendrils tumbling down. From sleeve to waist were billowing swags. She was nothing short of a fairy princess.

And Lars made an impeccable prince. In his evening jacket and dance shoes he looked as if he had stepped fresh off the Titanic. His hair was more formal than usual, slicked down Don Draper-style, which made it look darker than I knew it to be. He was making a perfect courtly lover for Kelly, who was glowing as a result of the gasps we all made on seeing her appear.

As the music began they started to move. They were so smooth it was as if they were flying. They spun through the extra space on the dance floor, seemingly owning it. The pair of them exuded nothing but confidence and grace. And yet …

I was looking at Lars' face when Kelly fell. I didn't understand what had happened until the moments afterwards when the fuss around them had subsided a little bit. All I saw was Lars leaning elegantly over her as if he had nothing but adoration for her, and then ... she lay crumpled on the floor.

'What's happened?' barked Chloe, anxiety pinching her face. She threw down her clipboard and ran to the couple. 'Matt! Call the medical team.'

I saw Matt, who had been at the other end of the stage, hurry off towards the exit, and I followed Chloe towards Kelly. She was breathing in through gritted teeth, wincing and holding her ankle.

'I caught my heel on the back of my dress,' she explained. 'It unbalanced me and I twisted my ankle.'

'Oh, you poor thing,' replied Chloe, already removing the fleece she was wearing to create a cushion for Kelly's foot. 'We've got the medics on the way. Just stay still.'

'How is it now?' asked Lars, who was kneeling by her head, and touching her tenderly on the arm. I noted the look of concern in his face.

'I'm not sure – I'm scared to put weight on it.' She looked up at him anxiously.

'Stay still until the medics comes.'

'Yes, stay still.' Chloe was exuding protocol from every pore.

'But we have so little time to rehearse with the band.'

'Don't worry, we'll think of something.'

Lars looked up at me. We caught each other's eyes. I had been doing my best to stay out of his way (without being unprofessional) since the Salsa Incident. It hadn't been easy, what with him becoming ever more popular on set and me being given ever more duties, but I was doing my best. This was my first run-in with him. It was every bit as discreet as my worst nightmares had let me imagine. What if he gave me away for my secret salsa?

The medics appeared, ushered in by Matt.

'Can we have some space around the patient please, everybody step back.'

We cleared the area surrounding Kelly while one of the medics examined her foot, gently asking what had happened and getting her to bend her ankle into various positions. After a couple of minutes he stood up and looked around.

'Right, it's a light sprain, nothing too serious. Kelly needs to keep her feet up for the rest of the today, but if she does that – if she does absolutely that – then she will be able to dance tomorrow.'

A stretcher was wheeled into the ballroom and the doctor, Lars and Matt helped her onto it.

'But what about the rehearsal?' said Kelly.

'I'm so sorry, Kelly,' said Chloe, gripping her clipboard once again. 'You only have ten minutes left of your rehearsal time now and we won't be able to do it tomorrow. The schedules for lighting are really tight now that we're not in the studio.'

'We really need to get things nailed down though,' said a voice from the band.

'It would be helpful,' seconded Lars.

'But you heard the doctor. Kelly absolutely cannot put weight on that foot today.'

'Could you mark it out alone, Lars?' asked another of the band members.

'What's the point?' Kelly's shoulders slumped. 'This is a disaster!' she wailed. She threw the broken shoe from the hand she had had it in since her fall. It landed on the floor in front of me. It was an exquisite, delicate shoe, and looked so sad with its broken strap. Kelly was clearly more preoccupied with getting the routine perfect than she was with not sustaining any further injury to herself.

'No, Kelly, it's not a disaster – the main thing is that you will be able to dance tomorrow.' Chloe was absolutely right, but I could appreciate Kelly's desire to nail this before the performance tomorrow night – the competition was getting ever tougher and no one wanted to be even that little bit unprepared. Theirs was one of the most technically difficult routines of the week.

Lars looked up again, more slowly this time. He glanced at me, and then turned to Chloe.

'Unless ...'

'Unless what?' said Chloe, now impatient.

'Unless we do the routine with someone else.'

'What do you mean?'

I could feel heat rising, first in my chest and then towards my face. I gripped and ungripped my hands. I didn't want to be seen blushing.

'I don't know, is there anyone else who knows the routine?' He was staring directly at me now. I lifted my chin.

'I do,' I whispered.

'You do?' Chloe looked confused.

'Yes, I've been watching the tapes all week ...'

'... and she can dance. She can really dance.'

'Thank you.' I looked up at Lars, who was staring at me expectantly. Kelly looked utterly perplexed. Her head snapped between the three of us.

'And you can do it to time?'

'I think so, yes.'

'She could do it before. I'm sure she could again.'

Just as Chloe was about to query what exactly 'before' might mean, Lars stepped in.

'I've seen her dance. She knows all the steps. Please, Kelly, Chloe, let's have our rehearsal. Amanda can help us.'

'Is this true, Amanda?' I had always expected that if Chloe found out about my dancing, she would be angry. But now her expression was more one of concern.

'Yes, I think I could help.'

'But are you prepared to?'

'Of course – I want the show to be as good as it possibly can.'

Kelly was now lying back on her stretcher.

'Guys, whatever helps.' She seemed neither jealous nor angry, but was slowly resigning herself to the fact that she was temporarily out of the equation. Lars bent over to her, his face filled with sympathy.

'We need Amanda, and she's prepared to help. Please rest, Kelly.'

'I know. Thank you.' She turned to me with a smile. I don't think I'll ever know how genuine it was. She is, after all, an actress with a lot of experience. Matt looked up at the others helping with the stretcher.

'Come on, guys.'

They carried her away with the doctor in attendance. 'Let's get an ice pack on that' were the last words I heard.

'She needs shoes,' Lars was saying to the others seated around. 'Amanda, what size are you? Wardrobe!'

'I'm a 37.' My heart was hammering. What had seemed like an enormous dance floor before now seemed infinite from my position in its centre.

'THIRTY SEVEN!' he shouted. Moments later one of the wardrobe girls reappeared with a pair of gold heels. They were basically my dream dance shoes: a heel but not too high, a small, delicate strap around my ankle, and then three stripes of gold leather spreading across my toes. They were dreamy, classic, elegant, and now they were mine.

'Here you go. How are they?'

I stepped back to the seats on the edge of the stage and tentatively tried them on. My hands were shaking. It took me three goes to get the prong of the buckle into the clasp. All those years of longing to have a pair myself. All those years of hoping that one day I would wear a pair with pride. And now I was shoving them on with a tense audience watching me, willing me to hurry up.

'They're fine, they're fine.'

I stood up, feeling ridiculous in my denim skirt and hoodie.

'Really? We can't have another injury.' Chloe's concern was touching.

'Are you okay?' Lars stepped forward and took my hand. I banished all thoughts of Cinderella from my mind. This was work. This was not a fairy tale. It was my career. I must remember that.

'Yes, I'm fine.' I took his hand. I forgot everything.

'Thank you, Amanda, this is very kind. Please, just do your best.'

'No problem'. I gave Chloe a ridiculous thumbs up.

'Stay here,' whispered Lars, before stepping across the to the band. He spoke quietly to the conductor for a moment, before returning to me. Yes. Returning ... to me.

The floor manager gestured towards the crew.

'Are we ready team?' Nods all round.

I heard the conductor count in to the beginning of the music. I couldn't feel my legs, my mind was entirely blank, I was quivering with nerves. I had no idea what was going to happen next – it was as if every anxiety I had ever had was suddenly rushing towards me. How could I get out of this now?

The song began. The American smooth began. My dance began.

At first I was shaking, but this time, unlike with the salsa, Lars was there. I wasn't dancing alone, I was in his arms. After the first few steps it was as if we had always been dancing together. The steps that I had been watching all week were no longer just taking place on a screen in front of me; they were coming from within me. To begin with my feet were moving, but soon my entire body was moving. And then, it wasn't just that my body was moving, but that it felt like a part of his. We were one – sinuous, graceful, elegant. We were no longer just creating shapes with our bodies, but with the space around us that we were inhabiting. I could barely feel my feet touching the floor any more. It was as if we were flying. It seemed that the dance shoes I was so honoured to be wearing were no longer even touching the sprung floor beneath me. I wondered if I would ever return to ground.

I felt Lars's body beneath me as the lift came beats closer. I had never even attempted such a lift, let alone succeeded at one. But suddenly – before there had been a moment for apprehension or doubt – there I was, held above his head. I could see the parquet of the floor beneath me. Lars tenderly released me from the lift and I felt filled with confidence. I could do this after all! I could be everything I dreamed of!

The dance came to a close. I dropped to the floor for the elegant finale. I stayed there, my head bowed; my eyelids clamped shut, breathing intensely to myself. It had been a dream, and I didn't want it to end. To open my eyes again would be to admit that it had.

And then … applause. I looked up, trembling. And saw that everyone surrounding the dance floor was standing, clapping wildly. Even the band were putting down their instruments and applauding, whooping and cheering. Chloe had her right hand clamped across her chest in a gesture of affection. Lars extended his hand to help me up, and once I stood he gave me the most enormous embrace. It wasn't a hug, it was an actual embrace.

For weeks I had idled away moments on the bus, at my desk, in the shower, dreaming about having my face clamped to that chest, and now I was there. With everyone watching. And yet, despite it all, it felt strangely intimate. I wanted to cry. I could feel my chest heaving up and down as a result of the intense emotion. Lars stroked my hair.

'Thank you,' he whispered. 'You were incredible. The best.'

Chapter 13

The applause was still ringing around us when Lars and I disentangled ourselves from each other. My usual response to so much attention – from my colleagues and from him – would have been to scuttle away as fast as possible and hide. But the dancing had filled me with a tantalising sense of what was possible. I could still feel the heat of his body radiating near to mine. Instead of wanting to crawl into the nearest hole I chose to stand there and let Lars lift me up, then parade me around the floor for a few seconds while the crew whistled in support for my unexpected skills.

I could feel myself glowing. But this time it wasn't shame burning in my cheeks but pride. All of those hours watching dancing, practising dancing, feeling like the nerd on the team for loving all of the technicalities so much – they had counted for something after all. I was experiencing my magical moment in the sun and I didn't care if my cheeks radiated under its heat. I had not only experienced a dream come true by dancing with Lars, but I had been genuinely helpful to my colleagues. I had stepped up and taken one for the team. I was part of something now.

As I realised that, I remembered that I was still at work, and that I might perhaps need to retain a little professional composure. For some reason I did this by brushing down my skirt, as if I were a 1950s housewife who had just baked a fresh loaf, and smoothing my hair. Then, I gave Lars a little curtsey, said 'Thank you' softly to him, and scuttled off the dance floor to stand near to Chloe again.

My heart was tight at the thought of what her response might be to my undercover skills. Would she be angry, thinking me more interested in dancing than working for her? Would she think my mind wasn't on the job? My anxieties proved to be entirely unfounded when, instead of frowning at me like a silly little girl, she put her arm around me, grinning from ear to ear.

'Well, Amanda. I had no idea! I don't think any of us did. No one ever doubted your enthusiasm, but that is quite a skill you have there.'

Emotion swelled up from inside me. *Please don't let me burst into tears in front of my boss. Please.*

She looked at me. 'Your mother would be very proud. And you should be very proud of yourself.'

'You have no idea how much that means to me,' I replied, swallowing fast to try and stop my tears from spilling out. 'I'm just glad I could help.' With that I stepped back to sit on a chair and began to unstrap my beloved sandals. Within minutes rehearsals had returned to normal, as if it wasn't the day that my dream came true at all. But I knew it had. And I hugged that knowledge to myself tightly.

As soon as I could take a break I scarpered off to the dressing rooms that make-up were working out of, and found Sally. When I knocked on the door of their room she was staring at her mobile with a look of total incomprehension.

'What's wrong with your phone?' I asked.

'Oh. OH. My phone is fine. My love life: another matter. Mister Date Hands has blown me out.'

'No way? I thought it had been established that he was totally Date Hands?' It did not pass me by that we were now joking about someone who had caused my only proper argument with Sally. This pleased me enormously.

'It was! He was all over me. We were a thing. But now he realises that this is not the time for him to be in a relationship. Ptcha! He is in a relationship: a relationship with his ego. Oh, the tedium. I really liked him. How could I have been so wrong?'

'I know you did, honey. But you weren't to know. What a crappy thing to have happened.'

As I put my arm around her, I felt Sally's shoulders shake. For all her feistiness and bravado, I could tell that she was really upset.

'I really liked him,' she mumbled, almost to herself.

'Yeah, and the idiot really liked you too.'

'He did. I really think he did.'

'No doubt, Babe. You know what, that was probably what scared him. The idea of having to step up to the plate and be a good enough boyfriend for you.'

'But I don't want a superhero.'

'Maybe not, but it's what you deserve. Honestly, everything you've ever told me the last week or so just makes me thing he's been stringing you along. Nothing more, nothing less.'

'Yeah, you're probably right.'

'I know I'm right.'

'Anyway, why are you so perky? What's happened? Someone given you your own salsa school?'

'As good as ...' and with that I launched into the story of what had happened to me that morning. From the shoes, to the applause, to the way that I had felt Lars's heartbeat against mine. It was intoxicating. I was trying to hold back so as not to upset Sally when she was already feeling down, but she seemed to realise how extraordinary the turn of events was too, and soon we had spent a solid fifteen minutes squealing at each other, grabbing each other's wrists and then trying to calm each other down.

'I can't believe it, dude! You totally got up on that dance floor!'

'I know, it was the most surreal thing ever. I'm so sorry to keep going on about it.'

'I want you to go on. It's just the best example ever of dreams coming true for someone who really deserves it.'

'Awww. Thanks, you.'

'Nah, no need to say thanks. You have cheered me right up.'

'Who's been in need of cheering and why? Do I have to get my clown shoes and red nose?'

Matt was at the doorway, his arms either side of the door frame, his body leaning in.

'Date Hands has ended it with Sally.'

'Idiot.'

'But I'm already cheered by hearing Amanda's incredible dance floor rescue story.'

A shadow passed across Matt's face.

'Yeah,' was all he said. 'Kelly's going to be okay. She's with the physio.'

'Oh good,' I replied. 'I'm just glad I could help.'

'I'm sure you are.'

'Don't start that again, you guys,' said Sally.

'Nobody's starting anything. Amanda? Nope, thought not. Anyway, I came to see who wanted to go down to the pier with me later. We won't be done here til it's dark but I'm up for making the most of things while we're here. Last time I barely left the hotel room.'

'Yep, me too.' Sally leapt on the idea. 'So I'm totally up for your plan. Better than staying in my room pressing refresh on my email in case Date Hands changes his mind.'

As night fell, the three of us hit the pier as promised. The wind was so fierce and so cold that it felt almost vindictive. The sea smelt incredible, the brine churning all around us. We were wrapped up in winter coats, scarves and gloves, and Matt and Sally were both wearing hats. Matt's was a massive beanie, pulled right down over his ears, and Sally's was a cute sheepskin affair with earflaps and a tie for beneath her chin. I was – despite Sunday's best efforts – ill-prepared for the cold, and was shivering. My only consolation was the pair of gloves that Matt had lent me on my first week on the show when I had been outside letting the studio audience in.

We got fish and chips and ate them quickly, huddled together, then decided that we needed doughnuts too, which we devoured until our faces were covered with specks of sugar. The sky was dark against the dramatic lights and there were very few people around. We walked down as far as we could, out onto the sea, and then took photos of each other with our red noses and wind-lashed hair. The lights flashed across our faces and created dramatic effects as if we were on stage all over again. Matt was incredibly patient as we took several of Sally, until we had a suitably devastating one. Then, it was immediately uploaded to her Facebook so that she could prove to the dastardly Mister Date Hands that she was having a wonderful time without him.

As the three of us walked back we saw an elderly couple, standing at close quarters, braced against the wind. They seemed both vulnerable and strong: an utterly united front as they stood together, protecting one another as best they could from the elements, and yet their age meant that they looked stooped and frail.

'Aww, look at them,' I said as we walked towards them. 'I bet they've been coming here for years. Just imagine, maybe they met here in the sixties or seventies.'

'Yeah, I love them. That's all I want.' And with that, Sally's ballsy exterior crumbled.

I glanced across to Matt with concern. He raised his eyebrows as if to say 'Well *I* don't know what to do – this is girl stuff.' But he put his arm around her instinctively.

As Sally's sobs took full flight, her phone went off. It was Mister Date Hands.

'Shall I take it?' She looked up at us, anguished.

'Not if he's going to be able to tell that you're crying.' Matt's tone was decisive.

'Oh screw that!' She wiped the tears from her eyes, straightened her back and pressed the green button on her phone.

'Yeah?' No one would ever have known how hurt she was from *that* tone of voice.

Sally walked across the pier to the other side, so that we could no longer hear what she was saying. Matt and I paused, leaning up against the edge, our backs to the sea. Slowly the elderly couple approached us, the woman reaching out her hand, encased in its sheepskin mitten, to her husband. We listened to the sea.

'You did great today,' said Matt, turning his face towards mine. 'I know what a big deal it must have been for you. You absolutely rose to the occasion.'

'Thanks. I know how you feel about him.'

'I don't hate him. I just want you to be careful. Dancers use their bodies differently to the rest of us. It doesn't always mean what it would mean if you danced with someone else.'

'Matt, I'm not an idiot.'

'I know. I would never say that. I would never even think that. It's just, I can see how vulnerable you can be. I just want you to be okay. You're special to me. You're my, you're my … well, you're my …'

His words were eaten by the wind but it didn't seem to matter. I turned to face him too, and suddenly felt warm. I didn't know why, and I didn't know what was going on, but it was one of those moments when all it would have taken was an inch. Just one of us to lean forwards an inch. I saw the elderly couple, now holding hands, in my peripheral vision. Suddenly a sheepskin-swaddled hand in mine seemed more romantic than all the sequins in the world. It was just … a matter … of an inch … You breath in … you breath out … you wait.

And then, just as quickly as the moment had overtaken us, it was broken. Sally was running towards us.

'DUDES! He has gone back to his GIRLFRIEND! I mean, I KNOW! I had no idea. Some people, they can just lie and lie. I had no idea. He even *told* me he was single!'

'No way!' I said, turning the full beam of my attention to her. 'Who would do that to you?' I looked back. Matt was staring at the couple. Whatever there had been between us was gone, caught on the wind and swept seawards, as ephemeral as the candyfloss being spun at the pier's entrance.

We put our arms around Sally and continued to commiserate with her until we found a pub back in the warm, and had a round of whiskeys to raise a toast to her deserved and fabulous new single status. One round was all we dared to have, given the day we had ahead of us, and it was only half an hour later that we were back at the hotel.

We arrived at reception, clapping our hands and stomping our feet against the cold. Matt and Sally were staying a floor below me and I had to buy a pass for the hotel wireless network as I wanted to email Allegra. While I was sorting that out another of the receptionists walked over and noticed that I had received a telephone message that afternoon. She passed it over, written neatly on a compliments slip decorated with the hotel's logo.

Please telephone Jen.

Curious, I thought to myself, before looking at my mobile. I saw that I had three missed calls from her. Unlike Sally I hadn't had my phone gripped in my hand so I hadn't felt it ringing in my pocket while on the windy pier. I noted the time; it was after ten. Jen wasn't really the sort to leave lots of desperate messages, but three missed calls was unusual. I put it down to her being super-keen to hear all about Blackpool. I had told her that I would be working all hours and that there was very little I could tell her about it anyway, but her enthusiasm knew no bounds. It was too late to call her back, so I sent a quick text while waiting for the lift. As I was tapping away the fire doors next to the lift opened and Lars appeared. No longer in his American smooth dinner jacket, he was now in his usual relaxed clothing – grey tracksuit bottoms, a deep v-neck t-shirt and a thin woollen cardigan. I wanted to know if it was cashmere. I wanted to reach out and touch it. At that very moment.

'Well good evening, Miss Smooth.' His smile was warm and genuine. There wasn't that edge, as if he was taking the mick out of me, this time.

'Hello there.' I tilted my head to one side, coyly. I felt myself do it, and immediately tried to straighten it in a vague attempt at maintaining my professional veneer.

'Bed time?'

'Well, I was just … Won't you be tired tomorrow? It's such a big dance for you.'

'There wouldn't have been a tomorrow's dance if not for you. Therefore, I think we should have a quick drink to celebrate your performance …'

'Um, I don't know if—'

'Come on, you.' And with that, he put his arm around my shoulders and led me to the bar. It was only seconds later that I was sitting in front of the barman, who was smiling at me expectantly. What was the right answer? *Obviously* I didn't want to be churlish. I *wanted* to celebrate our dance. The idea of basking in the glow of his attention was utterly exhilarating.

But what was the right thing to order? I didn't want to suggest something that would make me seem childish, or gauche. But I desperately wanted to be on top of my game in the morning as well. I wouldn't be able to work properly with a hangover, nor did I want to get caught in the bar with booze in my hand by one of the more senior members of the team. My eyes raced up and down the drinks menu in a panic. I couldn't deal with the pressure.

'Oh, just a white wine spritzer, please,' I said to the barmen. He nodded, turned and looked at Lars.

'A tonic water for me please.' I wanted to shrivel up and die. Why did I assume that going for a drink had to mean a boozy drink? I didn't even want any wine. It was too late. I had to deal with it now. I smiled graciously when the barmen placed the stupidly summery drink down in front of me at exactly the same moment that my chunky knit scarf fell off the back of my bar stool.

Ever the gentleman, Lars didn't even appear to have noticed what I was drinking, or that it was unusual. He swivelled around on his bar stool and raised his glass to mine.

'Cheers!' he said, chinking his glass against mine. 'Congratulations and thank you so much for your help!'

Having his attention on me full beam reminded me of the time I had been in an incredibly expensive sports car once. My legs felt like jelly, my mouth was going slightly numb and I was as excited as I was terrified.

'It's okay, it was a treat really. You must know that'.

There's no need to admit it, Amanda.

'Well I am glad that you had fun, but your help was invaluable. I knew you had a bit of a passion for dancing, but I had no idea that you had actual talent. You should consider taking it further.'

Breathe in Amanda, and don't forget to breathe out.

'I'll never be a professional though. I'm not like Kelly.'

'That can only be your decision. I think there is something in you.'

Ohmygodohmygodohmygod.

'She's lovely, but Kelly has had years of stage school experience. She's a professional. I don't dance because I want to make a living out of it. I dance because I love it. When I am dancing, I feel more confident, more powerful, closer to the real me. I feel more like the me that I like, that other people would like, that I want to be all of the time.'

Why are you telling him all of this? You've never told anyone.

'Why would anyone not like you? You're adorable.'

'I suppose I feel more alive when I'm dancing.'

I was tingling to the very tips of my fingers.

'You *are* more alive when you dance. Kelly is a sweet girl, but she has a lot on her plate at the moment. She is dancing to prove a point. She doesn't feel the dance; she doesn't live the dance. It is her anger and her hurt that is propelling her through the dance. With you, it is your passion for dance.'

208

'Don't be harsh on Kelly – she's only ever been kind to me. I thought you got on.'

'Oh we do, I adore her.'

'But … no romance?'

'No, not at all. Kelly is too recently hurt. She is in no place for love. She is rebuilding.'

How are we having this conversation? I'm not even drunk.

'And how about you, Amanda?'

'Oh, I'm, just, you see, well. It's confusing …'

Are you going to admit that you are single or not? Get a grip, girl.

I desperately didn't want to expose myself to embarrassment or rejection, but then, if Lars didn't know that I was single how could *anything* ever happen between us?

'… I try to keep, you know, work and stuff. I don't want to, with my career, but then – the right person—'

'I understand.' Mercifully, he had stopped me. 'It is hard, especially on a show like this. It is hard not to let the romance creep its way into your soul. '

'Yes!'

Okay, that reply was a little too emphatic.

I looked away, embarrassed. The barman had cleaned the entire bar, and seemed to be wiping things again. He was standing as far from us as possible, clearly trying to be discreet about how clearly he could hear our conversation.

'Well,' said Lars. He drained the last of his tonic water. 'I think it is time that we got our beauty sleep. Not for you, of course. Well, you can sleep, but what I mean is that you don't need to sleep for beauty.'

It was the first time I had ever seen him stumble or be awkward. He always seemed to know what to say. His commanding physical presence, his confidence on the dance floor, his calm nature – they all followed him off the stage and into real life. This was the only moment of weakness or silliness that I had seen in him. I giggled at him. And now he was the one tipping his head coyly.

'Come on, what floor are you on?' he said, his back against the swing doors of the bar. 'Good night!' he called to the barman as he held the doors open for me.

'Three.'

'Well I am on the ground floor, so I must bid you good night.'

He pressed the call button on the lift and while it whirred into action he turned to me, placed his huge hands tenderly on my shoulders and stared into my eyes.

'You were wonderful,' he said. 'Don't ever forget that. Ever.'

Then, as I heard the lift approaching, he bent down towards my face.

He's going to do it. He's going to kiss me. He's leaning in that extra inch.

The lift reached the ground floor, and as it did, he did lean in. He leant forwards and kissed me on the tip of my nose. The lift pinged, and the doors opened. I walked in.

The doors closed more slowly than any doors in history have ever closed. As soon as I was out of sight I had to hold the carpeted interior. I had literally gone weak at the knees. It was cool in there, and calm. I knew that it would be my last few minutes of peace and quiet for a few days. I inhaled, as if at a yoga class, and then faced the doors bravely as they opened. I could cope with this. A kiss from the man I had been dreaming of for months was fine. There was no problem here. And then I exhaled. You see? Totally calm.

Chapter 14

Saturday flew by in a blur of busyness for all of us. From the moment I woke up I felt as if I was trying to catch up with the speed of things, and I suspected that I wasn't the only one. There was no time for a leisurely breakfast bonding with our colleagues today. We were grabbing food and coffee, eating croissants and toast almost still standing, and some of us were still eating hotel muffins out of napkins on the bus to the Tower Ballroom.

I didn't even see Sally before heading out to get my coach but I made sure to text her as soon as I thought she was up.

Babe, you okay? Just finishing breakfast. My coach leaves in 8 mins.

Yes, hon. I'll be okay. My coach at quarter past. Thnx for everything last night. Gutted about that loser, but I'll get over it. So glad to be busy today.

At least we have that.

We'll go out soon when we're back, ys?

Oh indeed. And also – flatmate Allegra coming to
show in a week. She wants to bring guys, will tell her
to bring extra Italian 'distraction' for you, ha haa.

Oh yes please!

By the time we got to the ballroom, tensions were already
high. The dancers were anxious to make the most of the
new space, there was the tension created by Kelly and her
'injury' and Artem had hurt his shoulder during the week
as well. Every single one of us wanted to turn things
around, to make it the best show yet, to really give Blackpool the spectacle that it deserved. We were not going to
scrape by this week, just getting something on air as best
we could. We were going to be peacocks!

It was impossible not to feel infected by the buzz, to
sense that frisson of end-of-term excitement, to be spurred
on by the huge crowd in the Tower that night. As the music
to the opening credits began the crowd went wild. I caught
Matt's eye and he winked at me. Being part of this felt like
being on the crest of a wave, as the show began and the
sense of momentum swelled further and further.

The opening number was a sensation. As the professionals came out in their white and gold outfits to Viva Las

Vegas the audience erupted into cheers and applause. The men were wearing tight, white, Elvis-style jumpsuits and the women were in tiny outfits as much like showgirls as dancers. The energy was infectious and we were all tapping along.

It felt like a proper night out, the kind of entertainment that reminded me of years of being allowed to stay up that extra bit late as a child, so I could watch dancing programmes from my mum's lap. I thought of the generations that had danced on that beautiful floor, the romances that had begun, the romances that had ended and the romances that had never got further than someone needing to lean in that extra inch. It felt like a responsibility to do justice to the venue.

As I caught sight of Lars on the dance floor with the others I remembered his words about living the dance, not just doing it, and in that moment I felt as if he understood me better than anyone else in the world. He got the magic that dance could perform in a way that no one else I knew really did.

The show went off without a hitch. Perfect tens started to flow, Artem's shoulder injury held out and the judges even made a comment about the couple's perfect posture. And, of course, in terms of the dance itself, Kelly and Lars's American smooth went like a dream. It gave me a twinge of nostalgia to see them together on the dance floor, doing what I realised I had let myself start to think of as 'our dance'. Only about twenty people in the room had ever known I had done it, I reflected sadly as the audience rose to their feet in praise of the finished routine.

As the show drew to a close I could sense all of us starting to exhale and relax. We had done it! We had taken the show on the road and survived. No, we had more than survived – we had triumphed. I was thrilled for every single one of us.

But secretly, deep inside, there was a part of me that felt terribly sad as we headed back to the hotel. As I sat on the end of my bed, and then began to gather all of my belongings together, ready for the early start on Sunday, I felt a kind of homesickness. This couple of days had felt like a fairytale come true, and I was reluctant to let it end. I wanted the experience to last forever; I wanted to stay in the bubble of Strictly bliss that I had been in since we arrived.

The confidence, the glamour, the tenderness – I wanted to try and find a way to keep those things in my life.

But, no matter how tightly a ball I curled myself up into that night as I fell asleep, the alarm still woke me first thing, ready for the trip home. An hour later, I was on the coach next to Sally, flicking through the Sunday papers.

When I got home and turned my key in the front door, I remembered the state I had been in only eight days ago when I was desperate to have the flat to myself, only to discover Allegra was home. She had been such a good friend to me then that this time I turned the key hoping she was back.

When I opened the door I called out a loud 'Ciao!' and grinned when it was returned with an equally resonant 'Hallo there!'

As soon as I got into the living room I gave her a proper warm hug. 'You're home!'

We squealed at each other for a moment, before I sat down to catch up with her a bit.

'So how are things in Italy? How was the operation?'

Allegra's gestures were as contained as ever. 'The operation went well. It looks as if my father will make a full recovery. I am very glad that I went back though. My mother needed the help. She was so worried, but she was also looking after my younger brother and making food to take to my father on the ward. It felt good to be able to help them.'

'I can imagine. You've been so brave. Are you exhausted yourself? Are you behind with work?'

'Yes, I have fallen a little bit behind but, you know, I can catch up.' She nodded towards the table, which already had a couple of coffee cups on it.

'Don't exhaust yourself, just because you wanted to help your parents … Have you eaten? I'm going to make myself something proper later. I can cook for you?'

I had never offered to do this before and felt a sudden twinge of panic that Allegra would be appalled at the thought of my food. I wasn't an amazing chef, but I was keen.

'No thank you, Carina. I am going out for dinner this evening.' A pause. One of *those* pauses. She looked up and gave me a small smile.

'Oh I see! A friend! Well then, you won't need me cooking you own brand pasta then will you – and you don't need me cheering you up!'

'I will always need those things, Carina. And thank you for your concern.'

'No problem, Legs.' Was she going to let me get away with that nickname? I hadn't meant to test drive it – it had just been something that Sally had started to say on the way home.

'Ha!' In that moment I felt that we had transcended being mere flatmates: Allegra had become more than a curiosity and one of my real friends. I was excited by the prospect of her coming to the show the following week, and wanted to think of her as part of my group of friends. Also, the idea of her hot Italian friends, complete with her feminist approval, was very enticing, especially after what I had promised Sally.

I headed into my room to start unpacking, and as I did so I saw the blue glow of my phone ringing on the hallway table. I noticed that it was Natalie, but didn't feel up to telling her all my gossip just yet. I wanted to unpack, get settled and decided what my first proper Sunday supper – as inspired by Lloyd and promised to Jen – would be. But then, sometimes you see your sister's name and curiosity just gets the better of you.

'Hey Sis.'

'Hello Darling.'

'I've just got back! I have a mountain of news for you, sooooo can't wait for a proper catch up. I'm just about to unpack thought, still a bit all over the place. You okay if I call you back—?'

'Manda honey, I've got some bad news.'

'Oh my god. What? Is it Mum? Dad?' I closed my bedroom door and sat on the bed. Immediately I felt my pulse rate quicken and my chest tighten.

'It's Jen. She's really ill – properly ill. She's been taken to hospital and she's got to have a big operation.'

'No! Poor thing, is she going to be okay? What has happened?'

'She said she hadn't been feeling well for the last couple of weeks—'

'I saw her last weekend and she was fine!'

Even as I said it, I remembered how tired Jen had looked. With the clarity of hindsight I realised that she hadn't been fine at all, she was exhausted, and I had only seen what I wanted to. Caught up in my silly self-absorption and boy woes I don't think I even stopped to ask her properly how she was. My girlish anxieties seemed pathetically lightweight.

'Well she's not fine. She has something wrong with her liver. She's too weak for the operation at the moment, so she's in hospital for a bit to stabilise her systems.'

218

'I can't believe it, she's so strong. She's so healthy. How can she have something wrong with her?'

'It's just one of those things. It isn't anything she has or hasn't done.'

'So unfair.'

'I know, I know.'

'How's Mum? She must be devastated.'

'She's not great, to be honest. Obviously she's worried sick about Jen, but also she has never been ill or had to stay in hospital herself, so she's finding it all really stressful.'

'Yeah, Jen is always the calm one.'

'Exactly. Listen, do you want to come down for supper? Lloyd's cooking.'

Of course Lloyd was cooking. The day that Lloyd stopped cooking on a Sunday night was the day that the world stopped turning.

'I'd love to. It's one of those nights that I kinda want to be around my family.'

'Me too. See you sixish?'

'I'm there. Can't wait to give you a hug.'

I spent the next hour or so unpacking and generally nesting back at home. I put on a wash, I put away the several (almost countless) items of clothing that I hadn't worn in Blackpool and I did all of it while stopping and flicking through Sunday supplements, texting my friends and occasionally just plonking myself down on my bed with a heavy sigh, and staring into space thoughtfully.

When I emerged from my room an hour or so later, Allegra was making more coffee. I have no idea how she managed to be the calmest person I knew, while absorbing that much caffeine, but she was. And it made the house smell lovely.

She asked me if I was okay and I told her about Jen, aware of how trivial it might sound. Jen wasn't even my parent, and it seemed as if the doctors had everything under control, so I didn't want to seem to be hopping onto her sadness-wagon. But, as I should have expected, she was all-encompassingly understanding.

'Sometimes,' she said. 'It is not that they are ill, or that they might not get better. But it is the thought that they *can* be ill. It is so awful to see your parents frail, or even Jen in your case. Awful for them, sad for you and … the worst thing of all is that you realise that being a grown up just doesn't go away. You spend your whole childhood longing for it, and sometimes – I just wish I could get rid of it!'

I think it was at this point that I made a mental note to myself to start writing down everything Allegra said. How did she get to be so wise? I grabbed her forearm.

'You are SO right. I don't want Jen, or anyone, to be ill. But nor do I like the reminders it gives me that I am an adult, and that I just have this one life to make the most of.'

'Well, *I* am going to make the most of it. And I would like to know if I could have the cheek to make the most of my dinner wearing your top with the sequinned shoulders?'

'Ha! Of course you can borrow it. I call it my Strictly top – have done even before I started on the show.'

'That would be so kind.'

'Here, come and get it now. I'm going out to see my sister shortly.'

It was the first time I had seen Allegra nervous or asking for a favour and I was thrilled to be able to help her out rather than depending on her. She looked fabulous as she headed off to her date and I envied her confidence in how the evening might turn out.

Standing on Natalie's doorstep a little while later, I could barely believe that I had been staying there and desperate to leave such a short while ago. Now, I was filled with gratitude that I had family close by, and that I could spend my Sunday night with them instead of fretting at home while Allegra was on her hot date.

Natalie opened the door and gave me a giant hug, practically lifting me off the ground. I had never been so happy to have a big sister in my entire life. As I walked into the house Lloyd was opening a bottle of red wine and listening to a comedy show on the radio.

'Lil sis!' Another bear hug. 'Now then, ladies – a glass of wine.'

I looked at the glass. I looked at the wine. I looked at the carpet in the next room. And then, instead of panicking, I said 'Yes please, Lloydo.' Maybe I could handle being a grown up after all.

'So, how is she, Mum? Shall we call her?'

'Yes, I think we should for sure.'

Before long we were huddled at Natalie's kitchen table, talking into her iPhone which was on speakerphone. Mum's voice had that slight tremulous quality of someone who had either recently stopped crying or was trying not to cry.

'Oh girls, it's so good of you to call. Amanda you must be exhausted. How was yesterday?'

'Mum, I'm fine. I have so much to tell you, but it will all keep.'

I mouthed to Natalie that I would tell her everything later. She nodded and giggled.

'Have you been to see Jen today?' asked Natalie.

'Yes, she's okay. Spirits are high – she's such a trooper – but it's just so awful seeing her look so weak.'

'I can imagine. Do you know when she will be having the operation?'

'No, it depends on when she's strong enough; something to do with her blood levels. She didn't really want to talk about it when I went in. She wanted to chat about East-Enders and Kate Middleton and all of that kind of thing. She's no good at talking about weakness or admitting that she might need help.'

'Some people just aren't good at that,' said Natalie. I thought of Matt and his stoic way of dealing with things. 'It doesn't mean she doesn't love you, or that she doesn't appreciate what you're doing.'

'I know, it's just that we're so different. It's why we're friends I suppose. You need to surround yourself with people a bit different to you in order to keep you in line, don't you?'

'I guess so, Mum.' I felt unbearably sad for her, missing her friend and not knowing how to help.

'She is dying to hear from you, Manda, dying to hear all about Blackpool.'

'Can I go and see her?'

'I'll need to find out what visiting times are during the week, but I am sure that she would love that.'

Lloyd was now waving his arms around, trying to get us to create space for what he was about to get out of the oven, so we wound the call up and went into a brief flurry of throwing down mats and getting out plates, ready for Lloyd's Sunday-night extravaganza. This time, it was Beef Carbonade, complete with thick slices of French bread, smothered in mustard and plonked on top of the stew as giant croutons. It was the essence of comfort food, and felt like eating a hug.

Natalie noticed that the Strictly results show was on so we took leftovers and sat around the telly, with Natalie and Lloyd asking me all kinds of questions about the ballroom, the dancers and how everything was put together. Lars was not featured heavily as he and Kelly had cruised through to the next round, but my heart fluttered when he flashed up on Lloyd's enormous flat screen TV.

'I can't believe you've danced with him,' said Natalie breathlessly. I had told her the full story over dinner – or at least as much of the story as I dared to with Lloyd in the room. 'What does he smell like?'

'Oh amazing. Like grass and laundry, and man.' Lloyd looked horrified at the conversation we were having in front of him.

'Oh that's the best. I love it when a bloke looks after himself properly.'

'Yeah, lush.'

'I can't believe you were there.'

'I know, it seems completely unbelievable that I was in Blackpool this morning.' And with that, I suddenly felt very tired. I sat back on the sofa and curled my legs underneath me. As I nestled into Natalie's exquisite scatter cushions I realised how much my sense of time had become muddled. Whole days seemed to go on for weeks, while others flew by in a moment. There just didn't seem to be space in my head for everything. Lars's face flashed up on the screen again as part of the group dance. It occurred to me that I couldn't remember what he smelled like at all: I had just described Matt to Natalie.

'Look it's Lars again!' she shrieked, pointing at the screen.

'Three days 'til the Ashes ...' muttered Lloyd to no one in particular.

I stared at Lars. Seen through the screen, it felt almost as if I had never met him at all.

By the time I got to the tube station I realised that I had left my magazine on Natalie's coffee table, meaning I had nothing at all to divert me on the journey home. I stared around the almost-empty carriage. It was 10pm on a Sunday in winter. Most people were understandably at home, curled up on the sofa with loved ones, or already in bed.

In one of the double seats there was a couple, entwined with each other, apparently under the impression that they were indeed on their sofa at home. She had her legs looped up and over his, and he had his arm around her back. Something about the closeness, the urgency between them suggested that they didn't share a home at all. Were they having an affair? It all seemed a bit public for that. Perhaps she had flat mates or parents who did not approve of him, or vice versa. They looked younger than me, but perhaps not teenagers. Either way, they seemed enraptured by each other in a way that is only sustainable for a few months. The devotion that they were displaying was very different to that of the quiet attentiveness I had seen in that couple on the pier on Friday night.

To my left was an old man, holding a rolled-up newspaper and a walking stick. His eyes were closed and his head tipped back against the glass of the tube window. He looked tired, frail and perhaps in a little pain. I made a note to myself to keep an eye on him and make sure that he was okay when it came to getting out of the carriage.

My thoughts drifted back to wondering about how Jen was doing in hospital. I hoped she wasn't lonely, or nervous about the treatment. I thought about the week ahead, and felt relieved that I had Matt to confide in about Jen's illness. He had a unique ability to make me feel calmer, almost at once, and had always been so loyal to me at work. I hoped he was okay too, and I started to wonder about how he was spending his evening. I knew he had two flatmates, but I didn't know much about them. I didn't even know if he had family in London or not. I needed to stop thinking about myself so much and start investing in the people around me a little more.

I rested my head on the window behind me, closing my eyes and tilting my head alongside my gentleman travelling companion. The tiredness washed over me. It seemed that – without me asking – someone had switched my life from one being lived in black and white to one being lived in colour. I used to dream of a life this full, this exciting, this colourful, and yet always believed that it wasn't one that was available to me. But now I had it, it all felt as if it was a bit much. I wondered if I would be able to cope. Mum so worried, Jen so ill, the frisson between me and Lars, needing to make sure I continued to do well at my job – there just seemed so much to take in. Even the good stuff was almost overwhelming: Allegra, Sally and Matt and the emotions that these new friendships had created – it was all swirling and churning within me, and life was so busy I was barely able to keep up with processing it all. I felt as if I was a laptop, momentarily stuck trying to process data, too many applications opened too quickly at once.

The tube pulled into my stop and I braced myself for the cold as I swiped my Oyster card and left the station. At the same time, I braced myself. I didn't want to remain a spectator forever. I had had a taste of life on stage now, and I wanted a part of it. I wanted to dance through life. And now was the time to start.

Chapter 15

Through sheer force of will I began the week with a spring in my step, filled with determination to remember that life is short and I should live it to the full regardless of what it threw at me. I was going to take my place on the stage and get on with things. No more 'Oh boohoo, I'm experiencing too many emotions.' I was going to cherish each and every one of them, and be grateful that something was actually happening to me.

By lunchtime on Monday I finally got hold of Jen.

'Darling!' If I hadn't been told that she was in hospital, I would never have known it. 'How was Blackpool? I can't wait to hear all about it.'

'It was fine – no, it was wonderful. I can't wait to tell you all about it. But how are you?'

'Well, darling, I've been better.'

'I am so sorry to hear about it all. What are the doctors saying now?'

'I have to wait a bit until the operation, but they're not sure how long, which is the frustrating thing.'

'I can imagine. With a thing like that, you just want to know.'

'Exactly, I'm not much good at sitting around waiting to hear some news.'

'You poor thing. Is there anything I can do?'

'You can fill me in on all the gossip. Last time you were in an absolute state. What's changed?'

I knew it wouldn't keep, so I wandered outside the building, sat in a quiet corner, and told her all about the weekend. She listened to it all, thrilled by my moment on the stage but much more cautious about Lars than I had imagined she would be.

'Be careful, Manda. He is a guy who must have women throwing themselves at him. He sounds like he *is* a real sweetie, but you just don't want to get into any sort of a muddle, do you?'

'No, I know. I don't know what the frisson between us is about really. All I know is that he is the person who understands me most about dancing and so I don't want to let go of our friendship.'

'I understand that, I do. But remember – it's his job.'

How many more times were people going to tell me this?

'I know, Jen. But you don't know what it's like when it's just the two of us.'

As I was saying that I saw Matt crossing the courtyard carrying a cardboard tray of coffees. I lowered my voice, so as not have him hear me.

'Anyway Jen, when can I come and see you?'

'Well, Darling, it depends on when I have to have this operation. If it's sooner rather than later you might be able to come and see me at home, but then I might be crawling the walls with boredom and loneliness after a few days.'

'Urgh, boredom and loneliness, they're almost worse than being ill.'

'Well, I know what you mean but—'

'Oh no, are you in a lot of pain Jen?'

'I have felt better. There is no denying the fact that I have felt much better.'

'I'm so sorry. I wish there was something I could do.'

'There is.'

'What?'

'Just enjoy yourself. Squeeze every bit of fun out of every single day. For me.'

'Of course.' I was welling up. My breath was quickening in that way that means you're only using the very uppermost inch of your lung, lest you start sobbing. 'I promise that, Jen.'

The fire doors ahead of me clanged open and then shut, and Matt appeared from them, his coffees delivered.

'What's wrong?'

'Nothing. Nothing.'

'Why are you wiping your eyes with your sleeve then?'

'It's fine.'

'Clearly it isn't. Has someone upset you? Who was it? What did they say?'

'It's nothing like that, it's Jen.'

'Jen who I met?'

'Yes, she's really ill.'

'Oh my god you poor thing, that's tough. She means the world to you.'

'I know. She's in hospital waiting for an operation and it's all really heavy.'

'I'm sorry. Here, have a hug.' And he took me into his arms. I could have stayed there forever. I did one big sob into his chest and then held my breath to try and prevent a full-on snot-fest. I shifted my head up to look at him and smile.

'You'll be okay, Roberts.' He stroked my hair as I rested there another moment. Then, as quickly as it had happened, we de-hugged and walked back to the office.

'So, we need to go and talk to Chloe about getting the director tapes in.'

After that, the week started to progress as usual. After the enormous effort of moving the whole show up to Blackpool, things seemed unusually calm this week in comparison. I felt as if I had more time than usual now that things really were becoming second nature. With fewer contestants there suddenly seemed to be fewer people around generally, and I started to have the first creeping inklings of festive spirit. The Christmas lights were turned on in Westfield and around Shepherd's Bush Green and the end of the series was now in sight.

Something else that was helping my festive spirits was the amount of time and attention that Lars was continuing to direct my way. Whenever he saw me in the building he would offer to get me coffee, and we'd often sit chatting about how things were going with his routine, with Kelly and in my life.

I told him about Jen and he was very sympathetic, reminding me that 'it is easy to forget your pain on the dance floor'. I agreed, again shivering with delight that he understood how much dance meant to me.

His preparations for the week ahead were going well but Kelly continued to be a little erratic now that things were definitely over with Julian. The couple's popularity was starting to skyrocket in the press, and with it the swirling suggestion that there might be something between them. Despite Lars having told me outright that there wasn't, my stomach still lurched every time that I saw an image of them together, or read a piece about their 'burgeoning love'. I knew that it wasn't the case, but it felt as if he was cheating on me a little bit. My brain was completely on top of the fact that it was simply not happening, but my heart continued to march to its own beat, imagining a connection between us that he had never expressed. For a few days at a time I would manage to shove it to the back of my mind, but then I would sit behind a couple of schoolgirls on the bus and overhear them talking about how 'lush' Lars was, and feel the surge of possessive desire.

I managed to keep these things to myself though, as we sat clutching our hot drinks and talking through the coming routine. I was getting calmer about my job, but Lars's anxieties were only racking up. His success in the show was starting to take its toll: as much as he was buzzing with pride and excitement, he was undeniably tired. He confided in me about the increase in the work required and how Kelly's combination of ambition but lack of true passion for dance was starting to wear on him.

'I just wish she was as interested in the dance itself as she is in winning,' he said quietly, fiddling with the lid of his coffee cup.

'She is enjoying the dancing though – she has told me that, and she says it on air every week.'

'Oh she is, she loves the attention. But I feel as if every step is just meant as a token of revenge for Julian. I wish she could just enjoy life, and dancing. If she understood how beautiful she is and how happy she could be then every step would look different.'

Woah, this was confusing. What had started as a conversation that had left me electrified at how much I was being taken into Lars's confidence was now a chat about how wonderful Kelly was. Yes, I liked Kelly a lot, and I felt that she had been treated dreadfully by Julian. But I didn't want to sit around discussing her virtues with Lars.

Was something developing between them after all? Was he just sounding off to me because I was there? Because I was a compliant listener? Matt's words started to ring in my ears – I remembered his warnings about getting hurt through no fault of my own, and no real wrong doing on Lars's part.

'But you're still getting to be out there dancing,' I suggested. The audience doesn't know the difference; it's only really you that does.'

'I know, but it can feel lonely up there sometimes. It is like dancing with a stranger, even after all of these weeks. I am fond of Kelly, I am dearly fond of her. But she doesn't connect like others.'

His eyes flickered to mine. I said nothing. Lars suddenly stood up and shook himself against the cold.

'Brrrrrr. Let's head in.' I said.

Then Lars looked down at me. Those eyes. Those lips. His face was so close to mine. He leaned forward, and kissed me on the nose again. Then, very quietly, he whispered, 'Sometimes I wish I was dancing with you instead.'

Until that moment I had thought that swoons were something that only happened in novels. But I swooned. I felt it – the buckling of my knees, the flipping of my stomach, the sleepiness in my eyes. I even felt as if I could hear the word ringing in my head. SWOOOOOON.

It was one of those moments that I knew almost no one for the rest of my life would ever believe had happened. My excitement about that one dreamy instant meant that I pretty much floated through the rest of the week.

He wishes he was dancing with me. I would whisper it to myself when saw the tapes of Lars and Kelly in rehearsal. When I saw her rumba costume arrive from wardrobe as I was walking through the set with Matt I let myself remember it again. *He wishes that costume were for me.* And then, Lars and Kelly appeared on *It Takes Two* and I reminded myself once more. *He wishes that that was me on the sofa next to him ...*

Maybe my swoony dreamlike state was too obvious, or maybe it was too easily confused with the genuine anxiety I was feeling about Jen's illness and impending operation, but I felt as if Matt was giving me a slightly wide berth for much of the week. It seemed that he didn't really know how to approach me or what to say to me, and I didn't know how to reach out and bridge the gap either. It wasn't fair to keep on and on about Jen – even if he didn't talk about them much, I was sure Matt had worries of his own. And of course I could never go into details about my connection with Lars and how it was making me feel. So a strange politeness crept over us as the week progressed.

Show day was on us faster than ever before, and once again it met and exceeded all of our expectations. Artem, now fully recovered, was back on dazzling form with his partner, who had become firm friends with Kelly. Anton once again showed himself to be more than a gentleman with his routine. Paired with something of a national institution, we had all expected him to once again last only a few weeks in the competition. But contrary to everyone's predictions the couple were still in the show and seemingly popular with the viewers. Teasing his partner would perhaps have been an easy route to take, and one that the public might have enjoyed for a week or two, but Anton's dignity and discretion was becoming infectious and each week more and more members of the public were rooting for them. This week, the couple performed what nearly passed as a rumba, inspired by a blockbuster Hollywood movie. It was extraordinary, but somehow inspiring. While the applause rang out at the end of their routine I smiled at Matt who was standing next to me looking baffled. I nodded my head towards the couple and whispered 'You see, anyone can be a dancer.'

'That's not dancing,' was his reply.

'It doesn't matter,' I whispered with urgency. 'She is loving it – she doesn't care if she's good or bad. That's what I mean about having the courage to get up on the dance floor. You never know who is going to enjoy it.'

'I know I wouldn't.'

'But you don't. Not until you try.' I waggled my eyebrows up and down at him. He shook his head and returned his attention to the couple on the set, who were now receiving almost heroically low scores.

The show continued with few dramatic surprises. Aliona and Natalie looked as mesmerizingly gorgeous as ever, and I couldn't help but notice Matt noticing. And, as the closing dance of the show, Lars and Kelly performed a rumba that I found almost impossible to watch. It was incredible that Lars felt he had not connected with Kelly as well as he might have done – they looked every bit the couple falling perilously in love throughout the dance. Every bend, every reach and every swoonsome facial expression only served to reinforce the public's idea that the couple were at the point of embarking on the romance of the series. If I hadn't felt so wretched about seeing someone for whom my crush was now almost out of control, I would have wanted to watch the routine again and again. It looked effortless in its elegance and romance, and the judges agreed, scoring the pair three tens. Kelly was overjoyed and Lars smiled the quiet smile that I had come to know so well from our chats. I was pleased for them both, but felt the tug of jealousy at not being the one on the dance floor yet again.

As the show ended I finished up my duties, checked in with Chloe that she didn't need anything else from me, and headed out to the front gate with Sally to meet Allegra and her friends, as arranged. As members of the BBC Club we were allowed to sign in the group and have a drink in the building.

It was Arthur, Allegra's date, who caught my eye first. He was the very opposite of the kind of man I thought she would chose. He had something professorial about him, from the tweedy jacket to the fluffy goatee that looked as if it might have taken a month or two to cultivate. He spoke with a soft, gentle Manchester accent and seemed completely unable to believe his luck at having someone

237

like Allegra on his arm. I remembered that they had met at university, so I made the assumption that a night out at *Strictly Come Dancing* might not be either his regular nor his favourite way to spend an evening.

Allegra seemed besotted by him – there was rarely a moment when they weren't touching or whispering to each other adoringly. They seemed to be constantly sharing little jokes and reassuring each other in an almost unbearably cute way. There was little of the self-contained behaviour I had grown to expect from Allegra. It was as if she had melted, and turned into a limp-limbed victim of love.

Of more interest was the boy band's worth of hot blokes that she had brought with her. Unlike Arthur, her three Italian mates were cookie-cutter examples of Hot Italian Guys. They were named Sergio, Lello (short for Lionello) and Federico (or Rico, as he quickly asked me to call him). They were groomed to perfection, had immaculate hair and all smelled of expensive Farmacias. Great hair, sexy accents and scarves knotted in new and exciting continental ways. One look at Sally's glowing face showed me that Allegra had well and truly delivered the goods.

We headed up to the bar, chatting slightly awkwardly as we stood in a large circle waiting for the lifts. There were too many of us for conversation not to feel like a performance piece, but we didn't yet know each other well enough to break off into individual conversations. When the lift arrived it was a bit of a squash to fit all seven of us in, and suddenly we were cheek by jowl, uncomfortably close for people who had only known each other for a matter of minutes. It smelled delicious in there though.

As the group entered the bar I felt as if we were in a scene from a movie or a pop video. People turned to look at us, and it felt rather good. It was exciting to be seen with a stylish continental gang like this. Allegra and the boys immediately blended in with the international cast of dancers and celebrities, and soon we were just part of the party.

It was a real joy to see Sally and Allegra hit it off as instantly as they did. Their mutually feisty ways seemed to be bringing out the warmth in each other, and the boys were very relaxed company – especially in comparison to some of the nervous English boys I had dated over the summer before getting the job at Strictly.

The bar was buzzing. Some of the dancers were still stretching in the corner, while chatting to their friends and family. Lars was chatting with some of the girls, looking at a tattoo that one of them had recently had done. I couldn't help but notice that Chloe and Anthony, who I rarely saw exchanging a single word with each other during the week, were once again enraptured by each other's conversation. Was it just that the two of them were more shy than the rest of us, and didn't feel as confident chatting with random groups? Or was there a genuine frisson between the two of them?

Someone turned the music up and the lights down; the energy in the room was pulsing as much as it ever had done on a Saturday night. I was itching to chat, flirt and dance.

There was only one problem: I didn't fancy any of the boys. Not a single one of them. They were undeniably gorgeous, and perhaps at another time in another world I would have found them undeniably sexy too. But they just weren't doing it for me. They were so charming, and their European sense of gentlemanly conversation and manners was genuinely endearing. But I couldn't imagine myself kissing any of them, let alone anything else. Their hair might get ruffled – I couldn't take the guilt.

But, just as I was getting to the point of 'fessing up to Allegra that her 'bringing the hotties' master plan had failed on one crucial level, Matt came over, looking visibly disconcerted by our new pals. I had thought that he was heading home straight after the show this week but it appeared that there had been a change of plan.

His frosty yet slightly proprietorial demeanour suddenly inspired me to flirt with Rico in a way that I hadn't wanted to before. I wasn't quite sure why, but Matt's raised eyebrow over me hanging out with men who weren't him, or who were pre-disapproved in the way that Lars was, really got under my skin. Rico leant in to reply to me as the beat of the music got louder and I caught Lars's eye across the room. He raised an eyebrow and then winked at me. My just talking to Rico had brought about the same effect as if I had worn an exceedingly toxic new scent. Perhaps it was just old-fashioned jealousy …

* * *

The music seemed to be getting louder. I could feel my cheeks flushing, and I felt adrenaline flooding through me as Rico continued to make charming small talk with me. His hand was now in the small of my back, Lello was charming Sally, and the two of them were chatting with Allegra and Arthur. Meanwhile, Sergio was asking Matt about his job and his ambitions. As the music dipped, I overheard Matt telling him 'Yeah, I love this show and I'm not sure how I'm going to live without it next year. I've decided to explore documentaries and news next.'

Hmmmm, I thought to myself. *Is he just talking big again, or is he actually planning to do this?*

Sally read my very next thought.

'Guys! The bar here is going to close soon – let's go out. Just locally. I'm not ready for the night to end just yet and I reckon we should go dancing. What do you all say?'

Minutes later we were downstairs and out of the building, hailing cabs on Wood Lane to take us to a kitsch club on Shepherd's Bush Green. The night was freezing but we had all had enough to drink by then that it felt like an adventure not a hardship. Matt was with us, and a couple of Sally's colleagues from the make-up department who had caught a glimpse of our Italians.

By the time we had all paid and got rid of our coats I was starting to feel a little sleepy. The euphoria of an hour ago in the BBC Club had somehow trickled away, leaving me tired, anxious and slightly wishing that someone would turn the music down. My feet were starting to hurt and I was wondering how long I would have to stay before I could slip away home. It was almost walking distance after all.

It was Rico who saved me. I have no idea how he found out that they even stocked it in this dive of a club, but he was heading our way with two bottles of chilled prosecco and soon set about pouring it out to all of us. The music became ever more ridiculous and soon Sally had cajoled me onto the dance floor. Even Allegra was up there, all her attention focussed on Arthur, but making some serious shapes nonetheless. I don't know where the rest of the drinks came from but the small table that our group had commandeered never seemed to be without bottles and glasses. I think I bought a round; I must have done, but I don't really remember it. The music continued, and we were all sweating before long, our jaws stiff from giggling at each other. This was living each day to the full, I thought to myself as Jen fleetingly crossed my mind. She would be proud of me ...

I sat down for a moment, pausing to reflect on the evening. Allegra saw me and came to sit alongside me.

'You okay?' I asked.

'Yes! Having a fabulous night!'

'It has been such a laugh. Everything seems to be going well with Arthur ...?'

'Yes, he is lovely, and we are getting on so well. I adore him. I think it was borrowing your Strictly top that really sealed the deal for me though!'

'I'm so glad! I've never had any romance wearing it – I just like that it makes me feel romantic! But seriously – thank you so much for coming down. It's just what I needed after this week's news.'

'It has been fun. Now tell me, Carina – so Matt is the one you now like, yes?'

'What?'

'You decided that it was Matt you felt for, not the dancer?'

'What makes you say that?' We were having to speak so loudly to hear each other over the music. Allegra's accent seemed to be getting thicker the more she had to drink.

'The tension between you. It is quite obvious. Every time you laugh with Rico you check to see if Matt is looking.'

'No I don't.'

'Yes, you do!' She was giggling now. 'You don't notice it?' And then her attention shifted to over my shoulder. I turned my head to see what she was looking at, and before I knew what was happening Matt, who had been sneaking up behind me, grabbed me by the waist and dragged me onto the dance floor.

'Matt! What are you doing?'

'Dancing!'

'But you don't dance.'

'I do now.'

He had me in a mock ballroom pose and was swinging me around slightly unreliably. I was Tess to his Bruce, and

243

he was holding me close and spinning me round and round. As fast as he moved me, Allegra's words spun in my own head. It wasn't that I wasn't enjoying myself – in fact, the tingling that I had felt earlier in the evening was suddenly back. It was just that I felt unusual, overwhelmed again. Maybe it was just the booze.

And with that I fell to the floor.

Chapter 16

It was my head that woke me up. There was a dull ache where my neck met my head, as if there was a small animal, armed with a gavel, tapping away inside my scull. The first thing I felt when I realised I was awake was panic. Raw, shivering panic.

I started with my feet, slowly moving them to either side of me to check that I was definitely in my own bed, and that I was definitely the only person there. What had happened to me? How did I get here? What was going on?

I pulled the duvet up above my eyes to try and reduce the light, and then slowly, cautiously opened one eye followed by the other. So I was not in my pyjamas. I was wearing an old t-shirt. This uncomfortably suggested that I might not have been in a state to put myself to bed. The horror of what had happened to me could only be imagined. I peeked my eyes out from over my duvet. I could see my BBC pass dangling over the back of my chair. My coat was there too, and – mercifully – my bag.

Then it hit me. Matt! The dancing! That was the last thing I remembered. The room spinning, Matt spinning, me spinning. What had happened next? Had *something* happened? A hazy memory of my conversation with Allegra in the club came back to me. Instead of feeling appalled at the idea of something happening with Matt, I was filled with a cold treacly horror that I might have embarrassed myself in front of him. The truths I could have blurted out in front of him didn't bear thinking about. And yet ... I carried on thinking.

Was I one of those girls that the tabloids wrote features about? Was I part of Binge Britain? I tried to work backwards through the day. I was sure I hadn't had a shocking amount to drink – I had been too nervous.

I remembered arriving at the club and feeling sleepy, then having a glass or two of Prosecco and perking up. I remembered chatting with the Italians, Rico's easy charm and Matt's irritation at the attention we were paying each other. I remembered playing up to that. I remembered the show, my stomach twisting with jealousy at seeing Lars's rumba with Kelly, and Matt's non-committal response to what I said to him on seeing Anton's dance with his partner.

Finally, I remembered the key fact: the gnawing sense of anxiety I had felt all day about Jen and her operation, and the way that it had prevented me from wanting to eat anything from breakfast onwards. Ladies and gentlemen, there we had it – my body must just have hit a wall. A girl can't survive on adrenaline and caffeine alone, or at least not without a handsome fleet of servants and a top-class PR team.

Oh the humiliation. I must have collapsed, and everyone must have assumed I was a total drunkard. This was not the way I had been led to believe one seduced Italian men. I sat up and swung my legs around so that I was sitting on the edge of my bed. I felt my brain slopping around in my head, begging me to treat it with more respect today. My feet gingerly found the sheepskin slippers Mum had treated me with a few weeks ago. I was hit by the hunger of a thousand men.

I shuffled slowly to the kitchen and borrowed Allegra's stovetop moka to make myself a cup of coffee. While I waited, staring into space and listening for the comforting gurgle of coffee, I gingerly nibbled on some oat biscuits and realised that I was going to have to head out for some real ones. I ran a bath first. It was the only way.

When I got back to my room and shook out my duvet my phone fell to the floor, glowing from a recent text.

You okay Roberts?Mx

Instinctively, I moved my head away from the screen, as if trying to prevent Matt from seeing my sorry state from his phone. I punched out a reply – now was as good a time to deal with this as any.

Yes thanks. Sorry about last night. Was I a
nightmare?xR

Not at all. Was really worried about you. Mx

I winced, realising that I had to try and find out if anything
had gone on between us. Was it him who had put me to
bed? Or Allegra?

Did I get home okay?xR

Yeah. We got you back. You didn't make much sense
but you were being quite sweet. Mx

Oh man, there were approximately one thousand things
that that could mean. How could I find out specifics?
I bailed out, realising that I couldn't ask him, not with
my dignity in tact. I would have to wait until Allegra woke
up.

Thank you so much. And sorry again. See you
tomorrow. xR

I got myself dressed and headed out to buy food. It was
only when I reached the front door and saw a note from
Allegra that I realised she was not in the house. She had
got up and left already, apparently for a family lunch with
Arthur. I had had no idea she was even invited which made

me realise how fraught and self-involved I had been over the last week.

Eventually, I made it to the shops, then treated myself to a day of recovering. There was no way I was going to let another Sunday get the better of me. That was a solid gold fact. I read the papers, caught up on soaps I had missed, and had a long chat with Mum and Dad. I made myself a chilli that Lloyd himself would have been proud of, and texted both him and Jen to let them know that I had finally conquered my Sunday evening terrors and was 'one of them' now. When I heard back from her I gave Jen a call. She was still in hospital, with no news regarding her operation yet. Her spirits were lower than I had ever known them before, and I did my best to cheer her up with gossip and glitz from the night before. I let her know all about Allegra and the Italians coming to the BBC Club, and when she would have been roaring with laughter a few weeks ago, she sounded tired and drained. I tried to keep my voice cheery and light, but by the time I ended the call I had a lump in my throat and was struggling not to let it turn into tears. I stared blankly at my mobile for a couple of minutes after hanging up, more sad than panicked by what Jen had sounded like. I had had enough of Sunday, and was in bed before they had even announced who had been evicted from the jungle. Just as I had not heard Allegra leave in the morning, I didn't hear her arrive back at home.

I arrived at work on Monday filled with trepidation about confronting the loose ends I had yet to tie up after

Saturday night. But it seemed that no one really wanted to talk about it any more. Matt was behaving as if nothing at all had happened, and I didn't see Sally all day, despite texting her for a catch-up. Where was she? After what Allegra had said to me in the club I still had a nauseating paranoia that I had blurted something out to Matt in my fainting state. But that morning he provided no clues whatsoever. That formal distance that he had maintained over the last couple of weeks was back again. He was still lovely, but the chumminess of those early days on the series was gone. As for the Matt who had grabbed me around the waist and spun me around the dance floor without a care in the world: it was as if he had never existed. There could be no doubting that he *didn't* want to talk about what had happened on Saturday just as much as I *did*. It was clearly best to leave it altogether, and time to focus.

The competition was getting serious now, with very few dancers left, and the routines and sets getting more and more complex. I kept my head down for the next couple of weeks. I took to running for half an hour in the morning, eating properly and taking better care of myself. I didn't want to make myself ill with stress, especially not while Jen was ill. Seizing the day didn't have to be as hardcore as being helped home from a club exhausted. I called either Mum, Natalie or Jen every day to keep an eye on the situation and the rest of the time I worked harder than ever, focussing on the final, which seemed to be hurtling towards the team faster than a speeding train. It was set to be a spectacular show and our greatest test yet. And of course, it was set to be the last thing that we worked on together.

One thing that never seemed to even be a possibility was Lars and Kelly's not getting through to the next week. Their popularity was only growing and whatever reservations Lars might have had about Kelly were certainly not showing on the dance floor. They seemed as close as ever, but then again ... so were Lars and I. We continued to keep in close touch with each other, sharing coffees and chatting about his hopes and plans for the routines. Others among the team and the dancers would occasionally tease us for how close we had become, but there seemed no harm in it as we were both working so hard and getting our jobs done. Kelly, however, seemed utterly oblivious, only checking her press cuttings for news on what Julian was up to and how he was responding to her success.

I remained as bewildered as ever by Lars's continuing attentions. One minute I felt as if he was keeping me at arms length, and only out of a chivalrous sense of that being the right thing to do for as long as the show was on. After that, I sometimes told myself, he would reveal his true emotions for me. Other times, I worried that I was little more than a not-unattractive listening post. Maybe talking about dance was just a form of self-obsession for him? After all, if I were that gorgeous I would struggle not to be a little self-obsessed. One thing remained constant – he never gave me any concrete proof of his feelings either way, but seemed to be more fond of me than I could ever, ever have imagined. He remained the one person I could truly talk to about dance and how it made me feel.

No one was as shocked as I was when I woke up on the Saturday of the final to realise that the last day of the series was here already. I felt like the same girl who had been lying on the sofa at home believing that a job like this was far, far out of her reach. And yet so much had changed. My first job, my first flat, and the huge cavalcade of emotions that had come with the last few months. Then there was Jen, still in hospital awaiting her operation.

It was an icy morning, and I legged it from my bedroom to the bathroom as fast as I could the moment that I got up. I flicked the bathroom heater on and shivered under a hot shower until I was warm and ready for the day. When I finally emerged, swaddled in my dressing gown, hair in a towel, I was greeted by the smell of freshly brewing coffee and a smiling Allegra.

'Good morning,' she said.

'Morning,' said Arthur, who was wearing Allegra's dressing gown and seemed keen to get into the bathroom I had just vacated with as much speed and dignity as he could.

'I thought I would make you breakfast, to make sure you manage to stay on your feet all day,' announced Allegra, bringing a pot of jam and a pot of honey to the living room and popping them on the coffee table. 'By the time you are dressed toast and eggs will be ready.'

I felt a little teary as I closed my bedroom door. What a mate. And when I re-emerged there was a small, gift-wrapped box on the coffee table next to the spreads.

'What's this?'

'It's for you: an early Christmas present, as I might take mine to Arthur's house soon. But it's definitely yours.'

I unwrapped the box and inside was my gift – my very own moka. The warm glow that Allegra's morning treats had provided me with stayed with me until I got to work. The whole building was vibrating with excitement about the show. I felt as if all of west London knew it was the big night and was as excited as us. I got to the office, took my mobile from my pocket, and went over to the coat rack to hang up my big down jacket, knowing it would take up too much room if I slung it over the back of my chair. By the time I got back to my desk I had missed a call. I waved at Matt, who was walking in, and lifted the mobile to my ear. At first I was distracted by the distant smile that Matt had given me, and a little saddened that our friendship wasn't really the same.

'Hello, darling, it's Mum. Hate to bother you on your big day, but I didn't want to keep you out of the loop as Jen knows how wonderful you've been these last few weeks. She's called to say that she's going in for her operation later today. I'm not sure why, but the doctors have decided to bring the procedure forward. She wasn't keen to talk about it, and I'm not sure if the news regarding the

253

procedure being brought forward is good or bad. But she's in the best possible hands, and hopefully we can visit her tomorrow. Have a wonderful, wonderful show. We'll be watching of course, and thinking of you all the way through. Your father and I are so proud of you, I do hope you know that. Love to gorgeous Lars and of course darling Matt! Lots of love, Mum'

It was as if someone had taken all of the air out of the room. They were all moving around, as normal, but something was terribly different. How could this news have come today of all days? I appreciated Mum telling me but wished with all my heart that I had never found out. Poor Jen, having such a big operation while my biggest worries were errant sequins and gorgeous men. I felt so sick and so sad that I didn't even have it in me to cry. Thank heavens Allegra had made me eat first thing, or I would never have managed anything now.

I put my phone down and quietly asked Chloe if she would like a coffee.

'Never mind that, are you okay?'

'Yes, thank you.'

'You've just gone very pale. Have you had some bad news? Do you want to sit down?'

'It's okay, it's just my godmother. I've found out she is having a massive operation today. It's very sudden.'

'I'm so sorry. What an awful piece of news to receive today. Would you like to take a little break?'

'No,' I whispered. 'I have only just got here.'

'I know, but I don't want you to feel you have to carry on immediately after news like that. I know what this kind of thing is like.'

Chloe had come close to me now, and put an arm around my shoulders. I remembered her in those early days when I worked with her, always clutching at her BlackBerry, leaving me so unsure of if I was getting anything right or everything wrong.

'Do you?'

'Yes. I don't like to talk about it at work, but my mother has been seriously ill since the summer. I'm not going to burden you with the details now, but trust me – I understand the pressure of working on a live show while trying to keep an eye out for bad news. It's draining, but don't feel that you are alone in this. Come and find me if you need to today. You can always take five minutes, just let me know where you are. No job is more important than the well-being of your family.'

'Thank you so much.' Just having told her felt like an enormous burden had been lifted from my shoulders, but to find out so much else about her after all my months of doubts was mind blowing. I saw her in an entirely different light.

'And don't think I'm just saying this because I want the best from you today – of course I do – but working hard will help to keep your mind off things.' She gave me a little wink and patted my shoulders. 'Have a good day, Amanda, you'll be great.'

By the time the audience started arriving Chloe's words had proved to be right. We were all working hard as a unit, and instead of feeling left behind or overwhelmed by the pace and by what needed to be done, I felt swept along with the team, encouraged and strengthened by the support of the others.

Instead of being on the gates outside, checking people off the lists as I had done on my first show day, I was inside on set. Once the audience had all been checked into the green room, they started to make their way up through the building to the seats around the dance floor. I was there waiting for them, ready to make sure that everyone was in the correct seat for the coloured security pass that they had been given.

The audience began to filter in. Of course, a large number of people were family of the finalists – you could feel these loved ones' nerves as they took their seats. Everyone had made an extra special effort with their outfits – there was not a single woman who did not have sequins somewhere on her. Everyone was a riot of heels, ruffles, sparkles and colour. There were elderly couples who were fulfilling a dream by making it to sit in the audience at the final, there were mothers with daughters, holding hands, eyes on stalks, temporarily silenced by excitement, and there were groups giggling and chatting, infecting everyone around them with their high spirits.

Matt joined me with his clipboard and list.

'Seems to be going pretty smoothly, doesn't it?'

'Absolutely. Seems a shame that we have only just perfected our skills for the last show.'

'You've always been good, Roberts, and you know it.'

'Awww, thanks, man. Do you know what you're going to be doing afterwards?'

Matt continued to nod and smile as the audience members neatly filed into the rows of silver chairs, helping each other to find their places and making way for latecomers.

'Well, turns out I may be making my move to news after all.'

'No way! How come?'

'Chloe.'

'Chloe?'

'Yes, we had a bit of a chat last week, and she said how impressed she had been by me this series, and asked what I was looking to do next.'

'Wow, she asked you?' The impenetrable Chloe of the last few months, always staring at her phone, never seeming to notice anything around her, was fading further and further away.

'Yeah, she said that she has a friend in news who had been asking for someone of around my level, and would I be interested.'

'That's fantastic!'

'It is indeed pretty cool. Not in the bag yet though, Missus.'

'Of course, but that's just so impressive that she noticed.'

'The nicest thing was, she said that she noticed that I was outgrowing what I could do here at my level, but that she really admired how hard I was still working and the support that I was giving the rest of the team. What. A. Nerd.'

'No way, she was quite right. I would never have managed without you.'

'What can I say? I really do love the show – I need to protect it from the newbies like you.'

By now the audience was nearly all seated, and Matt and I, still standing on the dance floor, were facing them, in full view of everyone including the assorted cameramen who were now in position.

'Seriously, you've been amazing. I don't know how to thank you.' I didn't. I had no idea to show Matt how much he meant to me.

'I've had my eye on you from the start. I wouldn't let you mess up.' He made a tiny claw with his index finger and middle finger, pointed at his eyes and then my own. I smiled, and then, as if it was no part of me, my hand reached out to his. I touched it and squeezed it, while both of us looked at the list on his clipboard as if nothing was happening.

'Thank you,' I whispered. Matt carried on looking at the clipboard, and smiled. I had no idea who else saw our hands, and I didn't care.

Finally, everyone was seated, and the warm-up act took to the stage to chat to the audience for a while. Matt and I were standing in our usual positions beneath the gallery. I looked across the front row. There was a smattering of celebrities and contestants from earlier in the series, and previous winners. Everyone was looking super-glamorous, especially in the front row. There was a row of women who had been seated in the row below the judge's desk who were picked out for special attention by the warm-up guy and squealed with excitement when he made the point that they would be in shot whenever the judges were speaking. They fluffed up their hair, to the amusement of the rest of the audience, and stood up to show off their sequinned frocks. The sense of camaraderie that the audience members usually ended up feeling for each other after a night on set together seemed stronger than ever tonight. I looked back at the celebrities, and wondered if they were jealous that they weren't going to be on that stage tonight. And I cast my eye across the friends and family whose faces had grown so familiar over the last few months.

But at the end of the row, closest to us, was a beautiful blonde woman, about my age. She looked a little otherwordly, as if she were a character from a fairy tale who had been asked to wear twenty-first century clothes for the day. She seemed calm, placid and perhaps a little bemused by the chaos around her.

As the titles began to roll I leaned into Matt and nodded in her direction.

'Who's that? The blonde?'

'Where?'

'End of the row, wearing the pale blue dress.'

'Oh.' The theme music was reaching its crescendo now.

'That's Alicia.'

'Alicia?'

'Yeah, she's, um, from Sweden. She's ... Well, she's Lars's girlfriend.'

The music finished. Bruce and Tess took to the stage. The audience went wild.

Chapter 17

It was hard not to think of it as the audience clapping because I had just been told that Lars had a girlfriend. It felt like a cruel joke for a moment, until everyone simmered down and Bruce and Tess began their banter. I focussed on theat, and chuckled along with the rest to Bruce's jokes. I even rolled my eyes when Tess did, as if I were playing the part of 'me being fine'.

But inside I felt the shiver of shock still running through my body. It wasn't just shock at Lars having been taken all along, but shock at how I felt about it. It wasn't heartache, it wasn't even anything close to that. The simple fact was: I felt like an idiot for never even having considered it before.

All of those conversations I had had months ago: with Sally, with Jen, with Mum, with Allegra. As if Lars was really some kind of a possibility. It wasn't that I couldn't be with him – I could clearly see that I didn't want to be with him now – it was the crushing sense of the time I had wasted. All of that worrying, all of that staring into space, dreaming of gold shoes I would never have and steps I would never dance. And for what?

I was jerked out of my shock by the beginning of the first dance. The audience were immediately silenced. As the couple stood there waiting for the cue there was not a sound anywhere on set. The music began and the pair was set in motion. It was an extraordinary dance and we all knew it, bursting into rapturous applause. There were wolf whistles and shrieks from all over the set.

Next up were Lars and Kelly. I could see the corner of Alicia's face as Lars took to the stage. She was sitting forward anxiously, her hands clasped together in her lap. She bit her bottom lip. Even more nervous was Kelly, whose hand only stopped trembling as she took to her starting position in the centre of the stage. Her face was proud, imperious, as if she deserved to be there and she knew it. She was of course right – the couple had worked harder than ever to get their place in the finals. I had noticed Kelly's technique and confidence suddenly improve in the last few weeks. For her, the closer the final seemed, the further away Julian seemed. As far as this series was concerned, she truly was the butterfly emerging from the chrysalis. I was pleased for her. No woman should have to take on the heartache that she had so publicly, and she had done it with better grace than I could have done.

Their dance began: a tango. Lars was masterful, and Kelly as feisty as she ever was at her best. I admired their

262

beauty; the skill of their moves. But, as Lars scowled down over Kelly I saw that he was not a man who I would ever go on a summer holiday with. We were never going to sit down together for a glass of wine on a Sunday night. He wouldn't be able to take the day off work to care for me if I was ill. Our connection was about dancing, based on understanding and friendship, not romantic love. Matt had been right all along. Just because he could express great passion with his body didn't mean that there was great passion between us. And slowly it dawned on me: if that was the case with Lars, then the reverse could be true of Matt.

The tango was spectacular – there was nothing in it between the first two couples. I had become caught up in the excitement of what was going on on stage, and only remembered my own worries as the next clip of tape was played out to the audience.

I realised that I had not checked on how things had gone with Jen's operation. My phone – forbidden on set during broadcast – was not on me, and so I had no way of finding out. She would probably be in theatre now, as the operation had been scheduled as an emergency. I felt prickly, panicking heat rise throughout my body. My chest tightened with panic and I felt something like vertigo as I looked around. What was I doing here? With all of these smiling faces? While Jen was so ill in hospital? I took a very deep breath and tried to let it out as slowly as possible.

I looked down, trying to let my deep breath out with as much subtlety – and as little noise – as possible. My face must have been entirely at odds with those of the rest of the audience, who were now laughing at the comments of the next couple up as they larked around in rehearsals. It felt like a room full of sparkly Christmas anticipation and here I was on the verge of a panic attack.

Matt looked across at me and whispered.

'Turns out he's always had a girlfriend. I'm so sorry. I didn't even know.'

'What? Who?' I frowned. I had no idea what he was talking about.

'Alicia. Lars.'

'Oh. Oh *that*. That is so not what I was thinking about.'

I looked down at my feet. I felt more flustered than ever. I couldn't possibly start explaining to Matt what I had been feeling since seeing Alicia – it would make no sense to him. And I wasn't ready to bring Jen into the mix either.

The lighting changed as the next couple took to the floor. Suddenly the entire studio was plunged into total darkness. I couldn't see Matt's face at all any more, even though it was only inches from my own.

'It's okay, don't be embarassed. I knew you liked him and not me.'

My problem was that even though I now knew that not to be true, I had no way of convincing him otherwise.

What could I do, caught in the dark, with the man I wanted's face so close to mine?

'That's not true.' How long was this darkness going to last?

'You don't have to say that.' I could feel his breath on my face. His lips were so close.

'It's NOT TRUE.' My whisper was now urgent. Suddenly, the lights came up to show a dancer in position, centre stage, alone.

Matt's face was still obscured though. I couldn't see his face properly, but I could feel him looking at me. I leant in, very close to his face.

'I was thinking about Jen. She is having her operation today.'

There was no reply. The couple had now met on the dance floor and were doing a soft, romantic rumba. It was mesmerising, and I felt myself soothed and carried away from myself just watching it. This was the reason I loved to dance – it had transformative powers.

And then, in the dark, I felt Matt's hand in mine. It wasn't awkward, in the way that a nervous first date's hand could be, and nor was it unwelcome or imposing. It was just … there. He was holding my hand and I was holding his. Nothing else about us changed – we didn't look at each other, and neither of us shared a further word. Freed from obligations to talk about work, to dance or to impress each other, we held hands until the close.

I had no idea what this might mean. Was he simply comforting me because of what I had said about Jen? Or was this something else? Was it … a declaration? Suddenly everything that had gone on between us started to recontextualise itself just like it had with Lars at the beginning of the show.

Allegra had, as ever, been right about everything. There had been something between Matt and me all along. That kiss at breakfast in Blackpool – I had hardly been able to contain myself. The way he had been so angry about Lars. Dare I let myself think that that might be about me? Even the first show – when he had shoved his hand into my pocket to give me those gloves. That was the first time I had felt his hands on mine, and now here we were at the last show. Inseparable.

The audience broke into applause for the end of the next dance, and as they did so, Matt and I instinctively clapped as well. My nerves fluttered – what would we do when the applause ended? But I barely had time to worry before Matt had taken my hand in his again.

I had dismissed him because I thought that I only wanted a dancer, someone who could talk to me about steps and practise and the drama behind each routine. What I seemed to have missed about the whole situation was that to be a good dancer you need a compatible partner. And Matt had tried – I could see that now. That night in the club: trying to chat to everyone, keeping an eye on me. I remembered making Rico laugh, and as Allegra had rightly pointed out, Matt had been looking over at me anxiously with every joke. He had stayed late that night, long enough that he had worked up the courage to try and dance with me, and still I had managed to avoid noticing it with my own dramas.

I had invested so much in dancing that I had stopped using it to give me confidence and started to let it take over my personality. I didn't want to be that girl. I wanted to be someone for whom the whole dance floor was a place to express passion and pleasure, not some arena where I tested future dates. Urgh.

The final dance of the night began, and we were all on tenterhooks. Lars and Kelly took to the stage, this time in ballroom outfits, exuding romance from every pore. Kelly was gleaming with pride as she completed the routine to perfection, and as they stepped towards the judges, the audience rose to their feet in admiration. But was it enough? I was unsure. And so were the judges.

Everything seemed to pass in a blur after that and I found myself feeling relief that such a difficult decision didn't lie on my shoulders. Both couples seemed to be radiating nerves as they waited whilst the public votes were counted. They had done all that they could, all that was left now was to wait and hope. And then finally, the audience's breaths baited, Tess opened the envelope and read out the name of the couple who would remember this moment forever. The crowd went wild.

As we all stood to applaud, I knew that my hand and Matt's would have to separate once more. The panic returned, except this time I didn't have the comfort of knowing that the set would be nice and dark for us to hold hands in for a couple more hours. This was it, everyone exploding with festive cheer, and yet I felt that I was standing at the biggest crossroads of my life. I watched Lars and Kelly stand aside as Vincent picked up his gorgeous partner and span her around, Kristina and Anton shared a joke and kissed each other as the celebrations began, and the audience resumed their cheering for us all. But for every festive dollop of joy and pride in our achievements, I felt the responsibility as well.

It wasn't that I didn't want to have more jobs like this or that I didn't want Matt, but I had never had so much to lose before – and now I had it all. If I could have seen myself in this position six months ago I would never have believed it. But where would I be in six months time? I owed it to myself not to mess up now. And actually, I didn't just owe it to myself: I owed it to Jen as well. I had to take to my own dance floor, and show myself what I was made of.

Before joining in with the applause I squeezed Matt's hand – just enough that he might notice – and then I let go.

After all, if I didn't have the courage to let go, I could barely call myself a dancer.

Chapter 18

The explosions of tinsel fell from the ceiling, and the crowd was on its feet roaring with excitement. The winners were beaming with pride and relief. Meanwhile, Lars and Kelly were gracious in defeat, hugging each other and then hugging all of the other dancers as they flooded the ballroom floor to give their congratulations. The floor was a gorgeous mess of people crying, laughing and desperately trying to wipe the tinsel from their faces. The crew were still concentrating on getting those final key shots, but the rest of us were hugging and congratulating each other out of view of the cameras as well.

It felt like a combination of New Year's Eve and the end of term – a natural end to things, but also a reminder of everything we had been through as a Strictly Family. I couldn't bear that it was ending, but was determined to make the most of the night, and go out having achieved as much as possible.

As the cameras finally stopped rolling I surveyed the scene. Some of us were starting to walk towards the dance floor now, and Tess and Bruce were starting to talk to some of the audience members, thanking them for coming and making jokes with them. One girl who was there with her mother looked as if she was going to burst into tears, she was so overwhelmed by the excitement. It was as if I was looking at myself only a few years ago, so thrilled to be taken to West End shows. Tess waved at her and she beamed back. I wished for an inkling of her sense of magic, but my heart was undeniably heavy. I knew I had to go and check my phone as soon as I possibly could.

But first, I swallowed my pride and walked over to Kelly and Lars, who were still on the dance floor accepting congratulations and praise. I waited a few seconds until Kelly had finished talking to a grinning Anton, and then put my hand on her shoulder.

'Congratulations, Kelly. You were out of this world.'

'Thank you.'

'I'm so sorry you didn't win – it was ridiculously close.'

'You know what, I have nearly exhausted myself these last few months trying to win this thing, but now that I haven't …' She shrugged. Lars came up alongside her. 'Well, now that we haven't, I realise how much else I have gained. My confidence, new friends, a fantastic experience. The whole thing has changed me.'

'That's fantastic! I am so pleased for you.' I really did mean it. There was something softer beneath that brittle, hurt ambition. Kelly was just a girl like the rest of us, and now that she – literally – had a bit of a spring in her step, I could see that she would be fine.

'And congratulations to you too,' I said to Lars, as someone else interrupted and started talking to Kelly.

'Thank you, Amanda. I am glad you enjoyed the dances.'

'Oh it was more than the dances, you know I think the whole experience has meant as much to me as it has done to Kelly. Strictly – it's a game changer.'

As Kelly turned away to hug someone, Alicia approached behind Lars's shoulder. She was stunning, with a serene, clear face. Under the studio lights and even wearing minimal make-up, her gleaming skin and nearly white-blonde hair looked almost angelic.

'Darling!' said Lars, taking her hand.

'This is my good friend Amanda.'

'Hello, Amanda. It is a pleasure to meet you.' She extended her hand, her head tilted to one side.

So here we were, the moment I had been dreading for so long, and I didn't mind a bit. All those months and weeks of dreaming about being with Lars, wondering what was going on between him and Kelly, fantasising about our wonderful dancing life together, it wasn't real, he was just a good guy with a great sense of humour who had recognised and encouraged my passion for dance.

If you had asked me a month ago how I would have dealt with this situation, I would have run away sobbing, and now I felt nothing but affection for both him and Alicia.

'Oh, please excuse me – I have to help the audience off the set now.' I could see the others grouping together to ready the set for being cleared, and went to join them. Chloe saw me approaching.

'Any news?' she asked.

'No, I haven't been able to check since before we went on air.'

'Do you want to go and take a look at your phone now?'

'Don't you need me?'

'Amanda,' she gently placed her hand on my arm. 'I am sure we will be fine without you for five minutes. Family comes first. Just dip out now if you want to.'

'Thank you so much.'

I left the set as quickly as I could, so as not to get talking with anyone else, and ran to my coat, hanging over the back of my desk chair. I rummaged around and found my phone. Nothing from Jen, just a message from my mum.

No news yet, the show was like a dream. So proud of you for today. Much love and speak soon. Mx

I held the phone in my hand for a few seconds, as if I could somehow squeeze a bit of good news from it. But I took heart from Mum's sweet message that I had made her

273

proud, and thought about how much had changed since I got the job.

As I was returning to the set, I could hear the audience exiting and realised it might not be a good idea to go against the flow of excited, chatty human traffic. I took another turn down one of the elegantly curved corridors and headed straight to the bar area to see what I could do to help the team returning coats and bags to the audience.

Taking my shortcut, I saw Lars at the other end of the corridor, having just left his dressing room.

'Hey! Sorry I had to duck out just then. It was lovely to meet Alicia.'

See! I was behaving like an actual grown up and it was going *fine* …

'I'm so glad you could meet her. I was sure that you would get on. She is the only one who really understands how I feel about dancing apart from you. She is a physiotherapist, but she had a big job in Sweden this autumn.'

'She's lovely. And I just wanted to say before it gets busy again …'

'Yes?' He was relaxed, and smiling. It seemed amazing to me to see him just standing there, fresh from the biggest show of the weekend, and he seemed like … he was just a guy.

'Thank you for all of your support. You've been amazing – it has been so great to have a confidence boost from someone like you.'

'Oh Amanda,' he almost looked disappointed. Had I gone too far? 'It's not you who should be doing the thanking. Especially while you are waiting for news from your godmother. You have been a true friend to me this autumn, and I would never have got this far without you. I might have even got further with you!'

We both laughed. At first it was nervous laughter – were we both going to find that funny? And then, after all we had shared, we just broke into affectionate giggles.

'Yeah, right!' I said.

'You're the best. I hope we don't lose touch.' And with that he picked me up and gave me a giant hug. I squealed and asked to be put down.

'We have a party to go to!'

Behind me, I heard a clatter on the floor. Lars put me down and I turned and saw Matt at the end of the corridor. In front of him, at his feet, was a small cardboard box.

'Oh,' he said, quietly.

'Hey, Matt,' said Lars, oblivious to what was going on. 'You okay?'

'Er, yes thanks, Lars. Never been better.'

'Well, I'm going to go and get Alicia. She's on the phone in my dressing room.'

Lars gave me a jokey punch in the arm, and mouthed 'you okay?' at me. I nodded. He walked back to his dressing room.

'I don't believe it.'

'What?' I looked down at the box by his feet. Was that the heel of a shoe poking from it?

'So there was something going on all along.'

'Whaaaat?'

'You and Lars. I always thought so.'

'Well, Matt, yes. Actually there was something going on all along. A friendship. Lars has been supportive of me, and I have been supportive of him. I'm terribly sorry if that upsets you so much.'

He stared at me, blankly. 'That's how you manage your friendships is it? Kissing in corridors.'

'This is insane! You saw him hug me! Do you have any tiny idea how much of an idiot you sound, accusing me of this after the fuss that you made when I was mistaken about you and Sally? I give up. I give up. I thought you were my friend to, but apparently you're just some kind of morality monitor for me.'

'Don't make out that I'm the pious one here, Little Miss 'Oooh I'm Just Trying To Do the Best For the Show' when it's perfectly obvious that you just want to get up on stage with the dancers.'

He had kicked me where it hurt the most.

'That is so harsh. And completely unreasonable. You know how committed I am to the show, and you know how much I adore dancing. Don't you dare get the two confused when I have tried so hard to be professional.'

'From where I am standing it looks like you're the one getting confused.'

'Just back off. I am sick of being told what to do by you. You're not even my boss. My actual boss has turned out to be more of a friend to me today. Goodbye Matt.'

Even as I was saying it, I knew it wasn't strictly true, but I was so hurt by what he was saying to me that I felt compelled to strike back. I walked towards him to head back to the bar. As I passed Matt he was picking up the box from the floor. It was a shoebox.

I was shaking with anger by the time I reached the bar, but gritted my teeth, determined to have a fun evening. After a couple of glasses of wine, I suddenly felt the tiredness hit me like a truck. I tapped Sally on the shoulder and asked if she had a minute to chat before I left. We walked down to the office for me to get my bag, and I explained everything that had happened with Lars and Matt.

'Jeez, the drama! You're doing your own Life Salsa here, babe. It's an obvious one though, isn't it? He's into you, it's the only reason he cares like this.'

Sally was leaning on the door of the office, her back to it. The lights were off inside, and she flicked them on as she entered the room. There was a sudden shuffling at the other end of the room, and there were the startled faces of Chloe and Anthony.

'Oh. Hi there.' Chloe was flushed. But she also looked as if she was trying to conceal a smile.

'Just. Getting. My. Coat.' It was all I could think of to say as I grabbed my stuff and legged it out of the room. As soon as we were far enough away to be out of earshot, Sally and I exploded into giggles, and repeated exclamations of 'Who knew?!', 'I wondered!' and 'Proper gossip!'

We walked to the front of the building and Sally gave me my second enormous bear hug of the day. It was a Christmassy goodbye, but I knew that it wasn't an indefinite one as we had already planned to spend New Year's Eve together. I hugged her tight, told her how much I was looking forward to seeing her soon and went home to my packing.

A couple of days later I was back with Mum, Dad, Natalie and Lloyd. It was our least festive Christmas for a while – partly because Jen was still in hospital, although her operation had gone well, and partly because with no children around, we pretty much devoted ourselves to eating and watching telly. The Strictly Christmas special put a lump in my throat as I remembered the day we recorded it, nearly three weeks previously. I had felt as if anything was possible, rather than feeling anxious about the gaping void that the new year held.

But my gloom didn't last too long, as once the mulled wine kicked in we were all sitting on the carpet like children, playing a cut-throat game of monopoly. Old rivalries resurfaced as Natalie and I fought for everything from our favourite piece ('The top hat!' 'The iron!') to the best place to buy hotels. Lloyd started stealing the pink notes while no one was looking and we were hysterical before bedtime, as if we were fifteen years younger.

By bedtime I was curled up, hugging my knees with happiness that I had such a ridiculous family. I wondered what Matt was doing and how things were for him in Saffron Walden. I missed him, and felt horrible about how things had been left between us. It was as if I had a cut that hadn't been dressed properly – the pain just snagged at me now and again, usually when I was least expecting it. As for Lars, I did miss him, but in a totally different way. I missed my mate, but now I found myself thinking that he was the one I would be able to get in touch with if I was in trouble, not Matt. I shivered, and reminded myself that there was a new year ahead, and whatever it held I had proved myself stronger than I ever thought I was.

There were great plans for New Year's Eve – Allegra was away in Italy and she had offered Sally her room for the night, so that she could be with me and we could both go to a night being arranged by a members' club in London, up by the river. It was one of the most glamorous events I had ever been invited to, but several of us who had worked on the show had arranged to go weeks before. After working for so many Saturday nights up to Christmas we reckoned we deserved a big party, and I had meticulously saved enough money for taxis, drink, tickets and a new dress. I was determined that Sally and I wouldn't get stuck on a night bus so I had left shoes out of the budget. Madness, I know, but getting home, warm in shoes I had worn a few times, beat getting home by bus wearing heels that were giving me blisters.

Sally and I got ready together at my flat, with music on and a bottle of prosecco open as a nod to our new Italian friends. Lello was going to meet us there, and it was going to be the first time that he had come out with us without Allegra. Sally had high hopes.

I was wearing a new green silk dress, with a long zip down the back from the neck to the hem. I had bought it a couple of weeks before Christmas with a discount voucher that Natalie had found online and sent to me. I would never have been able to afford it otherwise. When I put it on I did feel special for a moment. It was no salsa frock, but it was the most ritzy thing I had owned for a while and I didn't think I looked too bad.

Ever glamorous, seconds later I was on my hands and knees at the bottom of my cupboard, looking for suitable shoes. I was eye-level with the boxes in front of me and found them reminding me of something. I remembered – the box at Matt's feet. Why was he wandering the corridors of TV Centre holding a shoebox?

The thought of him set the butterflies in my stomach back in motion. Sally had had confirmation that he was still planning to come to the party. We had not spoken since our confrontation on the night of the finals and I had no idea how things would pan out. I was still angry with him, but against my better judgement I still wanted to see him. I realised that he would probably be more nervous than me – after all, he was the one who had made the silly mistake. And of course he was about to attend a party full of people who were going to be dancing. It didn't really take the edge off though.

Once I had finally dived out of the bottom of the cupboard I turned and saw my phone on my bed, glowing.

Happy new year Darling! And guess what … I'm out of hospital at the end of the week! Beside myself, so excited. Strictly Christmas Special was all that kept me going!

'YEAY!'

'What?' Sally came running into my bedroom, her face looking like a 'how to' make-up demonstration – one half immaculately drawn, one half not.

'Jen's coming out of hospital! Wooohooo!'

'Oh now that is cause for this!' She ran back into the living room and grabbed the prosecco bottle. 'That is just the best news ever. I'm so happy for you. What a way to say goodbye to 2010!'

She was right. I felt as if a huge cloud was lifting from me. The weight of anxiety about Jen made me feel more free, made my sparkles feel more sparkly and made my heels feel higher. Tonight – regardless of what went on with Matt and me – I would enjoy myself.

Sally and I arrived relatively early at the party, but Chloe and Anthony were already there, now apparently happy to be seen as a couple. 'It was just until the series finished,' she whispered to me at the bar as she got me a drink.

When Matt arrived I took a deep breath (not just to suck in my stomach) and waved at him with a smile.

'Hi,' I said. 'Did you have a good Christmas?'

'It was okay,' he replied. 'Seemed a bit flat after, well, you know.'

'I know.' And we each went our separate ways.

But, to my fury, I found I still fancied him. How could he have gone from being a bit of background noise on my first day to being a good friend to now … being someone who could make my heart thunder like that? My new dress was tight, but when I looked down I could almost see my heart beating from within it. That's not normal. Someone who once represented comfort to me now seemed like a different man altogether. He was prepared to take chances, he had spoken out when he thought I was seeing someone else, he had stood up for himself. And his new shirt was gorgeous.

The music was getting louder, the beats were getting faster, and the room was filling up. Everyone had made a real effort and I was dazzled by what a good-looking bunch we actually were once we didn't have our grubby work clothes on. Finally, we had brought our own bit of Strictly to life!

I looked across the room. Sally, who was already practically sitting on Lello's lap, saw me and winked. She waggled her eyebrows at Matt and I giggled. Soon we were all on the dance floor together. This time, there were no choreographed steps, we were all just moving as one, smiling, waving our drinks in the air, our arms around each other. Chloe and Anthony were unbelievably cute, holding hands and keeping an eye on each other throughout. Sally took to the centre of the group at one point and did a hilarious dance, looping around in a kind of bizarre salsa. And then I felt it: Matt's hand around my waist again. He was on the dance floor too. Finally, he was joining in, moving with us to the beat, laughing with the rest of us.

I was so happy that I almost felt short of breath. Jen was getting better; the anger between Matt and me had dissipated; I was with my friends. It would be a good new year after all. I felt like a fool for ever having doubted it. As I lifted my hand to dance, I caught sight of my watch. It was nearly midnight. Matt saw me do it, and saw the time on my watch face. As I lowered my hand, he grabbed it.

Chapter 19

Matt half-guided, half-dragged me through the crowd and away from the dance floor. I could hear the DJ stoking everyone into a frenzy as midnight approached. People were trying to find their friends, tripping across the dance floor to the bar and the seated area, and vice versa. We kept crossing the paths of friends and lovers waving and reaching for each other. I felt flustered, but excited. Where was Matt taking me?

We left the main room and he pulled me over to the cloakroom area.

'Wait here, ' he said, as he handed over his token to the bored-looking woman behind the desk.

'It's a box. A white cardboard box,' he said to her.

'All right, love.' She shrugged and disappeared behind the rails of coats.

I could hear the crowd inside the main room chanting the countdown.

TEN ... NINE ... EIGHT ...

The cloakroom attendant arrived, carrying a shoebox. She slammed it on the counter, while Matt rummaged in the pocket of his trousers and produced a pound coin that he put in the tips dish.

SEVEN ... SIX ...

He turned to me. His face was tight with nerves.

'These are for you.' I recognised the box. I had seen it only a couple of weeks ago. And I recognised the one crushed corner that it had, where I knew it had been dropped recently. Matt held the box out towards me, lifting the lid away from himself so that I could see inside.

FIVE ... FOUR ...

It was a pair of gold salsa shoes. They were similar to the ones that I had worn in Blackpool, only more intricate and less functional. And ... for me. I looked at Matt.

'May I?'

'Of course, they're yours.'

I picked one out of the box. It was a pale gold, with a heel that was pinched in the middle and then curved slightly out again at the bottom. The leather was soft, and there was a small padded area at the front where my toes would rest. Above that, the five gold straps on each side splayed out delicately.

... THREE ...

I turned it around in my hand. Then put my palm flat out and placed the shoe on it to admire it properly, smiling at Matt. My stomach was doing a salsa of its own, and I

285

could barely move my hands properly for the tingling excitement that was running through my body.

'Thank you, Matt. Thank you for everything. I promise to wear them.'

'I am so sorry about everything that happened between us, Roberts. I would really like it if you still had these though. You deserve to dance. Even I can tell how wonderful you are at it. You deserve a dancer.'

… TWO …

'But …'

My voice was caught in my throat. What had seemed so wonderful only seconds ago was now crystallising into something else altogether. How was this happening? It felt as if he was ending something, not beginning it. Did he think I didn't want him now? Was this his final word on the matter?

Did I tell him the truth when he was sounding so final? Yes, I did. Because if Strictly had taught me anything it was that I had to stand up for what I wanted: I had to behave as if I was on the ballroom floor and I knew all the steps.

ONE!!!

'But I don't want a dancer. I want you.' I put the shoe back into the box and closed the lid. I reached out to take the box from him. His hands were still on it: it was connecting us.

The double doors to the dance floor swung open and noise flooded through as midnight struck. The shrieks, the

286

singing, the party poppers – they drowned out everything I had just said.

'What?'

I couldn't hear him. I was only lip reading; the cloak-room area was now as noisy as the dance floor itself.

I shook my head. We were both standing there, facing each other, each holding one end of the shoebox. I desperately wanted him to just lean forward. That extra inch. I opened my mouth to say it again, louder this time. *It's you I want. You. I get it now.*

'Amanda! Matt! Have you seen Anthony?'

We turned around. Chloe was at the doors, one hand in her hair, looking a little dishevelled. At first I thought she was tipsy but it soon became clear that she was actually panicked. Her hair was ruffled where she had been running her hands through it and her face was pinched and anxious in a worrying way – much more so than anything I had ever seen at work.

'I need your help.'

At that moment both Matt and I dropped the shoebox. We had each assumed the other had taken it, and the box simply fell to the floor in the space – the seemingly infinite, never to be bridged space – between us. We both kneeled down to rescue it.

'What's wrong?' Matt asked Chloe. 'Are you okay?'

'I think I have lost my wallet, my coat, everything.'

'That's what you get for trying to save on the cloakroom,' sneered the woman behind the counter. I glared at her.

'When did you last see them?' I asked. But I could barely concentrate: while maintaining eye contact with Chloe, Matt and I were both trying to get the shoes back into the box, our fingers repeatedly brushing against each other. Our faces were closer than ever before. I felt queasy with adrenaline.

'I had my coat on when we arrived – because it was still cold in there when we arrived.' Both Chloe and I cast a scornful glare at the cloakroom lady. 'I put it down on the back of the seating we were at, but now there's nothing there. My coat, wallet, keys, the lot. And I can't find Anthony.' Chloe's voice was rising now, she was choked with panic. I stood up and put an arm on her shoulder. Ordinarily I would never dream of touching her like that, but she seemed so distressed that the three of us couldn't just stand there as if we were in a meeting forever.

'Amanda, you stay here with Chloe, I'll go and find Anthony.'

Matt vanished into the room. I found a chair that was resting in the stairwell and offered it to Chloe.

'This is so embarrassing – it just isn't the kind of thing I do.'

'Well no-one means to lose their wallet – it's just bad luck. I'm sure Matt and Anthony will sort it out.'

'It's not about the money: it's my phone, everything. My mum is really sick now, and I didn't want to come out tonight. I only left my mobile for a minute – she really depends on me, you know? Anthony persuaded me that I

288

deserved a night to relax and now this happens. I feel such an idiot. And I know you'll think I'm being neurotic but I feel like I've let her down.'

'I don't think that at all. I think you're amazing holding it all together, and Anthony was right that you needed a chance to relax. Don't panic, I'm sure this can be sorted out.'

But moments later, Matt returned unable to find either Anthony or news of Chloe's belongings. Chloe seemed ever more distressed, and the staff at the club were completely useless about what they could do to help until the venue was cleared in a few hours. In the end, conscious that she needed to be back by her landline in case of news from her mum, and because it seemed unfair to interrupt Sally's night by asking her to come with us, Matt offered to take Chloe home and stay with her while she got her spare keys from her neighbour. It was the sensible thing to do and we both knew it. But as the arrangements were made, in what seemed like seconds I felt what had looked like becoming the most romantic night of my life draining away like dirty bathwater. I had wasted my chance once too often.

I watched Matt help Chloe into a cab, shivering outside in my frock as I waved valiantly, my heart wanting to break. I felt as if I was waving goodbye to Matt forever. I couldn't think of a way I could possibly get as close to kissing him as I had been when the clock struck midnight. I was Salsa Cinderella.

The dancing was still going on when I got back to the main room. Sally was having the time of her life, and I couldn't bear to break it up for her after my little drama. I resolved to have at least one more drink and enjoy myself properly, regardless of my romantic apocalypse. Twenty minutes later, just as I was finally about to suggest leaving, Anthony wandered in.

'Where have you been? We have been looking for you for ages. Chloe has gone.' My voice was coming out strangely shriekily, and I was addressing Anthony in a wildly informal way. We had barely spoken about anything but work in the past, but now I was hectoring him like an angry wife. I didn't care any more – as far as I was concerned, he had ruined both my night and Chloe's.

'What? Why? I've just spent the last twenty minutes looking for her! I've been calling her mobile and everything. She always has it on her but it's just going to voicemail.'

'She's had it nicked. And her coat and wallet and everything.'

'When?'

'About forty five minutes ago. She was devastated. We looked for you everywhere, but in the end she just wanted to leave because without her mobile she had no way of hearing from her mum.'

Anthony put his head in his hands. 'I don't believe it.' He was shaking his head now. I actually thought he might start crying.

'I only went outside to try and get a gift for her from the car. I wanted to give it to her at midnight, but I lost my bearings, turned down a street too early, and ended up the wrong side of the canal. What a cock-up. I've ruined absolutely everything now.'

I noticed that Anthony had a small jewellery box in his hand. My heart went out to him. He seemed like a really nice guy, and now he was as thwarted as I was. This evening was turning out to be the kind of fresh start you wouldn't wish on your worst enemy.

'Don't panic. She was okay in the end – Matt took her home to make sure she could get in. And she'll be on her landline now. I'm sure she'll still be up.'

I checked with Anthony that he had Chloe's home number and then waved him off as he trudged back to his car.

I headed to the dance floor once again, determined to fish Sally out and return home with her as soon as I could persuade her. But oh no, oh no no. There was no chance of that now as she was firmly entwined with Lello. Truly, she was at lip-lock central. It was as if Mr Date Hands had never existed …

I wanted to feel annoyed with Sally, but really I was thrilled that *someone* was having a good New Year's or I might have given up hope for all humanity. I stood at the side of the room for a while, pretending to check messages – nothing from Matt – and feeling more and more like the biggest nerd at the party. Finally Sally had come up for air long enough to come over and see how I was doing. I filled her in on the evening's drama, leaving out the key Matt Facts. I anticipated a minor battle to wrestle her away from her new beloved, but like the corker of a mate she had turned out to be, she leaned in to Lello straight away and whispered in his ear. Within ten minutes we were in the queue for taxis, and within the hour we were home.

We gasped with joy at taking our heels off, and it was only then that Sally noticed the box I had put on the coffee table.

'What's that?'

'Salsa shoes.'

'What? Where from.'

'Matt gave them to me. A Christmas present. From before.'

'WOW. That's big. Seriously?'

'Of course seriously.'

'So did you get it together?' I avoided her gaze. 'Why not? What's going on? You two are just being pathetic now. Why can't you just tell him? This isn't Jane Austen territory, you know.'

'Yes, I do know. And I did tell him. But that was when Chloe found us in a panic. And he had to take her home. I think he *wanted* to take her home. He was going to give me the shoes before, on the night of the finals. I saw them. But this time – it felt like more of a 'goodbye' gift than a 'hey how about it?' gift.'

'You're insane.'

'Thanks.'

'You absolutely have to make a decision about this.' Sally was now leaning against my kitchen counter, putting the two glasses of water she had just poured us in front of me. 'You have been too passive for too long.'

'I told him I wanted him. He said nothing.'

'But before or after Chloe?'

'At the exact moment.'

'So you don't even know if he heard?'

'Not really.'

'This is pathetic. As with everything, this is just a matter of confidence. So you don't know if he wants you – find out. You just have to ask. Then you could be together and stop wasting so much time. And let's say he doesn't, or even thinks that he doesn't because he's lost his nerve after all of the to-ing and fro-ing you've been doing – it's better if you know. You can either persuade him or get over him. You don't have to see him every day at work any more and you'll have lots going on in the new year that will mean you'll be over him in no time. Take control. Don't let him lead the dance.'

'You're right. I'll give it a week. If I don't hear from him I'll assume it's over.'

'No. That is letting him back in control. Ask him.'

'Okaaaaay. I will ask him. If I don't hear for a week. Deal.'

'Babe, you just made your new year's resolution.'

'You totally tricked me into it!'

'It's a lesson for life, doll. Keep dancing like you know the steps, and don't let anyone else drag you around the dance floor.'

'You're the best.'

'I love you.'

Maybe this wasn't quite the worst New Year's of all time, after all.

We spent the first day of the new year dancing as if we knew the steps to the rare yet elegant dance of 'eating one's own body weight in curry while watching the collected films of Nora Ephron'. You should try it. Anyone could pick it up. Training is very simple, and mostly consists of dialling a number, waiting for the delivery man, and then opening DVD box sets. It doesn't help you to lose weight as much as most dances do, but it is still one of my very favourites.

On the second day of the new year, I headed out to two job interviews, both of which were with people who seemed as startled to be back at work as I was to be out of a job. They gave me no indication of when I would be hearing from them, almost as if they were actively trying to dent my new year confidence. Ha! I wouldn't be defeated yet!

On the third day of the new year, when the boiler packed in and I couldn't get hold of the estate agent – or Allegra in Italy – until my lips were blue with cold, I started to feel my will to vigorously dance life's tango slip a little.

And on the fourth, the snow came. After seemingly endless warnings I finally woke up to the unique silence that can only mean that the world around you has been covered in a thick layer of snow. When I peeled back the curtains I was proved correct. My first worry was for Allegra, who was due to be flying home the following day, and my second was for myself. How on earth was I supposed to motivate myself to get anything done when it was now going to take at least seven hundred times longer than usual to get anywhere?

And so, it was day five when I found myself watching old movies in my tracksuit bottoms by four o'clock it the afternoon. At one point I went to the bathroom, and on re-entering the sitting room I realised what I had become. Teacups were on every surface, there were Mr Kipling wrappers everywhere and the room was starting to smell as if something might have died behind the sofa. This would not do. For the next hour I leapt into a frenzy of cleaning and then sat at the kitchen table to write myself a list of jobs for New Year: Day 6.

As I went to sit down, I saw the white cardboard box on the kitchen table. I lifted it and opened the lid. There they were: my salsa shoes. A reminder of everything I had achieved in the last few months. But more importantly, a reminder of what I still had to do. I picked up one of the shoes and placed it on the brightly coloured oilcloth on the kitchen table. Bad luck, I know, but I figured that at this point it was up to me to sort my destiny out. I hadn't even tried the shoes on yet – it seemed a crime to do so if I had no plans to dance in them. So I got out my laptop and spent an hour searching for local dance classes, rifling through drawers to find notes that people had given me about good dance classes in the area that the show's dancers recommended. I only had forty-eight hours left before the deadline to call Matt. I had to spend it wisely.

The next afternoon I left the house for Baker Street, allowing forty-five minutes more than I would normally need for the journey. I was wearing a hat, gloves, scarf and huge snow boots that I had bought on a trip to New York with Jen for mytwenty-first birthday. The pavements were treacherous in the residential roads surrounding my house, and I was convinced that I would have a broken ankle before I reached the bus stop. But despite my shock at being outside for the first time in a couple of days I made it onto a bus and was at the dance studio, my salsa shoes under my arm, with over half an hour to spare. I didn't really know the area, partly because it seemed so anonymous that I had never been particularly inclined to explore it. I wasn't sure what to do with myself, so I bought a copy of a magazine and went for a coffee as my anxieties about the class rose.

Would everyone in there be proper professionals? Or would they be a bunch of pensioners? Would I fit in? Should I tell people that I had worked on the show and risk them asking me indiscreet questions or would no one be bothered at all? I began to flick the pages of my magazine ever more briskly. It was an old issue, one that had come out before Christmas and was full of speculation about who might win the show. There was even a picture of Kelly leaving the set with Lars one day after rehearsals – I could remember the exact day it was taken. It felt like another lifetime. I didn't know whether I would experience anything like that ever again.

With a heavy heart, I realised that it was time to grab the new year by the scruff of the neck and skid across the pavement to salsa school. Gingerly, I walked from the coffee shop a little way down Baker Street, past the cinema and down the little alleyway to the entrance. My hands were numb and my boots where heavy with snow. I stood at the entrance, stomping my feet, hoping to shake as much snow from my boots as possible. I felt a hand on the small of my back, even through my thick down jacket.

'Roberts ...'

It was so cold that I could still see the word in the air once I had turned around. Matt. I thought of all of the other times I had felt his breath on my face. Images flashed past my mind. Him leaning over my shoulder as I sat at my desk. Him grabbing me and whirling me around on the dance floor after the show. Him standing in front of me at New Year, neither of us daring to lean in to the other. Over the last few days, as my hope had faded, I had begun to wonder if he was in fact a living breathing person, or just someone I had imagined.

But now, for the first time, I could actually see his breath. Little puffs of condensation in front of me as he stood there, smiling. I realised I couldn't see my own as I was winded by how happy I was to see him. I exhaled.

'What are you doing here?'

'I could ask you the same thing.'

'Salsa class, of course. I don't know if you've heard, but I have some magnificent new shoes.'

He smiled, a funny crooked smile that made my stomach lurch.

'And why are *you* here?'

'Well, Roberts, I don't know if *you've* heard, but apparently dancing isn't that bad after all. You should try it.'

'What?'

'You heard. I've been told – I can't remember who by – that I should give it a try some time, that it doesn't matter if I don't get it right at first, and that it might just turn out to be fun.'

'Seriously?'

'Seriously.' He took my hand in his and held me in a faux ballroom hold. 'It was my new year's resolution. Everything else about that night was so rubbish. I thought trying dancing couldn't make things any worse.'

'Everything?'

'No.' The word sat there in the air between our mouths. 'Not everything.'

I looked down. Our two sets of winter boots were there in the snow, facing each other. I looked up.

'Good.' And now I saw my word resting in the air, before evaporating.

'But—'

'Yes?'

'We never—'

'What?'

'We never got to dance. I would like to dance with you. I would like to show you that I can.'

'Well, we're both here now.'

'Yes, I suppose we are.'

'We could just go in. And dance. For ages.'

Our words were meeting in the middle now. The distance between our mouths was getting smaller and smaller.

I don't know who leant forward the extra inch in the end. We must have met in the middle. What I do know is that we never made it to salsa class that week. But we went the week after, and then the week after that. These days, we dance together even if we don't know the steps.

Find out what happens to Amanda next in

Strictly GLITTER

A Strictly Come Dancing novel by

Amanda Roberts

ISBN 978-0-00-742734-5

Out in Summer 2011